AF714512

Daityagarh

OrangeBooks Publication

1st Floor, Rajhans Arcade, Mall Road, Kohka, Bhilai, Chhattisgarh 490020
Website: **www.orangebooks.in**

First Edition, 2025

ISBN: 978-93-7426-287-0

DAITYAGARH

WHAT WAIT BENEATH

BOOK 1 - AWAKENING

DHARA SHAH

OrangeBooks Publication

www.orangebooks.in

Acknowledgements

It took me almost a year to bring Daityagarh to life. There were nights when the story refused to move, and days when it wouldn't let me rest. I researched endlessly, rewrote chapters over and over, and kept searching until the plot finally felt right - until the world of Daityagarh revealed itself the way it was meant to.

This journey has been a blend of love, patience, and quiet determination - and I owe it all to the people who stood beside me through it.

To my daughter, **Khushi Shah** - thank you for your endless love, your warmth, and for constantly motivating me to finish this book. You have been my strength, my reminder to keep believing, and the light that kept me going when the nights stretched too long.

To my husband, **Anand Shah** - my constant support, my calm, my backbone. Thank you for standing with me through every late hour, every rewrite, and every moment of doubt. Your faith has been the invisible hand that held me steady.

To **Shreeyan Bandkar** and **Aarya Phanse**, my first two young readers—thank you for reading Daityagarh before anyone else did, for your honest feedback, and for helping me refine, edit, and polish it with care. You saw this story grow—and your belief gave me courage.

And to all my dear friends—thank you for your constant encouragement, your kind words, and your faith in me through this long journey. You have been part of this book in more ways than you know.

With love and gratitude,

— Dhara Shah

Prologue

The fire had always obeyed.

Priests said it was the first covenant — older than gods, older than names, wood stacked in symmetry, ghee poured like molten sun, syllables bound into the wind until flame bowed its head in recognition. Fire devoured flesh, polished bone, lifted soul from soil, and surrendered the rest to the river. For centuries that pact had never faltered. But that dusk, something forgot its place.

At Dashashwamedh Ghat, pyres still roared, yet their hunger had thinned. Smoke curled downward instead of rising — a serpent unwilling to climb. The river's current seemed to hold its breath. A hush spread through the chants, too brief to be silence, too deep to be chance.

And then, one stone began to bleed.

Only a hairline crack, easy to miss — yet from it crept a single thread of red, deliberate, unhurried, sliding toward the water. The first drop met the river with a hiss, and from the smoke came a whisper that did not belong to men:

raṁ śaṁ kha-ratām… raṁ śaṁ kha-ratām…

The syllables pulsed like unseen tongues inside the heat. They brushed bone before they vanished. No mourner noticed. No priest turned. But those standing nearest to it shifted, instinct recoiling without reason. Only Aadhya noticed it.

Her scar noticed first. A pale spiral etched around her wrist — long dormant — flared alive as though molten metal had been poured beneath her skin. Heat surged up her arm, blooming in her chest like a second, ancient heart. The world leaned closer. Bells faltered. The mantras bent, half-forgotten mid-breath. And fire — faithful fire — stared back at her.

Then came the visions.

A skull, grinning through ash, refused to burn. Flames licked but yielded. Its sockets glowed with syllables, words that scraped like stone on stone. Smoke twisted, folding itself into a shape — a mirror made of flame, reflecting nothing.

Within it stood a woman cloaked in red. Spirals coiled her throat like serpents that breathed. Her eyes met Aadhya's, and she smiled — not in threat, not in welcome, but in recognition. The mirror burst apart. Its shards fell as sand.

The river was gone. In its place, dunes rose beneath a bruised sky. Anklets struck earth, sharp, deliberate — each step dragging fire up from beneath the soil. The desert itself trembled beneath her dance. From within that shifting land rose another voice, older than prayer—

vaḥrāṁ ōṁ ta-ka-sā… vaḥrāṁ ōṁ ta-ka-sā…

Every grain of sand trembled. Shadows bent unwillingly, carving themselves into shapes of obedience. Eyes bloomed across feathers — hundreds, blinking at once—watching without mercy.

Her body felt them all. The vision convulsed and split apart. The dunes sank into darkness. A house rose instead — wrong in every direction. The walls curved inward as if the house had forgotten how to stand straight. The corners melted into shadow, soft and uncertain. Lamps quivered in their brackets, spilling thin, nervous light across the beams, where ropes hung—some crumbling to ash, others still damp and glistening, as if something had only just let go. The air smelled of metal.

At the center stood a figure wrapped in pale light, motionless. In his hands — a rope that pulsed like a living vein. It tightened once. The air fled. Aadhya gasped, her chest collapsing against emptiness. Fever scorched her veins; syllables clawed up her throat, not words but memories of words. She fell forward. The stone beneath her was no longer stone but skin — warm, breathing. The scar on her wrist seared brighter. Images layered, bleeding into one another:

The skull that would not burn.

The woman in red smiling.

The desert that danced.

The house without corners.

The rope, pulsing like a heart.

The visions folded again. She was standing in a forest now — trunks pale and skeletal, roots writhing like salt-made serpents. From their branches hung skulls that swayed without wind, their sockets faintly glowing, their breath slow but alive. Beneath them, the soil gleamed white — salted, sterile, dead.

From that white silence rose the sound of drums. They did not beat — they grieved. Each strike emptied her chest a little more, until even her heartbeat felt borrowed. She stumbled toward the clearing and saw it: an idol formed of clay that glistened as if still wet.

Its face melted between forms — child, god, corpse, mother until it forgot which it was meant to be. The silence thickened, crushing. And then, from beneath the idol, something whispered.

tri-khaṁ nāra-daṁ… tri-khaṁ nāra-daṁ…

The chant spread like veins through the ground. The trees trembled. Blood seeped through their bark in slow rivulets. Faces formed upon the trunks, eyes half-open, lips moving too fast to understand. At their roots lay birds — dozens, wings folded inward, tongues split.

Aadhya fell to her knees, retching, the taste of iron in her mouth. Her scar burned again. From the darkness coiled the same rope — but now it burned, every strand alive with ember. It circled her wrist, her throat, her ribs, tightening. She gasped, clawing at nothing. Fire rose in her throat. Her vision dimmed. Then, just before the rope could close, her scar blazed — a spiral of light, defiant, refusing. The rope snapped, dissolving into smoke.

When her sight steadied, she was back at the ghat. The fissure on the stone had sealed. Only the faint scent of blood lingered, threading through the smoke like memory. The pyres burned again, obedient — but quieter, like creatures pretending to sleep.

Aadhya pressed her palm to her wrist. The mark still throbbed beneath her skin, alive. The air hummed faintly with that last syllable — ***nāradaṁ… nāradaṁ…*** — fading into the river's breath.

The wind shifted. The priests resumed their chant, unaware that the world beneath them had tilted. A single flame at the water's edge flickered, lifted its head, and went still — listening. The dusk deepened. The river drew in a breath.

And from somewhere beneath the ghats, something ancient stirred, remembering its own fire — the first tremor before awakening.

Table of Contents

Part – 2
Rajasthan
The First Seal

Part – 3
Himachal & Mumbai
Gathering Shadows

Part – 1

Varanasi Awakening

Chapter - 1

The Ghat That Bled at Dusk

Varanasi wasn't a city.

It was a memory wearing the mask of stone.

The first thing Aadhya Roy noticed as her cab rolled down the serpentine stretch of Chowk was not the crowd, nor the noise, nor the grime, but the smell, damp incense, charcoal, sweat clinging to the rot of the river. And beneath it all, faint, yet insistent, something metallic, like old blood that had seeped too deep into wood to ever be washed away. She rolled the window farther down, letting the hot wind knot her hair. The Ganga shimmered in the distance beneath its veil of smog, pale and oily, the slumbering skin of a god that refused to wake. Somewhere along the steps of Dashashwamedh Ghat, a conch groaned, its hollow cry threading through the labyrinthine alleys. It wasn't meant for her—not yet.

Twelve years had passed since she last walked these streets. The city no longer recognised her. But something older did. The spiral - shaped scar across her left wrist had begun to itch again.

She pressed her palm against it, closing her eyes as if to quiet the pulse beneath. She had told no one—not the hospital in Delhi where she worked, not her colleagues, not even the psychiatrist she saw each month—that her nightmares had returned. Always the same: fire, ash and a name she could never quite hold when she woke. The dreams had returned the moment she booked her ticket back to Varanasi. Now she was here, and the city had started humming again.

The cab jolted to a stop at Bengali Tola, the driver muttered something she barely caught, pointing toward a narrow gali choked with pilgrims, sadhus, tourists, and cows.

"Beyond that, no car goes . You will have to walk."

She paid him without protest and slung her tan duffel over one shoulder. The alley reeked of milk and stone, and something older still. Sandalwood clung to her skin like a second breath. She moved past a chai seller murmuring a chant, under his breath, a child drawing spirals in red chalk on the temple wall, and a white cow that stared at her, unblinking. Its gaze felt heavy, aware. She dropped her eyes quickly.

Her grandmother's warning surfaced, unbidden:

"In Kashi, the dead walk sideways. If a cow watches you too long, it may be someone remembering."

Her destination was an old guesthouse overlooking the river, barely a few hundred feet from the southern curve of Manikarnika Ghat. The building leaned slightly to the left, as though stone itself had grown weary of carrying secrets.

She signed the ledger under a false name—Rekha Sinha—and paid for seven nights in advance. "I'm here for medical volunteering," she told the woman at reception. The lie slipped too easily from her lips. That night, she didn't sleep. She sat on the narrow balcony of her room, watching the ghats below flicker with fire and the drone of chant. The funeral pyres of Manikarnika burned red against the black water, each flame wavering like a tongue that could not settle on a word. Though the guesthouse was hushed and the lanes had quieted, she was certain she heard a voice.

A deep one, rising from the river - calling her.

By morning, she had no answers. Only more questions. She woke with the taste of a mantra on her lips, one she had never known. Her bedsheet clung damp with sweat. And in the mirror above the sink, for the briefest instant, she saw not herself but a woman clad in red, spiral tattoos crawling up her throat like serpents.

She blinked. The vision was gone.

By noon the city was already molten with heat. Aadhya wandered through the twisting lanes, pausing for lime water, drifting near shrines she hadn't visited since she was seventeen. She wasn't sure what she was searching for. Until she found the old blind man at the ghat. He was seated cross-legged on a cloth mat beneath a banyan tree, his face tilted toward the river though his eyes were clouded like marbled glass. Three white horizontal lines marked his brow, and a rudraksha mala coiled thrice around his wrist. He looked like any other sadhu awaiting alms. She would have passed him by—except for what he said as she walked past.

"You've come back, Aadhrika."

The name struck like a blow. Her pulse stuttered, then thundered in her chest. She turned sharply. *"What did you call me?"* The old man's lips curved faintly, as though savouring some private jest whispered across centuries.

"I called you by your name."

"That isn't my name."

"Not in this life."

She stepped closer, her voice brittle. "Do I know you?"

"You did," he said quietly. "When you bled silver under the eclipse and the flames bent away from your bones."

Disbelief tangled with fear. "Who are you?"

"I am Pandit Mahadev Triveni; but names are only cloth here, child. In Kashi, only memory matters. And memory has teeth."

The river stirred behind him - rippling though no wind moved. Aadhya sank slowly to her knees across from him, compelled by something older than instinct. "How do you know my name?" she whispered. Instead of answering, he reached into a cloth satchel and drew out a black shard. At first, she thought it was polished stone. But when he placed it in her palm, she felt its weight. Obsidian. Smooth, flat, etched with a spiral at its center.

The same spiral carved into her wrist. The moment she touched it, her skin burned. Pandit Mahadev tilted his blind face toward the sun. "The city remembers you, Aadhrika. The river remembers. But something darker remembers too."

"Who was she?" Aadhya asked, her voice breaking.

"The one who was you?"

"Yes."

"She was a priestess," he said slowly. "A Daitya wearing human skin. The last of her kind who spoke to flame and commanded the silence between chants."

"I don't believe in reincarnation," she murmured.

"Your scars do."

Silence pressed close, heavy as ash. Then the priest leaned forward, his blind eyes faintly shining. "*When the ghat bleeds again at dusk, you will see what you were meant to forget.*"

A gust of wind lifted ash from the steps and scattered it into the air. When Aadhya blinked, the old man was gone. That evening, the sky burned the colour of dying embers. The air thickened, heavy with ash. Aadhya stood again on her balcony, the obsidian shard clenched in her palm. The scar on her wrist itched so fiercely it felt as though something beneath her skin clawed to be free. Below, the Ganga moved in strange eddies, ripples colliding as if some vast body turned restlessly beneath the surface.

And then, as the sun slid behind the temple spires, the ghat bled. A thin line of crimson seeped from one stone step of Manikarnika, trailing down like a wound reopened. No one else reacted. No one gasped. The mourners continued their laments, the doms tended to the pyres, and the city's chants carried on unchanged. But Aadhya could not look away.

A whisper curled into her ear, low and deliberate. **Come back.**

Her head snapped toward the mirror inside her room. The woman in red was smiling. The crimson line on the ghat below did not spread, but it glowed faintly in the corner of her vision—a stain that looked less like liquid and more like memory pretending to flow. Her pulse throbbed against the shard in her palm. The mirror woman's smile did not beckon. It did not threaten. It only lingered, as though she knew something Aadhya had lost. And then the reflection was gone.

Only Aadhya remained—sweat-soaked, eyes wide, her scar glowing faintly orange, keeping time with her heartbeat. She stumbled back from the balcony. The room had grown colder, though the fan overhead still creaked, its blades shivering reluctantly as if disturbed by the weight of air thick with memory. She wrapped a shawl tightly around her shoulders and sat cross-legged on the mattress, placing the shard on the floor.

"Who are you?" she whispered. The obsidian was mute, lifeless. But her scar burned hotter. Restless, she left the room. The guesthouse hallway was narrow, its bulbs flickering like fireflies nearing death. Silence pressed against the plastered walls, suffocating in its stillness. She descended toward the ghat.

Manikarnika still blazed with pyres. Smoke writhed upward, chants woven thick into the air. But Aadhya noticed what no one else did: no one placed a foot upon the bloodstained stone. They skirted around it unconsciously, perhaps unaware, perhaps unwilling. The stain remained. Dull red. Dry. As though it had always been there. She knelt beside it. The night was cool, yet when her fingertips brushed the step, it was warm. Not the warmth of stone sun-baked all day. A deeper warmth. Like something alive, hidden beneath. The patch pulsed faintly, like breath trapped in stone.

She closed her eyes. The sound rose immediately: not whisper this time, but chant. Low. Deep. A rhythm her spine seemed to recognize before her ears did.

"Vatnash… Ananta… Dah-vritti… Kaalbindu…"

The words from her dreams. The cadence she had murmured unknowingly in sleep. Her eyes flew open. No one else reacted. The chant was meant for her alone.

"You shouldn't be here."

The voice startled her. She turned sharply. A woman stood a few feet away, barefoot, hair uncombed, her eyes glinting unnaturally bright in the firelight. Ash smeared her face, her sari knotted roughly at the shoulder, tribal tattoos winding down her arm. A faint scent of salt and wet stone clung to her.

"Who are you?" Aadhya demanded. The woman smiled, tilting her head. "That, is not the right question." "Then what is?" The stranger stepped closer, gaze unwavering. "Do you remember the skull that did not burn?"

Aadhya froze. The words pierced her with the weight of recognition she could not place. Her gut twisted. The woman turned and began walking away, her bare feet soundless on the stone. She wove between sadhus and mourners like shadow given form. Without thinking, Aadhya followed. Past the pyres. Past the banyan roots. Into an alley drowned in darkness.

"I don't understand," she called, her voice shaking. "You will," the woman replied, without turning. "But only if you keep looking where the city tells you not to." At the alley's mouth, the woman glanced back once. "But beware. Memory may invite you, but it never lets you leave unchanged."

And then she was gone. Aadhya stumbled forward into emptiness, her chest aching with questions. It was past midnight when she returned to the guesthouse. She did not remember the walk back; her feet carried her on muscle memory, her eyes lost in thought. The shard still lay where she had left it. She picked it up, and froze. A second spiral had appeared—rougher, etched deeper, near the edge. It hadn't been there before. It looked unfinished. Like a fragment of a map.

The next day, she searched the lanes for the woman. She asked chai-sellers, sadhus, even a bookseller near Assi Ghat if they had seen a tribal woman smeared in ash, covered in tattoos.

Each stared at her blankly, shaking their heads. “No such woman,” one old shopkeeper muttered. “Sounds like a bhootni. The kind that comes to those who step where blood still breathes.”

By evening, she found herself beneath the banyan tree again. Pandit Mahadev Triveni was waiting. He did not greet her. He only extended his palm. In it lay a charcoal sketch of the same spiral carved into the shard. Below it, in curling Devanagari, one word:

Vatnash.

Aadhya’s throat dried. She sat slowly, folding her legs beneath her. “Tell me,” she whispered. “What is Vatnash?” Mahadev exhaled, long and measured, as though weighing how much of the flood to release. “A name,” he said. “And not only a name. It is a gate. A forgotten mantra. A curse turned backward.” Her breath faltered. “What does it want?” His clouded eyes turned faintly toward her. “You.”

The answer struck like a whisper with teeth. “I’m not a priestess. I’m not a Daitya. I’m just —” “Names don’t matter,” Mahadev interrupted. “Not here. Only blood.”

Aadhya’s chest tightened. She looked away, unsure if she wanted to laugh or scream. “Last night,” she whispered, “a woman came to me. Tribal. Covered in ash. She asked if I remembered the skull that did not burn.” Mahadev grew quiet. His expression did not shift, yet something in the air hardened.

“That was not a woman,” he said finally. Aadhya stiffened. “That,” he continued, “was memory itself. Seeking its vessel.” “Why me?” Her voice cracked. “Because you listened.” The air thickened with a silence that felt older than both of them.

That evening, she returned to the ghat. The stain remained, darker now, as though settling into permanence. She did not flinch when she touched it this time. She closed her eyes, breathing slowly, letting the chant coil through her marrow. And in the silence that followed, something shifted beneath the stone. A single sound. Faint. Like bone turning in ash. Like a skull stirring in its sleep.

The skull had shifted. She could feel it, though the city gave no sign. Around her, Varanasi carried on as it always had—priests chanting, doms stoking fire with brutal grace, pilgrims murmuring prayers they had inherited but never understood. The river gleamed with its usual smoke-smeared shimmer. Yet the step beneath her palm pulsed faintly, and she knew something ancient had taken a breath.

She rose unsteadily, brushing ash from her hands. The shard in her pocket grew warm, hotter than before, as if quickened by what stirred beneath stone. She didn't go back to the guesthouse. Not yet. Her feet carried her through winding alleys that smelled of milk gone sour, turmeric, sweat, and iron. Doorways sagged with garlands of lemon and chilies, their skins shrivelled, their protection long expired. Cows dozed in shadows; unseen eyes watched from latticed windows.

Without realizing, she returned to the banyan tree. Pandit Mahadev was already there. Always there, as though he had never moved, as if the city had pinned him to its roots for eternity.

"You heard it," he said, before she could speak. "Beneath the ghat. It turned." She sank to the ground beside him, exhaustion heavy in her limbs. "It's waking, isn't it?" The blind priest tilted his face toward the river. "Skulls are memory, Aadhrika. Those that burn surrender their pain. But those that don't… remember. And Kashi has more than one that refused the fire." Her breath caught at the name again. Aadhrika. It was beginning to sound more hers than Aadhya ever had.

“What am I supposed to do now?” she whispered.

“You listen.”

“To what?”

“To yourself.”

“I don’t want this.” Her voice trembled. “I came here for rest. I came here for quiet. I didn’t ask for any of this.”

Mahadev’s smile was faint, sorrowful. “No one asks for the truths they already carry.”

“I’m not her,” she insisted. “Not this priestess. Not this Daitya.”

“You are what you remember,” he said softly. “Even if you have not remembered it yet.”

Aadhya pushed herself to her feet, her chest tightening. “I need distance.”

“You cannot leave.” His voice was iron-soft, immovable. Her eyes flashed. “Excuse me?”

“You can walk. You can take the train. You can fly. But your blood will not allow it. Not yet.”

“Why not?”

“Because seven memories still sleep in this city, Aadhrika. Seven shadows that must rise before the silence in your bones unlocks. If you leave now, you will carry them with you. And they will burn wherever you go.” The words hit her like a curse. “What do you mean—burn?”

The priest leaned closer. “Each dream you survive, each chant you utter, each skull you disturb—it awakens what was buried not just in Kashi, but in you. The Daitya in you is bound to memory. And memory,” he whispered, “is the oldest curse.”

That night, her dreams were not dreams. She floated through corridors carved with flame motifs that glowed as if etched into her marrow. She wandered chambers half-flooded with black water, where lotuses bloomed in fire instead of petals. She walked through a forest of bones that whispered without mouths, chanting in languages her waking mind had never known. And in the center of it all was a throne. A throne fashioned from seven skulls—unburned, pristine, gleaming with a light that was not light at all. One of them opened its jaw and spoke.

Vatnash.

Aadhya woke gasping. Her bedsheet was marked with soot, not blood, though her palms were blackened as though she had plunged them into ash. The shard in her fist glowed faintly red before cooling into silence. She did not go back to sleep. At sunrise, Varanasi stirred into its daylight theatre: rickshaws clanging, pilgrims jostling, vendors hawking, pyres smoking as endlessly as they always had. But the air felt thinner to her, stretched like parchment, fragile under the weight of what she carried.

She stood before the mirror again. Her scar had grown. The spiral now branched outward, curling around her forearm in delicate lines like ink bleeding through water. Not random. Deliberate. She tore a page from her notebook and copied it down with a surgeon's precision, her hand trembling.

It was no scar. It was a map. That day, she walked the city differently. Not as a visitor. Not as a doctor on leave. But as something being led. She entered nameless shrines hidden behind leaning doorframes. She followed beggars who spoke in riddles, their rhymes half-prayer, half-warning. She lingered at funeral processions, watching to see if any of the mourners walked backward. At each turn, she felt it—the city answering her. A statue whose eyes gleamed wet for a moment. A bird that stilled mid-flight to watch her. A cracked wall that hummed faintly when her palm brushed it.

By dusk, she had seven notations sketched beside her scar. Seven points she could not yet decipher. Seven shadows pressing closer. That night, she returned to the banyan tree. Mahadev was not there. Instead, a garland of marigolds hung from the roots, fresh and fragrant. Below it lay another shard of obsidian. Crescent-shaped. Its edge carved with the same spiral—but reversed, as if mirrored. She picked it up. This shard felt different. Colder. But not dead. She closed her fist around it. The wind rose across the ghat, scattering ash into her hair. Beneath the noise of fire and chant, she heard something else. Not a voice. A song. Deep and rhythmic, older than the river. It moved through her blood. And below that rhythm came a whisper.

Seven skulls for seven chants. Seven memories for one awakening. Begin where fire refused.

Back in her room, she laid the two shards side by side. Their spirals aligned imperfectly, forming a symbol half-born, like an eye still closing. The air in the room was sharp, metallic, as though filled with breath not her own. In the mirror, the woman in red appeared again. This time, she was closer. Behind her. And in her hands, she carried a burning skull. A knock came at the door. Three taps. Slow. Ritualistic. Aadhya opened it cautiously. No one was there. But at her feet lay a folded parchment. She picked it up.

The paper was blank. Until ink rose across its surface, blooming like wounds opening in skin. When the third spiral forms, do not follow the cow that cries. Beneath Kashi lies the name you buried. Remember the skull that did not burn. The words seared into her. She turned back to the mirror. Her reflection was pale, sweat-stained, her scar glowing faintly orange. But behind her, the woman in red still smiled, her spirals alive and writhing.

Outside, the city was hushed. The chants had thinned, the pyres dimmed to embers, and the river reflected only smoke. But the ghat was bleeding again.

Chapter - 2
The Unburned Skull

That night, the spiral on Aadhya's wrist stopped being an abstract ache and became a heat that lived beneath skin—an ember lodged like a compass beneath bone, waiting for breath. She lay on the narrow cot of the guesthouse and watched the cracked ceiling rotate with the slow, resigned spin of the fan. Outside, the river whispered against stone in a restless susurrus. In the mirror above the sink the woman in red did not return; still, Aadhya felt an absence like a presence—inhabiting her marrow, hitching her breath. Sleep eluded her. At first light, she dressed on autopilot: the shawl wrapped tighter, obsidian shards secreted into the pouch at her waist. The fresh spiral, newly raised and tender, had scabbed at the edges; she no longer tried to hide it. Varanasi did not permit disguises—once the city glimpsed what lay beneath, it refused to unsee.

She drifted without aim through lanes that smelled of milk, wet stone, and clinging incense. Children ran barefoot, kites snapping through sunlit air. A snake-charmer crooned to a cobra in a basket; a vendor slapped dough with the practiced violence of trade. Her feet carried her until the air thinned of tourists and thickened with something older: Harishchandra Ghat. Lesser - known. Older. Quieter. Where, some whispered, death first learned to feed on itself. The pyres here burned low and private. The shadows felt less polite.

At the edge of the ghat, her skin felt the fire as a living thing. A man crouched near the third pyre, probing the blackened remnants with an iron rod as if searching for a story in wreckage. He was older than the soot on his cheeks; a scarf hid his mouth. When she spoke the heat rose.

"Excuse me," she said. He looked up, eyes narrowed. "No closer, didi. Bones still sing."

"Looking for what?" she asked. He jabbed the rod deeper into the heap. "What doesn't burn." A thrill of cold threaded down her spine. "What do you mean—doesn't burn?"

"Not every bone turns to ash," he said. "Not every skull answers the pyre. Sometimes something refuses. It stands through the fire." His voice was a dry rasp, as if memory had already eaten much of it. Aadhya hesitated. Then, she moved closer. "Has that been happening here?" He studied her, then tossed the rod away and wiped his hands on his dhoti. "Who are you?"

"No one," she said. "Just… someone who sees things." He inclined his head as if that explained everything, then jerked his chin toward a stone shed at the ghat's edge. "Storeroom. Behind the well. Ask Gopal. He'll show you, if you're brave."

She did not know why she followed the instruction. Perhaps it was the way the man had said the word brave, soft and practical, as if bravery were a task. Or perhaps it was the spiral at her wrist, pulling like a small compass. The storeroom squatted half buried behind sacks of dung and chipped idols.

The door hung ajar; inside, it smelled of sandal paste and old sweat.

“Gopal?” she called. A thin man emerged from the gloom, wiping a rag across a hand that bore black flecks. “Yes?”

“I was told you have something that wouldn’t burn.” His gaze dropped to her wrist and lingered. Not casual. Recognition.

“You know?” she asked. “I know enough to keep quiet,” he said, turning away and vanishing into the back. When he returned, he carried a wooden box: plain, nailed tight, the wood swollen with age. He set it on a rickety table and stepped back.

“Before you open it,” he said, voice low, “you should understand.”

“Understand what?”

“That what’s inside does not belong to this time. It refused fire for a reason.” He pushed a crowbar toward her like an offering more than a tool.

She took it and pried the lid, slow as if haste might break something sacred. Dust sighed up. Expectation tangibly increased in her chest. Inside rested a single object. A skull. Whole. Unburned. Its bone was darkened, not with the crust of flame but with a sheen like old oil; it reflected light awkwardly, as if embarrassed. Most unnerving of all: a spiral was carved deep into its forehead—the same spiral that looped beneath her skin. She stepped backward. The room wavered, then righted itself. “No one touched it?” she asked.

Gopal shook his head. “We kept it, when we didn’t know what else to do. It came with a burning—two nights ago. The registers? The name got smudged. As if the man never lived.” He coughed. “We kept it. It’s… not for us.” The hollow eyes of the skull seemed to collect the light and hold it. For a moment Aadhya thought she saw movement in them—a suggestion of pupils. Then a whisper threaded from the bone, so soft she thought her own anxiety produced it.

"Vatnash… Aadhrika…"

Her hands closed on the crowbar. Heat spiked along the spiral on her wrist; a metallic tang filled her mouth. She slammed the lid shut, the bang of wood a poor punctuation for the reeling in her skull. "What do I do with it?" she managed. Gopal said nothing. From the doorway, a voice as familiar as the river said, "You listen to what it remembers."

Pandit Mahadev had followed her here. Aadhya hadn't noticed his approach, although how he came to be at the storeroom in this moment held its own sort of inevitability. He moved as if the room and its objects were his innate province; Gopal stepped aside as if by habit. Mahadev knelt by the box and unclipped a small square of red cloth. "Laal kapda"(red cloth), he murmured. Gopal handed it over like a suppliant. Mahadev wrapped the skull reverently, as one would swaddle an infant, then turned toward her. "Come," he said. "To where?" she asked. "To the well of spirals. It must speak before the sun bleeds again."

The city shifted with a thin, almost audible consent. They threaded back through lanes that reeled with morning commerce, vendors hawking, goats bleating, tourists clicking photos unaware that underfoot another narrative beat like a heart. No one noticed the blind priest carrying a skull wrapped in red. The animals did. Dogs lifted their heads with low, offended growls; a crow snapped its rhythm over rooftops; a monkey shrieked and fled from Mahadev as if recognizing a memory better left un-awakened.

They stopped in an abandoned courtyard, ringed by crumbling walls and fig trees; in the center yawned a small circular well, moss-clotted, without bucket or rope—the hollow of it falling into darkness. Mahadev handed her the bundle. “Place it on the edge,” he said. “And listen.” Her hands trembled as she unwrapped the cloth. The skull lay there, solemn and obscene. For a breath nothing happened. Then wind crawled up from the well, cool and smelling of old damp and iron. The air carried a voice—the sound of a mouth shaped at the bottom of the world. It spoke in tones that blurred with her own memory.

“The fire rejected me,” the voice said, and the timbre was hers and not hers. “Because I remembered the betrayal. The river tried to drown me. But the spiral held. You must find the others. Before they burn the name again.”

Aadhya’s palms felt suddenly slick. “Who—are you?” she whispered. “I am what you forgot,” the skull said. “I am what they silenced.” A hairline crack raced down the temple, like a fault line waking. From the spiral a single bead of dark blood—impossibly fresh—oozed and fell onto her palm. Mahadev, steady as a tide, took her hand and held it until the world stilled.

“That is the first vow,” he said softly. “The blood has returned to the name.”

The sky dimmed. A conch sounded, low and ceremonial. The blood droplet on her palm did not soak or run - it pulsed—an extra heartbeat beneath her skin, not running, not soaking—simply present, a small spiral of life, a second heartbeat beneath the epidermis. It neither dampened nor dried; it pulsed, a metronome of memory. Aadhya wanted to laugh or to flay the absurdity from the world. Instead she stood frozen, because beneath the panic there was a stir: something ancient in her answering a summons it had never known belonged to it. The skull clicked softly, as if amused or pleased. Mahadev’s hands, blind but sure, covered the bone and the sound ceased

“This one has remembered,” he said. “Now you must find the next.”

“Six more?” Her voice broke against the stones.

“Six,” he confirmed. “They will find you as the fire remembers them. The spiral will draw you. Stay close to it.”

As if on cue, the spiral on her wrist flared, an itch that was part compass, part demand. They walked back through the courtyard in near silence. The city’s light had gone copper; shadows hung longer. Even the air felt thicker, dense with ash and expectation. Mahadev guided her to a narrow door near Meer Ghat.

“This is where you will stay now,” he said. She frowned. “This isn’t my guesthouse.”

“It was for who you thought you were,” he said simply. “This is for who you will be.”

The door gave with a whisper. Inside a low room warmed faintly by a single lamp waited: a mattress, a brass water pot, a cracked mirror. On the far wall a faded mural depicted a woman wreathed in flame, a spiral blooming from her brow. It was not merely an image. It was a recognition. Aadhya did not need the priest’s words to know the figure’s name. That night she unwrapped the skull again and set it beneath the mural. She lit a diya and kept vigil. Sleep came in shards. Her dreams stitched themselves of field and ash: bodies curled like ruined dolls, a sky spangled with red lights, and a horned figure whose staff claimed the shape of a skull. He spoke with the wind, not his lips:

“Seven must return. Seven must be named. Or the gates of Vatnash open hungry.”

She woke with a scream stranded in her throat and the diya guttered out. At dawn she carried the wrapped skull back to

Mahadev. "It's yours now," she said, handing it across. "No," he corrected, placing it at his feet. "It is yours." Her fingers grazed the cloth and she could feel the small, steady pulse within—like a heart hidden inside bone. Outside, the river kept moving as if nothing had altered. But the city, the places of flame and ash, had rearranged themselves around a memory recollected.

"You received your first vow," Mahadev told her. "The vow of remembrance."

She tried to be a rational surgeon in that moment—to catalogue, to measure, to name what anatomical or neurological event might explain the sensation of blood that did not flow. The medical part of her rattled frantically. But the other part—older, less eager for explanation—stilled and listened.

"Where does this path even lead?" she asked. Mahadev's blind face tilted toward the river as though he were listening to its currents. "Toward what you buried," he said. "And the spiral will remind you when you forget." She flexed her hand and felt the tiny raised line beneath the skin—no longer merely a scar, but a summons. Outside, the city continued, indifferently, as if nothing at all had been returned to life. Aadhya stared at the wrapped skull in her hands. Her pulse refused to calm; her own breath sounded too loud inside her chest. "Is this what I've become?" she whispered to no one in particular. "Some vessel for a memory I didn't choose?"

Mahadev's head tilted, the blind eyes seeming to regard her more acutely than any sighted gaze. "No," he said softly. "You are not a vessel for what was forced. You are becoming what you buried." The words should have comforted, but instead they terrified. She wanted to scream. She wanted to reject this marrow-deep inheritance and run. But her body stood still. Because even beneath panic and denial, something hungry had begun to turn in her blood. The skull rattled faintly, clicking against the stone floor as if it applauded the recognition. The sound wasn't violent—it was rhythmic, deliberate, like two bones clapping in time with a mantra. Mahadev stepped forward and placed both hands upon the skull; at once the clicking ceased. His voice dropped lower, almost reverent. "It stirs because another waits. The spiral will not let you rest until it is found."

Aadhya's voice cracked. "There are more?"

"Six," he said, as if the number were sacred. "The city hides them in fire. You'll know when you are near one—the flames will refuse." Her throat tightened. "How can I even begin? Where do I look?" Mahadev stood as though unfolding from centuries rather than years. "You don't look," he said. "The spiral will. It has always shown the way." As if hearing him, the scar on her wrist flared with an insistent itch, a compass beneath the skin. She pressed her palm against it but the heat seeped through her hand regardless.

The air in Varanasi felt heavier when they stepped outside, as though some vast chest exhaled from beneath the streets. The shadows clung longer before dissolving; the light bled copper. She clutched the skull against her body, wrapped in red silk that now seemed less like cloth than a shroud. The weight was deceptive—light in substance, heavy in meaning. At a bend near Meer Ghat, Mahadev slowed. His blind head tilted, as if the air itself had shifted. Aadhya followed his silence, her eyes drawn to the wall beside them. The plaster was cracked, blistered with damp, but as she stepped closer, the surface seemed to move—pulsing faintly like flesh. She pressed her back against the stone before she could think better of it.

The wall exhaled. Something warm slid free from the crack, dropping at her feet with a dull clink. She stooped, trembling. A tooth. Human. Yellowed at the root, but wet with fresh warmth as if it had just left a living mouth. Her stomach lurched. Mahadev bent without hesitation, his fingers brushing it before lifting the object to her palm. “It belongs to you now,” he said. Her hand closed around it involuntarily, the heat of it seeping into her skin like an ember. She wanted to fling it into the Ganga, to scream, to deny—but her body disobeyed. Her wrist spiral burned, and in the pit of her stomach something answered, hungry. Before she could protest, the house beside them groaned. The warped wooden door creaked open of its own accord, as though inhaling her presence. No wind had moved it. No hand had touched it.

Mahadev turned his face toward her. “The city chooses when you are ready,” he murmured. Inside, a low room glowed faintly orange, walls close and breathing with warmth. A brass pot of water sat against one wall, a narrow mattress against another. On the far wall a mural, faded by time, depicted a woman engulfed in flames, a spiral blooming from her brow like a third eye. Aadhya’s chest constricted. She didn’t need to ask the name. She knew. **Aadhrika**.

That night she unwrapped the skull and set it beneath the mural. The tooth lay beside it, obscene in its ordinariness. A single diya lit the room, the flame trembling as though afraid of its own duty. She kept vigil until exhaustion betrayed her.

Her dream was no dream. She stood upon a battlefield blackened with ash. Bodies lay curled in grotesque stillness, blue fire flickering in their wounds. Above, the sky trembled with red stars that blinked in rhythm with the spiral on her wrist. From the center of the desolation a tall figure emerged—horned, robed, his face veiled in ash spirals. He carried a staff crowned with a skull. His voice rode on wind, not lips:

"If the dead are unnamed, the pit will open its mouth. If the spirals are forgotten, the hunger will not."

The words bled through her bones, and when she jolted awake, they still clung to her teeth like the taste of ash. The diya was out. Only darkness breathed in the room. By morning, Aadhya felt as though the city itself had begun breathing through her skin. The skull and the tooth weighed down her satchel unnaturally, pulsing with a rhythm that was not her heartbeat. Mahadev sat unmoving by the riverbank, crows perched around him like watchful sentinels, but when she drew closer he did not reach for the relics. Instead, his blind face tilted toward her. "You carry them now. And they carry you." The words lodged in her chest like a stone. She realized there would be no giving back, no passing the burden. The vow she had accepted had welded itself into her marrow. The thought hollowed her stomach, but she could not argue. Beneath the terror was something worse: a hunger, ancient and insistent, threading through her veins. Mahadev's silence pressed on her, patient and terrible. The city, too, seemed to listen, as though the river itself waited for her next step.

"You are not alone in this, Aadhrika."

"It doesn't feel that way," she whispered.

"Others are coming," he said. "One is already here." Her head snapped up. "Who?"

"You'll know him soon enough. His father once saw the seal—and was never seen again." Her stomach lurched. "What are you talking about?" He did not answer. Instead he turned his blind face toward the sun. "Go to Nagwa. There is a shrine hidden near the broken bridge. Few know it, fewer keep it clean. They call it the temple of the headless goddess. The second vow waits there." Her throat constricted. "What kind of vow?"

"The vow of fire."

Her pulse hammered. "You said the next skull hasn't burned yet."

"It won't," he said. "Unless you leave it there." He turned to her fully, his voice sinking into her bones. "You must choose. Burn it—or let it remember."

Twilight found her at Nagwa, where thorned trees hunched like sentinels and the temple sagged under centuries of neglect. Its steps were cracked; its idols mutilated. The murti inside had no head. Not from time's erosion—someone had severed it. The stone neck still bled red dust. A single diya, flickered weakly in one corner, flame bending low as though ashamed. The air was cold without wind, filled instead with the stillness of a place that waited. Aadhya stepped forward, cradling the skull against her chest like an offering. Before the headless murti, a shallow kund blackened by forgotten rituals waited, rimmed with ash hardened like iron. Her choice stared back at her. Burn it now, and the vow would end. Or place it here and listen. She stood trembling. And then, unbidden, words rose up her throat. Words her mouth had no right to know.

"Aag ko yaad hai, Jo mitti bhool gayi.

Jalne se pehle, Naam phir se bol." (The fire remembers what the earth forgets. Before it burns, speak the name again)

The spiral on her wrist glowed faintly red, and in her arms the skull exhaled. Not a metaphor, not an illusion—breath. Warm, human air pressed against her chest. Its jaw clicked shut. Aadhya didn't drop it. She didn't flee. She only whispered back: "I remember."

The vow sealed. The weak diya surged without touch, its flame turning blue, steady as a star. Outside, the thorned trees shivered, and something vast shifted in the shadows. She didn't return to the guesthouse. The moment she whispered those words, the city folded differently around her, as though Varanasi had been turned inside out to reveal an underside. She wasn't a visitor now; she had entered its breath. The skull in her satchel pulsed faintly, like a heart hidden beneath layers of cloth. Every step along the narrow alleys seemed guided. Cows lifted their heads as she passed; street dogs lowered theirs. At a temple gate a sadhu muttered a verse she caught in fragments:

"Jo jala nahi, Wo yaad ban gaya. Jo yaad ban gaya, Wo lautega…" (The ones that didn't burn became memory. And the ones that became memory will return.)

By the time she reached the mural room by the eighth ghat, the conch had blown three times. Her hands trembled as she set the skull beneath the painted figure again. This time the diya did not flicker—it blazed blue. The flame of remembrance. She lay awake through the night, listening to whispers from behind the mural. They braided together until they formed one word, again and again.

Vatnash.

At dawn she found Mahadev seated beside the Jnanavapi tank, encircled by crows. Seven of them, black and still, their eyes reflecting no sky. Her voice shook as she sat beside him. "It spoke again," she said. "The skull."

"What did it say?"

"One word. Vatnash."

Mahadev's mouth curved faintly, though his hands twitched as if with effort. "Then it has begun."

"What has begun?"

"The summoning." Her skin prickled. "I thought this was about memory. About vows."

“It is. But every vow is also a call.”

“To what?”

“To where the curse began.” Aadhya’s pulse quickened. “Vatnash is… a place?”

“Yes. And a name. And a wound.” His blind eyes turned toward her with uncanny precision. “You must understand, Aadhrika. The seals were not made to trap evil. They were made to bury truth.” Her breath stalled. “What truth?”

“That the Daityas did not die. They were rewritten.” The words lodged like ice under her skin. “You’re saying all of history—what we’ve been taught—is false?”

“Not false,” he corrected. “Designed. The victors wrote verses. But beneath the verses, the blood never dried.” She turned her face away, unable to meet him. The skull in her satchel seemed heavier, as though it had overheard. “What happens when I find all seven?” she whispered. “Then you choose,” Mahadev said. “To open the path to Vatnash—or to burn it shut forever.”

“But I don’t even know what it is.”

“You will.” He rose, his silhouette sharp against the tank’s reflection. “And the next shadow has already stirred.” The day lengthened with an odd heaviness, as though the city itself strained to breathe. Aadhya wandered near Manmandir Ghat, her body moving ahead of her mind. The air here was different—less frantic, less congested. Pilgrims sang in low voices beside the water, their chants weaving with the river’s slow sigh. A cow slumped beneath the shade of a neem tree, chewing as though time itself had thickened into fodder. She did not know why her steps had led her there. Until she saw the boy. He couldn’t have been more than ten, dressed in a torn yellow kurta. Alone, he sat on the steps, his knees tucked up, a small bundle in his lap. He wasn’t crying. He wasn’t restless. He was only watching the river, as if it were telling him a story.

But his eyes—Aadhya froze at them. They weren't a child's eyes. They were ancient. Heavy. And spirals drawn in ash looped faintly along his forearms, coiled in deliberate lines. She approached cautiously. "Hey… what's your name?" The boy didn't look at her. His voice came soft, steady. "They buried my father under the wrong name." The words chilled her. "What do you mean?" "They burned him," he said. "But not all of him. A tooth wouldn't burn." He opened the bundle on his lap with careful fingers. Inside was a tooth—blackened, but whole. Untouched by fire. "I took it."

Aadhya's skin prickled. "Why?"

"Because it speaks," the boy said simply. His gaze finally shifted to hers. Too calm. Too knowing. "Do you hear it?" Her throat felt dry. "Hear what?"

"The tooth," he whispered. "It keeps whispering names I don't understand."

The world around them continued as always—pilgrims washing their feet, priests chanting, a vendor hawking marigolds. None of them saw what she was seeing. None of them heard. Aadhya knelt slowly, lowering herself to his level. "Why are you alone?" He shrugged, as if it did not matter. "They told me not to speak of the spiral. They said if I kept showing it, I would go to the fire too." Her chest constricted. "Where's your mother?" The boy's voice didn't waver. "She left before the river came."

"The river?" He looked at her then, eyes glinting with something unfathomable. "She's in the breath now." The spiral on Aadhya's wrist pulsed hot, as though answering him. She swallowed, extending her hand toward the cloth bundle. "May I hold it?" He nodded once. The tooth was heavier than it looked. And the moment her skin touched it, the ghat dissolved.

Stone walls rose around her—damp, enclosing, carved with symbols she didn't recognise but instinctively knew. A pit yawned before her, swallowing light. Screams echoed up its throat, chained figures dragging themselves against iron that sang with anguish. The air was filled with a chant:

"Aag mein jo bacha, Wo sach ban gaya…" (What survives the fire becomes truth).

The vision snapped away. She was back on the steps, gasping, the tooth biting cold into her palm. The boy tilted his head. His mouth curled faintly. "It likes you." Her hands trembled. "Who are you?" He didn't answer directly. His voice was calm. Certain. "I'm the second vow." That night, Aadhya brought the tooth to Mahadev. They placed it beside the skull beneath the mural of Aadhrika. The moment the two touched, the diya flared. Not with oil. Not with wick. But with memory. A second flame burst into being—blue, high, sharp as a blade.

Mahadev's hands shook almost imperceptibly. "The second has spoken," he murmured. "The fire is learning your name again." Aadhya sat cross-legged, her palms pressed to her knees to still their trembling. The room pulsed with heat, though the night outside was cool. The skull and the tooth seemed to resonate in tandem, their spirals vibrating with a soundless rhythm—as if memory itself had learned how to breathe.

"Where are the others?" she asked, her voice breaking. Mahadev exhaled slowly, as though weighing how much truth she could endure. "Not in places. In echoes. They will appear to you as the fire remembers them. But be warned." Her eyes snapped to him. "Warned of what?"

"The closer you move toward the seventh, the more the city will resist."

"Varanasi?" she whispered.

"No," he said, his blind gaze unnervingly direct. "The other city." Aadhya frowned. "What other city?"

"The one beneath this one," Mahadev said. His hand rested lightly upon the skull, almost affectionate. "This city was built atop another. One the Devas feared. The spiral is not only a mark. It is a map." Her voice lowered to a whisper. "A map to where?" His answer was a blade hidden in velvet. "To the bones of Vatnash."

That night, her dreams altered again. No battlefield this time. She stood at the lip of an immense pit that cracked open beneath a blackened moon. Smoke coiled upward, not with the violence of fire but with the grief of something weeping. Below, chained figures writhed. Their faces were concealed behind burning masks, each one shaped differently—animal, human, hybrid. They screamed, but no sound emerged. Their agony was silent, deeper than voice. Above them floated seven flames. Each bore a spiral that throbbed faintly, like wounds that refused to close. As she watched, one flame flickered. And vanished. She woke with a jolt. Her pillow was damp—wet with blood. She touched her face. A nosebleed. The mirror across the room shimmered with condensation. No—not condensation. Something darker. She stood, trembling, and wiped her hand across its surface. Red streaks marked her palm.

A word was written there. Remember.

The morning brought no relief. The city itself seemed to acknowledge what she carried. The headlines in the newspaper piled at the corner tea stall made her heart stop. "Skull Refuses to Burn at Manikarnika Again – Fourth Case This Month."

Aadhya circled the words with shaking fingers. Her scar itched, raw and hot beneath the skin. The city was waking. So were the bones. And in the deep pit of Vatnash—the city beneath the city—something had stirred. Watching. Waiting. For the third flame to return.

Chapter - 3
The Call of Vatnash

The city had begun to stutter. Not in the obvious rhythms—bells clanging, vendors shouting, scooters coughed through alleys—but in some deeper cadence buried beneath the stones. Something under the ghats, under shrines, beneath the bones of the streets had shifted, - a tectonic remembering that made pigeons start at no breeze and shadows linger a second too long after the sun had passed. Aadhya Roy felt it in the small betrayals of perception: her reflection lagging a half-beat in the cracked mirror, as if the glass itself was relearning how to be her.

On the floor of the little mural room, the skull and the tooth sat in companionable silence. *The blue flame in the diya had not died in three nights - it needed no wick, no oil.* It burned on what it fed upon—forgotten names, husks of prayers, and the silent commerce between ash and memory. Aadhya folded her legs and sat before them with the steadiness of someone trying to habituate terror. The spiral on her wrist was beginning to peel at the edges, the skin refusing to hold the design any longer, as if it were trying to shed the map etched into her flesh.

At noon, a voice came. Not loud - not spoken to the world. It rolled in the hollow places, a low vibration that seemed to come from behind the eyes.

"Vatnash."

It was a sound like thunder muffled by earth. The skull shifted, not in the way of animate objects but in the way an old story turns its mouth toward you. Its carved spiral pointed, impossibly, toward Aadhya's heart. "Stop," she whispered to the room. "I'm not ready." But readiness is not a door a city will open; it is a threshold the city flings you across. She returned to Mahadev before dusk. He was at a narrow shrine, cut into the ghat steps, an obscure niche nobody visited. Its idol was faceless, half-erased by water and time, its sanctum clogged with riverweed. Mahadev handled it like a patient tending a relic.

"This is where the chant was first stolen," he said without turning - when the Devas made language theirs." Aadhya stood behind him, arms folded, the small man-made gestures of someone bargaining with what she could not yet name. "You keep saying things like that," she said. "Stolen. Rewritten. What do you mean?" He paused, fingers rearranging the black flowers he had offered. "Memory is not simply recollection. Memory is resistance. And what resists is what remains." She looked down at the crinkled petals and the burnt camphor. "I hear the name," she said quietly. "Vatnash. It's in my head now." He nodded as if that confirmed a pattern. "Your vows call it," he said. "Vows are voices the past uses to find its way."

"Is it a place?" she asked. "A spirit? A being?"

“It was a city,” he said. “Then it became a prison. Then a, chant. It took on whatever shape the world preferred to believe.”

“That makes no sense” she said. She wanted the practical, the anatomical explanation: why a skull whispered, why a tooth murmured names. Logic felt small and fragile here.

“Neither does your heart keeping time with a bone,” Mahadev replied. “And yet it does.” She sank beside him and watched the flame tilt obsessively sideways, as if trying to find a doorway in the air. “Tell me everything,” she said. He breathed out, a sound like a slow prayer. “Vatnash was the repository—Daitya memory made city. Flame there did not punish; it remembered. Names were kept. Histories folded into ash and housed like scripture. The Devas did not merely raze it. They transcribed it into other stories. They made words into fear, altered songs into curses. They buried the bones beneath new cities.”

“And Vatnash?” she asked. “Where did it go?” He did not commit immediately. “It vanished and left echoes: marks, a calling spiral, and fragments of unburned truth.” She told him of the pit in her dream: chains, burning masks, nameless screams. He listened without surprise. “Then Vatnash has chosen you,” he said. Chosen. The word felt like a verdict. “Chosen me for what?”

“To remember it,” he said plainly. That night, the call changed register. It came out of water. She had crept to a lesser-used bathing ghat just before midnight, the moon low and blemished with red. The Ganga lay black and patient, and the moment her feet submerged, the water warmed against her skin with an unnatural tenderness. The name came again, not as human speech but as a pressure in the bones of the river itself.

"Aadhrika."

The sound did not travel across the surface; it pulsed through the muscle of the ghats, through stone and tendon and the marrow of those standing nearby. Aadhya dropped to her knees in the shallows, breath small and ragged. "Where are you?" she whispered, though she knew answers were less likely to come as fact than as invitation. Beneath the water something moved. a chant surfacing as if a throat had been pressed beneath sand. She put her ear to the rippling skin and heard it clearly—three syllables drawn out with the slow spiral of ritual.

"Vatnash... Vatnash... Vatnash..." The sound wound itself through her body like a thread. She rose from the river soaked and trembling. Her reflection in the mirror that morning was not outright monstrous—no horns, no palisade of flame—but something about her face had lengthened, cheekbones sharpening, pupils widening in a way that made her look not fully human. When she touched the mural on the far wall that depicted a woman wreathed in flame, her fingers smeared a new grey-black across the painted eyes—ash, not paint. Her hand had done the smearing while she slept; she could not remember making the mark. The city's public pages reacted with anxious smallness. The headlines at the tea stall clustered like insects:

"Temple Bell Rings Without Touch—Dashashwamedh Ghat."

"Priest Claims Ghost Walked Into Morning Aarti."

"Another Skull Refuses to Burn."

Patterns self-assemble in human minds. To Aadhya they read like constellations forming around a single bright star: the dead were refusing the pyre; something was returning its name to the living. She took the skull and tooth back to Mahadev. When she reached into her satchel, she found another object she did not remember packing: a thin curved bone, not quite a rib, scored with faint incisions. She held it up—Mahadev's fingers brushed the etching as if they could read language by touch. "Not a rib," he said softly. "A vow-stick. We carved promises into bone before paper. The body becomes the ledger." He traced one of the shallow notches and read aloud, his voice reverent and pained:

"The third will come when the chant is heard by blood, not ear."

She thought of the river's voice the night before and felt the skin slide away from her scalp. "That's what happened," she breathed. "It was in the water."

"The flame is calling you back," he said. "Piece by piece." A letter arrived that evening—no stamp, no sender—only a spiral of red wax sealing its flap. She opened it with the same shaking fingers she'd used to pry the storeroom box. The paper inside smelled faintly of rose and ash and bore a terse summons:

You're not the only one remembering. Some of us never forgot. Come to the House of Mirrors at midnight. Alone. Bring the third.

No signature. No explanation. Her wrist's spiral warmed like a soft ember. Far across the ghats a bell tolled seven times; the sound entered her like punctuation. She wrapped the vow-stick among the skull and tooth, slid the bundle into her satchel, and folded the letter into the inner pocket of her shawl. The city readied itself the way an animal narrows before a leap. She stepped into the lanes at eleven-thirty, the night formerly ordinary now a corridor that smelled of clove, soot, and iron. Lanterns winked in empty windows. A blind been-player coaxed a hollow tune for somebody long dead. Children drew eyes in chalk on doorsteps, as if they could ward something with a gaze.

The House of Mirrors crouched west of Nepali Mandir, a swallowed – up haveli with a red curtain at its arch. Vines threaded its stone like a network of old scars. Inside, mirror shards tiled the walls, each reflecting her back but wrong—in one she was younger, in another her lips moved, though she spoke no sound, and in a third she stared back as an angular stranger she barely recognized. At the room's centre, a veiled woman sat cross-legged, spiral tattoos like inky vines climbing her fingers.

"You sent the letter?" Aadhya asked. The woman nodded but did not remove her veil. Her voice came as if from a cracked shell. "I heard the fire remember your name." The woman—Dhooni, she would later tell Aadhya, though names here were fractured things—produced another carved bone and offered it to Aadhya's palm.

"You have the third," she rasped. "But the fourth is in ash. *Burn what does not burn.*" Before Aadhya could ask more, the veiled woman gestured to a mirror and said with shuddering certainty:

"There's someone here who remembers you. He's been waiting."

When Aadhya's hand met the glass, the room dissolved into a place of black pillars and floating, watchful flames. From the inky dusk, a figure emerged—tall, bare-chested, spirals crawling across his torso, eyes like cooled cinders. He spoke as if through smoke.

"I am Agnivrat," he said.

The name landed with the gravity of myth. Memory has faces as well as rules; Agnivrat's was carved from them. He called what she carried a map and warned her that the spiral on her wrist would guide her home if the fire continued to speak. She woke back in the House of Mirrors on the floor, the veiled woman above her.

"She was one of the Ash-Keepers," Mahadev would later say. "Guardians of lost flame." Dhooni pressed a longer bone into her palm. "The fourth is in ash," she whispered before vanishing, her body crumbling like dust. The spiral on Aadhya's wrist bled a faint red as if the line were a vein suddenly opened. By dawn, when she reached Mahadev, the old man was already chanting by the tank. Crow after crow lined stone ledges, watching in silent congress. The vow-stick pulsed in her hand like a heart. "The seals are weakening," Agnivrat had told her in the mirror-vision, and the memory of that sentence crawled over her skin. Mahadev listened to her breathless report and said, the words heavy with knowledge:

"The third flame will try to rise tonight. If we fail to bind it, it will consume more than recollection—it will consume time."

She looked at him, the syllables lodging in her throat. "Time?"

"There are things in Vatnash sealed outside of time," he answered. "If the wrong one finds your scar, it will not stop until the spiral brings it to the seventh."

A cold, animal fear condensed in Aadhya's chest. She felt suddenly less like the proprietor of her life and more like the vessel someone else had intended to fill. The vow-stick warmed in her hand, an accusing, insistent pulse. Outside, the ghat breathed low and patient. The city stuttered on—but now those faltering beats had a direction. Vatnash, the name that had at first sounded like myth, had teeth. It had drawn a path, and it was calling her to walk it. The House of Mirrors was no house at all. It was a ruin that remembered itself, a husk of stone and glass trying to reassemble a memory that no longer fit. Every shard caught Aadhya at a different angle—her smile half a second late, her eyes turned inward, her body thinner, older, sometimes with spirals pulsing faintly on her throat. The further she walked, the more wrong she became.

At the room's centre the veiled woman sat cross-legged, humming a mantra without tune, without rhythm, yet heavy with intent. "Dhooni," the name fell from her cracked lips as if torn from soot. Spiral tattoos climbed her arms, black and pulsing-like veins that refused to die. "You carry the third," she rasped, her voice a brittle shell. "The vow-stick woke because the river remembered you." Aadhya clutched her satchel. "Who are you?"

"What was left," the woman answered, tilting her head. The veil shifted, revealing the scorched texture of skin branded with spirals that glowed faintly red. "Ash does not vanish. It lingers. We were made into story. But stories leak." She stood with surprising force, limping toward one of the great mirror panels. Her veined fingers tapped the surface. The glass quivered like water. "There's someone here who remembers you. He waits still."

"For me?" Aadhya's throat tightened.

"For the priestess wearing your skin," Dhooni said.

Before Aadhya could ask, Dhooni pressed a bone into her palm—longer, notched in rings like the grooves of an ancient instrument.

"The fourth is in ash," she whispered. "Burn what does not burn."

Then she gestured to the mirror. "*Step in.*"

"In?"

"Your memory can walk where your body fears."

The air dropped colder, the mirrors swelling with a pulse that felt like breath. Aadhya lifted her hand and placed it against the glass. It burned. For an instant she pulled back—but the spiral on her wrist flared, and the glass dissolved. She stood beneath a sky of cracked stone. Pillars of obsidian rose from ash-soaked ground, endless and uneven. Suspended flames hung above, hovering like sentinels, watching without warmth. The silence here was suffocating—not absence, but the pressure of a thousand unspoken names. From behind one pillar, a figure emerged. Tall. Broad-shouldered. Bare-chested. Spirals carved across his torso in jagged lines, as if fire itself had branded him. His eyes glowed like cooled cinders.

"You shouldn't have come yet," he said. Aadhya stumbled back. "Who are you?" He bowed his head with ritual calm.

"I am Agnivrat." Her breath caught. The name was one Mahadev had only spoken with the restraint of someone afraid to let history loose. Agnivrat, the Daitya warrior who guarded Vatnash until the seals closed.

"You're real," she whispered.

"I am memory," he said.

"And memory is more real than flesh."

He stepped closer. The air around him warped faintly, heat rising though no flame touched. "The spiral on your wrist is not just a scar. It is the map back. It glows now because the fire has begun to speak again."

"I need answers," she said, her voice shaking. "You will not find them here," Agnivrat replied. "Only warnings."

"What kind of warnings?" He raised one arm. The obsidian sky above them cracked wider, bleeding tar. Black liquid hissed as it dripped down the pillars. "The seals weaken," he said. "Not because you remember. Because others do. Others who never forgot. They stir now, gnawing at time itself." Her pulse hammered. "Who are they?"

"You will know them," he said, retreating into shadow, "by what they burn." The pillars shuddered. The hovering flames blinked out, one by one. The world cracked. Aadhya gasped awake on the floor of the House of Mirrors. Glass rained from the walls, shards scattering around her like fallen stars. Dhooni stood above her, one hand faintly glowing, as though she had pulled Aadhya back from drowning. "You saw him," Dhooni said.

Aadhya's mouth was dry. "Agnivrat. He said the seals are breaking. That others… are awakening." Dhooni nodded once. "The fire does not have one child."

"What do I do?" The veiled woman pressed the longer bone into her hand. "Burn what does not burn." Her body began to unravel, her form crumbling like ash lifted by wind. "Wait—!" Aadhya cried. But she was gone. The mirrors reflected only Aadhya—alone, the spiral on her wrist glowing blood-red. By dawn, she reached Mahadev. The blind priest was already waiting at the ghat, a line of black powder circling his body like a drawn ward. She spilled the story—the mirrors, Dhooni, Agnivrat's warning. Mahadev's face darkened. *"She was an Ash-Keeper," he said. "One of the guardians of the lost flame."*

"You knew of them?"

"Some knowledge cannot be told. It must be earned."

He held the longer vow-stick with shaking fingers. "They are appearing faster. Time itself is collapsing around the spiral."

"What happens when I find them all?" Aadhya asked, her voice trembling.

“You won’t need to,” Mahadev said gravely. She stared at him. “Why?”

“Because Vatnash will come to you first.”

Her skin prickled cold. That night, the third flame stirred. Mahadev led her to the southern edge of Manikarnika, where no pyres ever burned. The stones there were blacker, slick with something deeper than soot. A well sat chained with rusted tridents driven into the ground, the air rank with lime and iron. “Why don’t they burn here?” she whispered. “Because this place already remembers too much.” He handed her a bowl of lime and salt. “Circle the well. Do not let the spiral break.” She obeyed, tracing the boundary with trembling hands. The ground quivered beneath her feet. Mahadev’s chant rose, guttural and raw, not Sanskrit but something older—a tongue dragged out of fire’s marrow, molten syllables rasping like stone against bone. Her wrist burned. The chains rattled. And then it came.

A scream. Not human. Not beast. Metal shrieking as if torn underwater. The well cracked. A fissure split its sealed mouth. Ash poured out in a choking wave. From within it, a hand emerged—charred, spiralled, its fingers clawing toward her. Aadhya staggered back, heart pounding. The spiral on her wrist seared as though trying to answer.

“Hold the circle!” Mahadev shouted. She tried. The bowl shattered in her grip. The line broke. The hand reached higher.

Then—The skull in her satchel ignited. No wick. No oil. Just truth. A scream ripped the air—not from Aadhya, not from Mahadev, but from the hand itself. White fire climbed its arm like a reverse flood, devouring upward. The ash recoiled, collapsing into itself. The fissure sealed with a shudder. Silence fell. Only the skull burned, white and pure, its hollow sockets lit with memory. Mahadev dropped to one knee, his voice hoarse. “The third flame has passed.” That night,

Aadhya lay awake in her room. Her journal trembled in her lap. Where she had drawn spirals the day before, words now bled across the page in ink she had not written.

When seven chant as one, the gate will bleed again.

Beneath it, a second line: *The fourth lies where names are buried, but bones remain.* She stared until the letters swam. The spiral on her wrist throbbed like something alive beneath her skin. The night had not ended, though dawn seeped pale at the edge of the river. Aadhya sat on the floor of her room, her journal spread across her knees. The pages no longer obeyed her hand; they wrote themselves in spirals, words forming like veins beneath the skin of paper. The skull still burned white in its place before the mural, its light cold, almost surgical. It wasn't fire—it was memory given shape. And memory had teeth.

Aadhya's reflection in the cracked mirror unsettled her more than the flames. She was still herself—hair tangled, eyes ringed with sleeplessness—but the woman in red was there too, faintly, superimposed. For the first time, the figure wasn't smiling. She was crying. Black, tar-like trails streaked down her face, dripping into spirals that crawled across the glass. Aadhya reached forward, palm flat against the mirror. Heat singed her hand. She snatched it back. Then came the writing. Three words appeared across the glass, as if etched by an invisible hand:

It Comes Tonight.

The letters glowed, then bled into dripping blackness. Aadhya staggered back, knocking over her stool. Her breath caught in her throat. The room throbbed with the hum of the skull, low and insistent. She pressed her fingers to it—the vibration ceased. She pulled back—it returned. Like a heartbeat she couldn't silence. By three in the morning, the city outside had gone unnervingly still. The ghats below flickered faintly with dying pyres, but the usual cadence of chants and bells had hushed. The silence was not rest—it was vigilance. As if the city itself was waiting. Aadhya stood at her balcony. The air smelled of burnt cloves and copper. Her mouth tasted of iron. And then, at the far edge of Manikarnika, she saw it:

A figure. Tall. Motionless. Watching her. Its body looked charred, as though carved from blackened wood. The face shimmered faintly, molten, shifting like metal just pulled from the forge. It raised one hand—slowly, deliberately. The sky above the ghat flared flame-red, then collapsed into pitch black. Aadhya blinked. The figure was gone. At dawn she found Mahadev. He was waiting, barefoot, a line of black ash drawn around his feet like a seal.

"What did you see last night?" His voice carried the weight of someone who already knew. Her throat tightened. "I think… it's trying to come through." He nodded once, his blind eyes milky yet severe. "Then we must bind the gate."

"What gate?" Mahadev lifted the vow-stick Dhooni had pressed into her hand. The notched bone trembled faintly in his grip. "When fire first walked as memory, it carved doors in the bones of cities. One of them lies beneath Kashi. Beneath the ash you pass each day." Her stomach turned cold. "You mean… Manikarnika?"

"Yes," he said softly. "The well where ash does not rest. That is where it will claw first." She felt dizzy. "That's where I saw the blood. Where it began." He raised his face toward the river. "The third flame will rise tonight. If it is not bound, it will not only consume memory—it will consume time." Her voice faltered. "Time?"

"There are things buried in Vatnash that were sealed outside of time itself. If one of them finds you before the spiral is ready, Aadhrika…" His tone sharpened. "It will not stop until it devours the seventh." Aadhya's knees weakened. She gripped the edge of the shrine wall for balance. "How do we stop it?" Mahadev's expression was unreadable, but his voice was certain. "Through fire. Not the fire that destroys. The fire that remembers." That night, they returned to the southern-most edge of Manikarnika

The ground was black, slick with something that had soaked too deep to clean. The chained well loomed, sealed by rusted tridents, lime crusting its mouth like old salt. Mahadev gave her a clay bowl of powder. "Lime and salt," he said. "Circle the well. The spiral must not break." She bent low, scattering the mixture in trembling arcs. Her wrist throbbed with heat. The ground shivered. The chains rattled. Mahadev's chant thundered—an ancient tongue that ground against her ears like molten rock scraping. The well fissured. Ash surged upward. A scream tore the air—not beast, not human, but metallic, jagged, like a blade being ripped through water.

A blackened hand pushed through the seam, spirals carved deep in its flesh. "Hold the circle!" Mahadev shouted. Her bowl cracked, scattering powder. The line faltered. The hand rose higher, fingers clawing toward her chest. Her spiral seared. Her breath caught. Then—

The skull in her satchel ignited. No wick - No oil - Only memory. White fire burst forth, roaring into the night. The hand shrieked as the flames consumed it, not upward but inward, devouring the very ash it was born from. The fissure closed. The chains clanged shut. Silence. Only the skull burned—its sockets glowing with white fire, its spiral lit with unbearable brilliance. Mahadev fell to one knee, his blind face wet with sweat.

"The third flame has passed."

Later, in the small hours, Aadhya sat with her journal open. Her hand had not moved, yet the pages filled.

When seven chant as one, the gate will bleed again.

Beneath it, another line unfurled:

The fourth lies where names are buried, but bones remain.

Her pulse stuttered. The spiral throbbed against her skin like a second heartbeat. A knock broke the silence. Three sharp raps against her door. She froze. Every muscle tensed. Another knock. Slower. Measured. Her hand hovered over the satchel, fingers brushing the skull through the cloth. She forced herself to rise. The latch clicked. On the threshold stood a man. His hair was unkempt, his jaw sharp. Thin spectacles perched on his nose, and a satchel hung from his shoulder. His boots were scuffed with dust, as if he had been walking the city for hours.

He blinked at her, adjusting his glasses as if uncertain. "I'm… looking for Rekha Sinha?" Her heart lurched. The alias. "Yes," she said slowly. He extended a hand, polite, a touch formal.

"I'm Dr. Advait Rana, he said. I believe we're supposed to meet. Someone named Triveni sent me." The name cut through her chest like a blade. Mahadev. She stared at the man's hand, then back at his eyes. Something in them unsettled her. He was steady, rational—but beneath, there was the same pulse. The same searching hum she had begun to feel within herself. The spiral burned under her sleeve. She stepped aside, her voice steady despite the tremor beneath it.

"Come in."

Chapter - 4
Seven Names in Ashes

Aadhya stared at the man in the doorway, her mind struggling to reconcile the impossible calm of his face with the inferno still smoldering in her bones. The spiral etched on her wrist had not stopped burning since midnight. It pulsed faintly now, as if recognizing him before she did.

"Dr. Advait Rana," he repeated, his voice measured, extending a hand toward her. "I was told to look for Rekha Sinha - a room near the river. You're… her, I assume?" The false name felt suddenly brittle on her tongue. For a heartbeat, she considered maintaining the lie, but the heat in her blood betrayed her. She took his hand cautiously. His skin was warm, rough with calluses-and she noticed the grit beneath his nails, the fresh abrasions across his knuckles—as if he had been clawing at stone or earth. He looked every inch the archaeologist Mahadev had described, though she could not shake the question: Why send one now? Why him?

"I'm Aadhya Roy," she said finally. "Rekha was just a name I used." Advait raised an eyebrow, though his hand lingered in hers a fraction too long before letting go. "Mahadev neglected to mention you had aliases."

"He neglected to mention you at all," she countered, her tone sharper than intended. A small laugh escaped him, dry and tired. "That sounds like him." The air between them thickened with silence, neither certain how much to reveal. Finally, he tilted his head toward the narrow cot. "Are you going to let me in?" Wordlessly, she stepped aside. The guesthouse room was dim, its yellowed plaster walls flaking with age. A single diya burned near the balcony, casting restless shadows across the mirror and the floor. On the bed lay her journal, pages filled with frantic spirals and half-legible mantras. And on the stool beside the balcony—the skull.

Advait's eyes caught it immediately. He crossed the room in two steps, crouched low, and peered at it. His expression shifted from curiosity to something harder, darker. "Is that real?"

"Very." His hand hovered, then settled on the bone. He traced the faint spiral etched across the temple ridge, his face tightening with recognition. "I've seen this before," he murmured. Aadhya's breath stalled. "Where?"

"Vindhya foothills," he said, still studying it. "Collapsed cave wall. We thought they were tribal glyphs at first, but…" His gaze rose to hers, sharp now. "What is this, really?" She lowered herself onto the bed across from him. "Tell me first—what do you know about the Daityas?"

"The demon clan from the epics?" His tone was skeptical. "They fought the Devas. Lost. At least, that's the version we're permitted to believe."

"And what if some didn't lose?" she pressed. "What if they weren't destroyed at all, but sealed—scattered in fire and ash, waiting for someone to remember?" His eyes lingered on her, searching. "Are you telling me this skull belonged to one of them?"

"I don't know," she admitted, voice tightening. "But something—or someone—is calling to me through it. And Mahadev said you were meant to help." Advait let out a humorless laugh, rubbing his temple. "I study dust and bones, Dr. Roy. I don't decode voices from the dead." Her eyes darkened. "Then you may not have a choice. Because this isn't just about me anymore. It's about this city. Something is pushing its way back through." The candle flickered as if in warning, and a faint hum threaded through the silence—a low, rhythmic pulse that neither of them could place. The air felt charged, like static before lightning. For the first time, his arrogance faltered. The bravado in his eyes dulled, replaced by an unease that made the shadows in the room seem to lean closer.

They sat together until morning, the silence filled with scattered words, exchanged truths, and hesitant trust. Advait finally unrolled a long strip of cloth from his satchel. On it were rough sketches—symbols, glyphs, fragments of script copied from rock faces. One image made Aadhya's chest tighten. A circle. Seven spirals branching outward like spokes of a wheel. "This was buried beneath a site near Mirzapur," he explained quietly. "A burial mound older than any written history. We called it the 'Memory Wheel.'"

"There are seven spirals," she murmured. "Exactly."

"Seven names," she whispered. "Seven that refuse to burn." His gaze snapped up. "What do you mean?" She told him everything. The vow-sticks. The House of Mirrors. The woman called Dhooni. The Daitya warrior who had spoken through glass. The skull that whispered and the tooth that hummed. The bleeding stone at Manikarnika. She told him of fire that refused to consume, and cloth that carried voices instead of ash. By the time she finished, Advait's skepticism had eroded into something else entirely—recognition, or perhaps fear. "I've been hearing things too," he admitted at last. His voice had lost its steadiness. "In my dreams. Always the same three words." He shut his eyes and said them.

"Vatnash. Wakes. Again." The sound hollowed the air. Aadhya's blood turned cold. "That's what I heard," she whispered. "In the river. In the mirror. Even in the well of spirals." The temperature in the room dropped. The flame of the diya thinned to a blue line. Somewhere outside, a conch blew—but it sounded wrong, drawn out, like breath escaping a dying god. The weight of those words settled between them like ash too heavy to scatter. By afternoon, they were walking together along the cremation steps of Manikarnika. They stayed on the public side of the ghat, where chants rose ceaselessly, pyres cracked, and mourners wept. Yet beneath the rituals, Aadhya saw it clearly: the ash was no longer random. Symbols were appearing—letters older than any alphabet, curling inward like traps.

"They're multiplying," she whispered. Advait leaned close. "Where?" She pointed to the half-burned mound of logs. Amid the smoldering embers was a word—not Devanagari, not Brahmi, but something older. Curved. Almost serpentine. He inhaled sharply. "That's the same script carved on the wheel." Before they could approach, a small hand clutched Aadhya's wrist. She spun. A boy stood there—barefoot, skin streaked in ash, his eyes milk-white with congenital blindness. He said nothing. Only pointed toward the word in the cinders, then pressed his fingers against the spiral on her wrist.

It flared hot under her sleeve. "He sees them," she whispered. Advait crouched to meet the boy's eyeless stare. "What's your name?" The child did not answer. Instead, he reached into the pouch tied at his hip and placed a charred strip of paper in Aadhya's hands. She unfolded it carefully. A drawing. Seven figures stood in a circle, each holding a flame. Beneath them stretched a black line of ash. And under the ash—eyes. Dozens of eyes, wide and watching. Aadhya's throat went dry. "Who drew this?" The boy turned without a word and vanished into the smoke.

The river wind followed his absence—a cold exhale that brushed Aadhya's cheek like a hand made of mist. Somewhere in the pyres, a flame popped, and for a moment, the fire burned black. They walked in silence for a long while after leaving Ramesh Das's hut, following the sloping path behind the cremation grounds. The smoke here was thicker, clinging not just to air but to memory itself. The chants from the main pyres dulled into a low, ceaseless hum, like the city's pulse pressing against their ribs.

"Are you sure we can trust him?" Advait asked finally. "No," Aadhya said. "But sometimes madness sees more clearly than reason." Advait didn't argue. The boy's drawing, the corpse-wrapped spirals, the names that refused fire—it all pointed to one thing: death in Kashi was never absolute. Not for everyone. Not for the ones the flames rejected. Her scar pulsed faintly as she walked. The wind hissed between the stone alleys, carrying fragments of chants—half-formed, unfinished. They sounded as though the dead were trying to remember their verses. Mahadev's words from the banyan tree echoed back to her: *Look for the man who buried names in ledgers, not pyres. He still breathes, barely.* The path led them down into a crumbling corridor, once the service alley for the cremation ghats, now half-swallowed by banyan roots and moss. At its end, hunched in shadow, stood a sagging colonial-era building. A rusted iron sign hung crooked at the entrance:

Varanasi Nagar Nigam – Mortuary Division.

The structure leaned like a corpse refusing to lie still. Its bricks sweated damp, the plaster peeling in curls that resembled skin. Inside, the air was stale—camphor and mildew, the aftertaste of rot. Wooden racks bowed under the weight of ledgers bound in twine and leather, their pages bloated with humidity and gnawed at the corners by insects. Aadhya hesitated at the threshold. It felt less like an office than a mausoleum for words. Advait brushed past her, his lamp beam cutting through the gloom. "Come on." They found him in the back room. An old man, skeletal, wrapped in two wool shawls though the air was thick with heat. He slept upright in a chair, his head bowed, lips parted. The name *Pannalal Mishra* was stenciled faintly on the cracked wall behind him.

"Sir?" Aadhya said gently. His eyes opened slowly, milky and red-rimmed. He blinked as if waking from another century. "Haan…?" His voice rasped like dry paper. "We need to see old cremation records," she said. "Backdated. Special cases." His rheumy eyes narrowed. "Why?" Advait stepped forward, voice low. "Because something from those cases isn't gone. It's still here. And it's waking." For a long moment, the old clerk stared. Then, with surprising steadiness, he said: "People come here for peace. Some don't find it. But peace isn't searched for—it's forgotten."

"We're not looking for peace," Aadhya said firmly. "We're looking for names." That changed something in his expression. He rose unsteadily, shawl trailing, and shuffled down a narrow corridor lined with shelves. The air grew damper, heavier, as though each ledger carried the weight of centuries. Each footstep echoed differently—like the ground beneath them wasn't entirely solid, but layered with something softer, something that remembered. He pulled a red-cloth-bound volume from the bottom shelf. The cover was tied with black thread, stiff with age.

"No one asks for this one," he muttered. "Not even the priests." He untied the thread with fingers that trembled but never faltered, and opened it carefully on the desk. Each page bore the same structure: the deceased's name, date, pyre time, final rites. Most entries were ordinary. But every twelfth, sometimes every tenth, bore a red spiral scrawled in the margin. Small. Faint. Some smudged into near invisibility. Aadhya leaned over the desk, her pulse thrumming. "What does it mean?" Pannalal's mouth was grim. "It means the fire… paused."

"Paused?"

"The wood caught. The ghee hissed. But the flames refused for a breath. Sometimes a blink. The fire hesitated, as if testing the flesh. Some burned at last. Others…" His eyes darted toward the walls, lowering his voice. "Others remembered." He flipped toward the back of the book. There, circled in thick black ink, were seven entries. Unlike the rest, these weren't written neatly. Some looked carved into the page with a nail. One had been scratched so hard the sheet had torn. Each bore a different script: some Devanagari, some curling glyphs neither Aadhya nor Advait recognized.

"These seven," Pannalal whispered, tapping the page with his yellowed nail, "would not burn. The pyres were stoked three times over. The wood snapped. The flames licked. But the bodies stayed. Ash beside them. Fire around them. But them? Still." His voice trembled—not with fear, but awe. As though even the memory of those nights had teeth. Aadhya's breath came shallow. She pointed to one entry—just a circle with three dots. "What happened after?"

"We wrapped them again," he said. "Placed them back. Again and again. Some took three nights. Others were never consumed fully. Their eyes lingered. Their teeth shone through ash. But the priests…" He gave a brittle smile. "In Kashi, you do not ask the river why it flows crooked." Advait's voice was taut. "And their names? Were they recorded?" Pannalal shook his head. "Not the names. Only their refusal." He closed the ledger slowly. "Seven names. Seven pauses. That is all I can give you."

The sound of the ledger closing was too loud—like a coffin sealing shut. Even the flicker of the hanging bulb dimmed as though the room exhaled. When they stepped out of the archive, the sun was already lowering, and the river shimmered like molten glass. The air tasted metallic, like copper coins pressed against the tongue. "We have the names," Advait said. "No," Aadhya corrected softly. She held the copy of the ledger against her chest, the ink still damp. "We have fragments. Traces. Their true names are buried."

"With who?" Aadhya stopped mid-step, her gaze turning inward, as if the scar on her wrist itself whispered the answer. "The ones who cleaned them," she said. Her voice barely rose above a whisper, yet it carried the weight of revelation. The evening wind shifted, and from the ghats below came the sound of something heavy being dragged across stone. The path led them to a temple courtyard on the river's edge. Here, beneath a banyan tree, linen sheets floated in a stone basin, stained with turmeric and rosewater. A woman sat nearby on the lowest step, her hands cracked and dark with years of work. Her left eye was blind and milky, the right a piercing pale blue. A scar cut across her temple to her jaw, as though something had once tried to silence her face.

She looked up as they approached. "You're late," she said. Aadhya stiffened. "Do I know you?"

"You don't," the woman replied. "But you've seen me. In fire." Advait stepped forward cautiously. "We were told you might know about the ones who wouldn't burn." The woman's lips curved bitterly. "I remember their cloth."

"You cleaned it?"

"I tried."

"What do you mean?" Aadhya asked. Her one good eye fixed on them. "Every shroud from Manikarnika passes through water. Even the half-burnt. Even the forgotten. But seven…" She gestured toward the basin. "Seven came back black. Not from soot. From memory." Aadhya's mouth was dry. "You mean they bled into the cloth?"

"They spoke through it," the woman said. Her hand lifted to trace the scar across her face. "One whispered a name that gave me this."

"What name?" Advait pressed. She didn't answer. Instead, she limped to a bundle of cloths tied with jute and pulled out one bound in three knots. Slowly, reverently, she unwrapped it. Inside lay a long strip of linen. Blackened. Charred. Yet one section remained untouched. Along its edge danced seven marks—spirals, eyes, waves, a tongue cleaved in two.

"Only one of these is a name," she whispered. "The others… shadows. But I do not know which."

"Can we take it?" Aadhya asked. The woman nodded, though her voice turned cold. "But if it begins to burn again, you must return it. Or it will wake the one who listens beneath ash." The air around the basin seemed to thicken, and for the briefest second, the water rippled without wind. Aadhya could have sworn she saw the reflection of a face staring back from beneath the surface—a face made entirely of smoke. They walked back in silence, the cloth wrapped in jute and pressed against Aadhya's chest. The evening wind carried flecks of ash that stung her cheeks. Advait's voice was tight. "This feels like more than records. More than history." "It is," she said softly. "We're not chasing data. We're opening locks. And every lock remembers the hands that forged it."

Above them, the last light of day dimmed behind the temples, and somewhere in the distance, a conch shell wailed once—long, low, and broken halfway through, as if the sea itself had forgotten how to breathe. The woman's warning clung to Aadhya's mind long after they left the courtyard: *If it burns again, return it. Or it will wake the one who listens beneath ash.* She carried the jute-bound cloth as though it might breathe in her arms. Each step back toward the guesthouse felt heavier. The night deepened fast in Kashi—one moment the lanes glowed with lamps, the next they seemed to close in like ribs. Inside her room, she laid the cloth carefully on the bed. Even wrapped, it seemed to pulse faintly when she exhaled. Advait leaned against the window, his arms folded, his face hard. "We should catalog it. Photograph, digitize, run through the Indus script index. Maybe even spectral analysis." Aadhya shook her head. "This isn't data, Advait. These aren't symbols you crack with code. They're locks. Living ones."

"Locks to what?" She met his gaze. "To memory." Her scar itched, throbbing faintly as though in agreement. She reached out and traced one of the spirals on the cloth. For the barest second, it twitched. Like muscle beneath skin. She pulled her hand back quickly. Advait's voice was quieter now. "What are they sealing?" Aadhya whispered, "Not what. Who." The air seemed to tighten. The ceiling fan stilled mid-rotation, its shadow frozen on the wall like a black sigil. From the street below, the usual clatter of bells and distant prayers had stopped—as if the entire city held its breath. The lamps in the guesthouse sputtered out one by one. Outside, dogs howled in low unison, then cut off abruptly, as though silenced. The cloth lay between them, bound once more, yet its weight filled the room like a third presence. Advait broke the silence first. "We need help."

"From who?" He hesitated before answering. "You're not going to like it." She gave him a tired look. "Try me." He reached into his satchel, pulling out his phone. No signal, but he opened a saved file: a voice note. "I didn't show you this before," he admitted. "I wasn't sure what to make of it." He pressed play. A woman's voice filled the room—crisp, fast-paced, touched with a Goan lilt: "If you find overlapping spiral frequencies in burnt residue, that's not contamination. That's signal memory. Daitya code. It embeds like trauma. You're not listening to a name. You're listening to a survival scream." Aadhya froze. "Who is that?"

"Divyakshi Naik," he said. "AI researcher. Signal-mapping. Mumbai. She stumbled on spiral patterns in cremated remains months ago. Didn't know what she was seeing."

"And now?" "She disappeared." Her stomach dropped. "Not dead—not officially. But the last file she uploaded was titled *Daitya Core: Name 1 / Vatnash.* And then silence." The cloth seemed to pulse harder between them, as if the name itself had heard. "She knew," Aadhya whispered. "She knew one of the names." "Maybe that's what saved her," Advait said grimly. "Or what took her." Aadhya rose abruptly, clutching the cloth. "Then we'll do what she couldn't. We'll find it. We won't speak it. But we'll face it." Advait picked up his satchel. "Where do we start?" Aadhya's gaze drifted to the river, shimmering black under moonlight. "Below."

The word seemed to echo longer than it should have—as if the city itself repeated it from underground. Manikarnika's public cremation tiers had deeper layers—the old sub-chambers once used during monsoon overflow, now sealed. Her grandmother's warning returned: *When the ghat floods, the forgotten names rise from underneath. That's why the lowest chamber stays sealed. It remembers too well.* By midnight, they reached the hidden steps behind ruined temple walls. A stray dog followed them partway down, barking twice, then whimpered and bolted when Aadhya stepped into the archway.

The air grew warmer as they descended. Not the warmth of summer—but breath. As though something vast was sleeping just below the stone. The door awaited them at the bottom. Thick wood, braced with rusted iron. Red threads and knotted strings dangled across it—old protections, brittle now. Aadhya reached into her satchel and drew out the obsidian shard Mahadev had pressed into her palm days ago. Its spiral flared faintly. The locks shivered. One by one, they clicked open. Advait stared. “How—?”

“It knows me,” she whispered. The door groaned open. The sound wasn’t wood against stone—it was wet. Like a mouth opening after centuries of thirst. The sub-chamber was cavernous, the walls scorched black. A single platform rose in its center, burned nearly smooth by centuries of fire. A thin shaft of moonlight pierced the collapsed ceiling, a blade of silver slicing into the dark. Everything here was ash. Not gray, but gray-blue, as if laced with something crystalline. The dust shifted faintly when they stepped in, like it was breathing. Advait lifted his flashlight. The beam caught faint markings on the slab. Not etched, but scorched—spirals, jagged glyphs.

Aadhya’s pulse quickened. Her wrist burned hot. She unwrapped the linen cloth slowly and laid it across the platform. The stitched symbols lined up perfectly with the scorched grooves. “They match,” Advait murmured. “This isn’t just a chamber,” she whispered. “It’s a seal.” As she spoke, the ash stirred. Not from wind—but recognition. Each grain seemed to tilt toward her, as if drawn to its maker. Advait circled the platform, his lamp cutting arcs through the dust. The ash on the floor wasn’t scattered randomly. It formed a pattern—a faint ring of seven figures, arms extended toward the slab's center.

"Ritual," he muttered. "Containment." Aadhya placed her palm against the stone. The moment her skin met its surface, the air went deathly still. Even the ash froze. Then—fire. Not visible flame, but something deeper. A pulse that roared through her bones like memory set alight. The vision hit her like drowning in heat. She saw a woman in red, standing amidst a battlefield littered with broken Deva banners. Her mouth was sewn shut. Her fingers dripped with ash as she carved spirals into her own skin. Seven names bled across her arms and throat as the sun collapsed into eclipse. When the woman turned— The face was hers.

Exactly hers. The eyes were not human. They burned without light—like the memory of fire that never cooled. The scream that tore from Aadhya's throat didn't sound human. She stumbled back. Advait caught her, gripping her shoulders hard. Her pupils flashed spirals, her lips trembling with words she didn't recognize. "Aadhya!" he shouted. "Look at me!" She gasped, clutching her chest as though her ribs themselves burned. "It wasn't a name," she whispered hoarsely. "It was a person." Advait's eyes widened. "Who?" Her throat tightened. "Me." Her voice cracked on the word, and for a heartbeat, the air around them seemed to whisper it back—hundreds of her own voices, layered through time, calling from beneath the ash. They staggered out of the chamber before dawn, sweat-soaked and shaken. Neither spoke on the climb back, though both knew something irreversible had occurred.

Aadhya Roy was no longer only a surgeon, or a woman tangled in visions. The chamber had recognized her. The name written in ashes was not a stranger's. It was hers. And now, something else recognized her too. That night, she dreamed of mirrors. A circular room made entirely of reflection. Seven versions of herself stood in a ring. One burned endlessly, nothing but flame. One was bone and socket. One had no face at all. In the center stood the woman in red. This time, her sewn mouth had come undone. Her lips curled into a smile.

"One name down," she whispered. The mirrors cracked outward in unison, and the voice that followed wasn't hers anymore. It was the cities.

"Six more to burn."

Chapter - 5
The Mirror Ritual

It began with the mirror. Not the one above the sink—the small glass that had first betrayed the woman in red—but a different mirror that arrived the morning after Aadhya's sleepless night. A boy no older than thirteen stood in the doorway, framed by the alley's light. He wore a red thread on his wrist and a Hanuman locket with a cracked glass shard. Without meeting her, he propped the mirror against the far wall and said, in a voice like wind through a temple bell, "From the owner. For guests who stay more than three nights." He turned, and was gone before she could ask who had sent him, leaving behind a faint, persistent scent of camphor and turmeric.

The mirror was oval, its brass frame curling in the shape of an ouroboros—a serpent swallowing its own tail. The glass was not true; it was slightly undulated as if water had frozen mid-ripple. When she looked at it, she did not see the room so much as a delayed echo of the room: movement a beat behind, responses borrowed from an instant already passed. When it finally reflected her, it showed not who she was in that moment but who had been, or might be. It made her blink to catch the discrepancy: smiles that her mouth had not formed, eyes closed although she was awake, a slow, unsettling mimicry.

By afternoon, the mirror had become an insistence. She shoved it into the cupboard, shut the door, and walked away. When she returned minutes later, it leaned against the wall where she'd left it, as if the room itself had returned it. She breathed through the trauma technique she'd learned in therapy - inhale three, hold, exhale five -a trick to teach the body to forget its own panic. The technique steadied nothing. The mirror remembered. Her wrist flared with heat. The spiral under her skin pulsed, ever the compass. She went downstairs. Advait sat in the courtyard scribbling notes, sun burning a band across his forehead. When she told him, he stood before she finished: a scientist's curiosity softening into something almost like dread.

"You, okay?" he asked. "No," she said. The answer came blunt and honest. "The new mirror in my room—it's wrong." He frowned. "Not the small sink mirror?"

"No. This one. It came this morning." He moved with the cautious certainty of someone who had handled fragile relics at excavation sites. Up the stairs, past the cracked corridor, into the small room with its single diya flickering. The mirror sat where the boy had left it, catching the light with a wicked patience. "It's antique," Advait said after a measured silence. "Possibly colonial, maybe older. See the edges? Hand-cut. The serpent motif—" He trailed off, watching the glass as if it might rearrange itself. "It shows things that didn't happen," Aadhya said. "Or things that haven't happened yet."

He turned slowly, and in his face, she read something that surprised her: belief without theatrical doubt. "I thought you'd want me to laugh," she murmured. "No," he said. "I believe you." The confession was small but significant. It shifted the room. He reached into his bag and produced a thin silver strip—the prototype his late mentor had designed in a forgotten university lab in Delhi, a device meant to read what stone remembered. "If this is imprint - memory," he said, "I want to see its footprint." He ran the scanner across the glass. For a long moment nothing registered but the hiss of the diode. Then the needle shivered, the device producing a faint, metallic whine. It stopped, leaving the two of them listening to the after sound.

"Not a broadcast," he said finally. "A response. To us." They sat with the mirror between them, a notebook open on the bed like a small island of rationality. Advait traced the serpent frame with a fingertip as if reading braille. "In some tantric traditions," he said quietly, "mirrors were not merely reflective objects. They were membranes—thresholds between the living and the remembered. Ancestors could be invited in, or echoes trapped." Aadhya folded her arms against the heat of the midday air. "So, you're saying it's watching me." "No," he corrected. "I think it's remembering you."

She had always learned to resist sentimentality. Years in surgical theaters taught a clinician the economy of words and the discipline of skepticism. Yet the mirror tugged at a deeper ledger - the ledger written in blood, story, small stubborn rhythms of a grandmother's tales. "I had these dreams as a child," she confessed. "Fire. Spiral marks. A voice calling—Aadhrika. My mother blamed fever; my grandmother said memory leaked through." "Why did the dreams stop?" he asked.

"They didn't," she said. The admission held a bitter honesty. "I simply stopped listening." Advait produced the linen from his satchel—the cloth with seven marks they'd found at the washerwoman's. The edge with the spiral still warmed faintly when they touched it. He turned it in his hands as if it might reveal new seams. "What if the mirror is another seal?" he suggested. "Like the stone chamber - but intimate. Personal."

"Like a private conduit for the vow," she said. He looked at her, suddenly very steady in a way that made her want to trust him. "Then we don't smash it. We sit with it. Let it show us whatever it will." That night they did not leave the room. They extinguished all but one lamp and lit a ghee diya. The bed's thin mattress made a hard stage. They sat across from one another, the mirror angled toward the moonlit window so its glass caught a slender knife of light. The room contracted into the three of them—the bed, the mirror, and the silence between breaths. At first there was only their reflections and the ambient chorus of Varanasi: distant bells, the river's slow breath, a dog's single discontented bark. Then the glass darkened. Not with shadow, but with something thicker: recollection condensing.

Aadhya's reflection blinked. Once. Twice. Then did not blink at all. The woman in the mirror wore her face but not her time. She was older, mercilessly precise: high cheekbones like a carved mask, eyes rimmed in kohl, a sari dusted in ash. The spiral on the woman's wrist glowed like a coiled ember. The reflected hand rose; so did Aadhya's. But only one palm held visible flame. The mirror did not speak with sound - it spoke in montage: quick images stitched with the urgency of prophecy. Flames licking a blackened river; an idol submerged in bone; a crowd chanting a syllable until their mouths bled; two figures standing on the precipice of a cliff—one with fire, the other with doubt. The images flew like sparrows, impossible to catch and awful to miss.

Aadhya's nails dug into the sheet. Her breathing went ragged. Advait whispered something - her name? a prayer? The sound reached her like a voice under water. Her hands burned though nothing touched them. A hairline fissure threaded across the mirror's surface - a thin line that spider webbed into an almost invisible crack. The images ceased. The mirror cleared. The lamp guttered. Air returned to the room like someone hesitantly breathing again. She sat stunned, every cell feeling as if it had finished running a marathon. Her wrist's spiral cooled from an angry red to a faint ember. Advait sat with his breath returning as well; the damp of his collar testified to the night's intensity.

"What did you see?" he asked when he could speak. She did not lie. "Myself," she said. "But not who I am." "Who then?" he pressed. "Who I was. Who I might become," she answered. He reached toward her wrist, hesitated, then touched the scar with one finger. The contact was light, clinical almost, but it steadied her. For the first time in months she did not jerk away. The mirror's crack remained like a hairline scar, pale in daylight, sharp in moonlight.

She slept fitfully, while Advait's steady breathing eventually surrendered the room to something like a fragile peace. When she woke with the dawn, the wall beside the mirror bore a new mark - faint, charcoal-gray at first, then growing more distinct as the morning light strengthened. A spiral had been scribed upon the plaster, but this one branched like a fevered tree: seven limbs unfurling from the trunk. One limb pulsed faintly, a thin thread of red as if something under the wall had answered. Aadhya's fingers slid to her own scar, the sensation like a key turning in cold metal; the mark on the wall was a map, not a mirror. Under the plaster she felt a low, patient hum—not sound but intent, the city picking up a rhythm she had only just started to hear.

The guesthouse had started to remember.

Downstairs, the woman who ran the place muttered over a string of mala beads without looking up. In the common room, the incense clung like a second fog. Outside Room 3, a soft scratching sounded—nails on wood, obsessive and quiet. A professor they'd met yesterday knelt on the floor and carved spirals into the planks with his fingernail, blood beading where he pressed too hard. His eyes were silvered; when he turned his head, it went a fraction too far, as if his neck had forgotten its joints. His voice, when it came, did not belong to him. *"You've opened one name. Now six stir. Some scream. One remembers you."*

He collapsed into himself like a blown candle. They rushed to him - pulse faint, breath thin. Advait and Aadhya moved with the practiced swiftness she'd honed in operating theaters, yet this was a new kind of triage. They did what they could, called for a local doctor, and returned to their room to find a fragment of cloth on the pillow. It was a square cut from the same linen: the same characters stitched in threads that crawled like veins. When Aadhya read the shape—not in any script she recognized—an involuntary sound filled her head. A word. *Vatnash. The name landed like a stone inside her.* She recoiled. Advait caught her arm. "Same as Divyakshi's last file," he breathed. "The first name."

The guesthouse seemed thinner, as if the walls had folded to make less room for the living. The boy who brought the mirror never returned. The woman at reception stropped her words into water patterns and said nothing. On the wall the spiral-tree had grown another limb, where the plaster glowed a faint, angry red. They did not part that night. The mirror lay shrouded in a bedsheet but its presence pressed through cloth like heat. They sat on the floor, backs against the wall, one lamp between them. Neither had the small courage to turn the cloth away.

"What if this keeps happening?" Aadhya asked, in a voice stripped of bravado. Advait looked at her, the scientist's mask slipping to reveal something raw: worry, fear, and a tenuous compassion. "We find the names," he said. "We mark them. But we do not speak them." She nodded, though a portion of her tensed with a hunger she did not yet understand. The mirror had shown her what she was and what she might be. It had demanded a recognition that felt nearly like homecoming and twice as dangerous. Outside, the city breathed as if steering a great lung. Inside, the whispering began in threads—beneath floorboards, behind plaster, down the pipework of the building. Not language so much as rhythm: Vatnash, Vatnash, a heartbeat not hers.

Aadhya pressed her palms to her ears but the name threaded into her throat no matter what she did. She met Advait's eyes. "We follow it," she whispered. He nodded. They would go below, to the place's names were buried and the past had been bound. The mirror, for the moment, remained a mouth half-open behind its sheets—waiting.

The whispering did not end. It deepened. All night it crept through plaster and stone, through the grain of the wooden beams, through the bedsheets themselves. It was not sound in any ordinary sense, but a pressure—like something small and persistent pressing into the skull from the inside. Aadhya lay awake against the wall, back aching from the hard floor. Every time she shut her eyes, she felt her own breath stutter to match the rhythm of the whisper. When she opened them, she found Advait awake too, his jaw tight, staring at the shrouded mirror as if by looking long enough he could prevent it from speaking again.

By dawn, exhaustion blurred into delirium. She had not slept, only drifted in and out of shallow half-dreams: rivers running in reverse, bodies walking unburnt from pyres, her own face repeating in spirals. The light outside shifted from black to violet to gray, and still the whispers clung. When the first temple bell of morning rang, the voices fell silent. The silence felt heavier than the sound. Advait rubbed his eyes. "We can't stay here another night."

"We can't leave either," Aadhya replied hoarsely. "It will follow. You know it will." He didn't argue. He simply packed his notes, every page covered in sketches of spirals and sigils, his pencil strokes growing darker with each one as though he had been pressing against resistance. When he looked at her, his eyes seemed older. Not tired, but burdened. "We need proof," he said at last. "Not just visions. Something tangible. A record."

"Where?" she asked. He hesitated before answering. "Mahadev once told me—whispered, really—about a place beneath Mandar Kothi Temple. An archive for the unclaimed dead. Not the names sung by priests or carved into stone, but those left behind. Ash that had no family, fire that could not finish its task." She wrapped her shawl tighter around her. "And if those names are written?"

"Then we'll know who refused the fire." They left just as the city began to stir. The old woman at reception didn't look at them, her lips moving silently over some private tally. Aadhya paused at the desk, waiting for a word, but none came. The woman's fingers moved through invisible beads, and for the briefest moment Aadhya thought she saw ash smudge the woman's cuticles, as though even she had been sifting through remains.

The streets were damp with night's condensation, and dogs prowled restlessly, their eyes too bright, their tongues lolling in silence rather than panting. The alleys narrowed the further they walked, winding like intestinal passages, every turn carrying a smell: turmeric from a kitchen, stale milk from a locked dairy, the acrid tang of old incense ground into walls. Advait led, chalk in hand, marking the stone as they passed—protective spirals, though faint, as if he didn't entirely trust the ritual yet. By the time they reached Mandar Kothi, the sun had barely cleared the horizon. The temple had long ceased to function, swallowed by banyan roots that reached like skeletal arms across its crumbling facade. Two stone lions guarded the gate - one headless, the other eyeless. Its sockets were dark and waiting. The doorway bore no padlock, only cords of turmeric-stained thread knotted into a complicated pattern. Seven knots, like small hearts tightened and hardened by time. Aadhya touched one lightly and drew her hand back. It was damp, though no rain had touched it.

"It remembers," she whispered. Advait produced a blade from his satchel. "And it wants to be unremembered." He cut one knot, then another. On the third knot, the cord bled. A single drop, dark and viscous, falling to the earth. It hissed when it touched the stone. Aadhya shuddered. Advait's jaw tensed, but he didn't stop until all seven knots fell limp. The door opened by itself, timbers groaning like lungs emptied of air. The descent was narrow and spiral, stone steps slick with moss. Their lamp cast a trembling amber halo that exaggerated every shadow. The air thickened as they descended - the temperature neither warm nor cold but wrong - the kind of air that felt as though it had been sealed away for centuries, stagnant but restless.

At the base, the chamber revealed itself. Shelves were carved directly into stone walls, lined with scrolls and cloth bundles. The place had once been a fire-ritual sanctum; its corners still bore remnants of brass bowls and charred wood. But the bowls were blackened with something older than ash. Not burnt ghee. Not camphor. This was bone-dust, ground so fine it shimmered faintly under lamplight. The shelves breathed like old lungs; the dust lifted and fell in a rhythm that pretended to be wind. The dead were not sleeping—they waited. "Scrolls catalogued," Advait whispered. His voice echoed strangely, stretching too far. "Each alcove marked by sigil. See? Spirals, curves, lines—"

Aadhya moved closer. The central pedestal at the chamber's heart was bare. But when she laid her hand upon it, she felt warmth. Stone had no right to pulse like this. Not after centuries. The spiral etched into the pedestal's center glowed faintly when her palm pressed against it. The chamber exhaled. Dust lifted from the shelves. The stone cracked down the middle, and from within rose a scroll bound in red thread, as if birthed by the pedestal itself. Advait caught her arm. "Let me." His tone was careful, almost reverent. He untied the thread. Inside lay a single sheet of parchment, darkened with age yet vivid as though written that very morning. Ink curled across the surface in spirals and strokes.

Three lines. One mark. And a name. Neither of them spoke it, but it rang in their bones regardless. Vatnash.

The chamber groaned. Shadows collapsed inward, pressing toward them. One shelf cracked open with a soundlike ribs breaking. Ash spilled out—not loose, but shaped. A skull tumbled forward, striking stone with a dull crack. It was not cleanly burned. Flesh clung, blackened and shriveled. In its sockets, something pale pulsed—soft, obscene. And from the spiral branded into its forehead, red threads unspooled like veins, reaching outward. Aadhya stepped back instinctively. "Is it—?"

"Yes," Advait whispered. "Unburned. A name without fire. A soul still waiting." The skull lifted slightly, as though breath stirred dust beneath it. Aadhya froze. Then came the voice. Not through air. Not through sound. But directly into her marrow.

You opened it. You bled it. You are the vessel. And the flame remembers. Her wrist seared. She gasped, clutching at it. Her lips parted involuntarily, breath shaping the first syllable - "Vat -"

“Don’t!” Advait seized her, yanking her back. The word strangled in her throat. At once, the skull shuddered and collapsed. The half-burned skin flaked into ash, scattering like insects fleeing light. But the presence remained. It had heard her almost-name. It had marked her. On their way out, the temple rewarded—or cursed—them with a relic. In an alcove near the door, where vines had hung limp when they entered, now rested a mask. Ancient, metallic, its surface dark but faintly glimmering. The face it bore had no eyes and no mouth: only smooth, terrifying anonymity. A Daitya war-mask. Advait reached out, hesitated. It’s for you, ‘he said softly’

“No.” Her voice was firm, but already her hands disobeyed. She lifted the mask. Cold at first, then warm, as though weighing her. When she angled it toward the lamplight, her reflection glared back—but not her. A woman with fire in her hair. Ash across her cheeks. A name lodged in her breath.

Aadhrika.

The name burned without sound, pressing into her. She lowered the mask quickly, but its weight lingered in her hands. They left the chamber before sunrise. The streets outside were quiet, but too quiet: even the stray dogs had hidden themselves, leaving only shadows along walls. A cat followed them briefly, its pupils spiraled into coiling patterns, before vanishing into an alley. The old woman at the guesthouse scribbled shapes in water on the floor as they passed. She didn’t look up. She didn’t need to. In her room, Aadhya placed the mask in a locked drawer, though she knew locks meant nothing. The scroll she wrapped in three layers of cloth and buried in her satchel. Still, the mirror hummed faintly through its sheet, like a mouth behind gagged cloth. And when she finally closed her eyes, she burned—not in agony, but in recognition. In becoming.

Somewhere in the labyrinth of her half-sleep, she whispered into the dark: "One name." And in the silence that followed, something listened. *Six more.* The guesthouse no longer felt like shelter. By the time they returned from Mandar Kothi, dawn was breaking—but the building seemed to resist light. The courtyard was damp with shadows that refused to recede, clinging to pillars like bruises. The old woman at reception did not greet them. She sat motionless at her desk, lips pressed shut, her fingers moving rhythmically across an invisible mala. On the counter before her rested a shallow bowl of water. Spirals floated on the surface—not drawn, not inked, but forming and reforming by themselves, vanishing as soon as the light touched them.

Advait tugged Aadhya gently toward the stairs. "Don't look at her," he murmured. But Aadhya couldn't help it. The woman's one open eye caught hers for an instant. It wasn't blind. It wasn't even human anymore. It was silver. In their room, the mirror still shivered faintly beneath its shroud. The cloth covering it twitched like skin breathing. The air was heavy, metallic, as if the walls themselves were sweating iron. They collapsed onto opposite sides of the bed. Neither spoke at first. The scroll wrapped in red thread lay on the table, and the mask remained locked in the drawer—but their presence pressed into the room as palpably as breath. Finally, Advait broke the silence. "If the name itself can reshape this house, what happens when we find more?" Aadhya pressed her palms against her temples. "It doesn't reshape. It remembers. Every surface is becoming memory. That's why the walls breathe. That's why the old woman's eye turned." Advait leaned forward, voice low. "And if the guesthouse remembers too much?"

She didn't answer. They tried to sleep through the day, but rest was impossible. Every few minutes, Aadhya woke to small sounds—the scratching of nails on wood, whispers that rose from floorboards, the faint creak of doors opening though no wind stirred them. When she rose once to wash her face, she found her reflection delayed again, half a second behind, mouth opening when hers had already closed. She covered the sink mirror with her shawl and returned to bed trembling. By dusk, they both gave up. Neither could bear another night within those walls. Advait paced, restless. "We can't keep reacting. We need answers. Documentation. Divyakshi might have known more than Mahadev ever told us."

Aadhya frowned. "You said she disappeared."

"Yes," he admitted. "But not before leaving fragments. Datasets. Spiral traces encoded in crematory ash. If anyone can show us how deep this goes, it's her." He pulled his notebook closer, flipping through scrawled diagrams. "Her last message said: Daitya Core: Name 1 / Vatnash. She saw what we saw. Maybe more. If we can find where she was working—" "—then we'll know what took her," Aadhya finished quietly. That night, before leaving for the station, they decided to check the guesthouse one last time. Not out of obligation, but necessity. If the house had become a vessel for the first name, they needed to see how far it had spread.

Room 3—the old professor's quarters—was quiet. Too quiet. The door creaked open at Aadhya's touch - a sound too alive for dead wood. He was still there. On the bed. Breathing shallowly. His eyes no longer silver, but dull, clouded, as if whatever had spoken through him had receded. But the walls… The walls were covered. Not with chalk. Not with blood. With ash. Fine gray streaks, curling into spirals across plaster, gathering into patterns that resembled maps. Some led inward. Some branched outward. One wound directly around the professor's body, a coil drawn tighter and tighter, as though preparing to crush.

Aadhya touched the mark nearest the door. Ash clung to her fingertip. It was warm. "He won't last long," Advait whispered. She pulled her hand back. "Then we shouldn't be here when he doesn't." They returned to their room only to find it changed again. The spiral etched into the wall the night before had grown. No longer just branches. Now a tree, its limbs reaching toward the ceiling, each tipped with a glowing ember. Two burned red. The rest pulsed faintly, waiting. Advait's jaw tightened. "It's counting with us." Aadhya couldn't take her eyes from it. She felt the pull in her bones—the longing, the recognition. It wasn't threat. It was memory clawing back into flesh.

She whispered, "What happens when all seven burn?" The room didn't answer. But the mirror shuddered beneath its shroud. They left at midnight, satchels heavy with the scroll and the mask. Neither spoke as they walked through lanes slick with damp. The city had shifted. Dogs followed them without barking. Pigeons turned in slow circles above. On the ghat, a Dom's torch flared blue before sputtering back to normal flame. When they reached the station, Aadhya felt her wrist sear once more. She turned, half-expecting to see the woman in red standing among the crowd. But there were only pilgrims, chai-sellers, travelers yawning into the night. Still—her reflection in the train window smiled back at her, lips moving in silence.

They boarded just before dawn. The whistle pierced the air like a ritual blade. Aadhya pressed her forehead to the cool glass, watching Varanasi recede into the mist. She should have felt relief. But instead, she felt tethered. This city wasn't done with her. Its ash clung to her breath, its flames followed in the mirror of her blood. And though she was leaving, she knew with the certainty of fire: she would return. For now, the train pulled forward. Mumbai awaited. Advait leaned across the aisle, speaking low so no one else could hear. "If Divyakshi was right—if the spirals are code—then we're not dealing with superstition. We're dealing with something woven into the memory of matter itself. Something alive in signal."

"And if she was wrong?" Aadhya asked, voice steady though her wrist burned. "Then we'll find her body," he said grimly. Aadhya closed her eyes. For a moment, she almost drifted into sleep. But just before she did, she heard it. Not outside. Not whispered from walls. From within. A voice threading directly into her marrow.

"Six remain. And one remembers you still." Her eyes flew open. Advait was already watching her. He hadn't heard it. The train thundered on, carrying them westward. Behind them, Varanasi smoldered. Ahead, another city of fire waited to be unmasked.

And in her chest, the spiral pulsed like a second heart. The sound of the train dissolved. The whistle, the rails, the wind—all gone. Aadhya opened her eyes to the same dim room, the same half-spent diya trembling near the mirror. The shroud over it was still, yet the air thrummed faintly—as if it had exhaled the dream back into her. She had not left Varanasi. The journey she'd seen was the mirror's doing—a glimpse, a warning, or perhaps a memory yet to occur.

Chapter - 6
Skulls That Whisper

The whisper hadn't stopped. Even after the mirror cracked, after the woman in red dissolved into smoke and silence, Aadhya could still hear her—thin as a thread, curling behind her ears, brushing the nape of her neck like cold breath. She tried sleep. She tried silence. She tried the old landlady's suggestion: burning camphor by her bedside. Nothing worked. If anything, the camphor only sharpened the voices. The smoke seemed to make the whispers multiply - and now the skulls themselves were shifting in ways she could not dismiss.

They sat at Manikarnika in rows - half-buried in ash and time, fossilised in the soot-lined alcoves behind the pyre steps. She remembered them from childhood visits: blackened things, long stripped of meaning, sometimes hawked by priests to gullible tourists as "blessed relics." Objects of trade, not reverence - until, two nights ago, a subtle motion made the relics feel less like props and more like witnesses. She was walking past the ghat, scarf pulled tight against her face to keep out the river smoke, when one of the skulls turned. Only slightly. A tilt, barely perceptible - yet enough to notice;

sufficient to change everything. She hadn't told anyone. Not Advait, whose presence had become strangely anchoring—the steady cynicism, the way he lit cigarettes as though defying the city itself. His quiet made her feel less adrift. But some part of her knew this wasn't delusion, wasn't exhaustion. What she felt was a slow realignment of the city's boundaries: someone—or something—was learning to look back.

That morning she returned. Alone.

The fires still burned. Another body lay consumed, its ribs collapsing inwards like a house in ruin. Priests scraped the remains with long iron rods, pushing ash into the Ganga with a dispassionate rhythm. The air was thick—human smoke, sandalwood oil, and the wet breath of the river. Aadhya walked behind the platforms, ducking under a rusted iron chain into the ossuary alcove. The skulls were piled there, dozens upon dozens, stacked like discarded offerings. Jawbones missing. Cracks like veins of marble.

And one was humming. Not loud, but low—an unbroken bone-deep vibration, like a temple bell rung underwater. She pressed her palm to the grill - the iron burned cold. At the center of the pile, one skull trembled, a small one with a fracture carved across the right eye socket. Her throat tightened. She took a step back. Behind her, someone cleared their throat. Aadhya turned. An old woman stood at the edge of the alcove, her saffron shawl stained with damp smoke, a crooked stick in her hand. Her eyes were cataract-clouded; toenails yellow and curling; lips cracked in a permanent, crooked smile.

"They've chosen you," the woman rasped. Aadhya froze. "Who?" The stick tapped against the stone. Once. Twice. *"The Vaatika."*

"I don't know what that means."

“No,” the woman said. “You don’t. That’s why you’re still standing.” Then she turned and began walking away, her stick clicking out a rhythm that echoed against the ghat steps. Aadhya’s chest tightened, but she followed. They wound deeper into the old cremation quarter, past locked shrines whose doors had been nailed shut, past pyres blackened by old rains. Dogs barked in the distance, a chorus of alarm. The air shifted. A scent rolled over the stone—singed cloth, sour milk, something that didn’t belong to the living. The old woman stopped near a wall overgrown with moss. She tapped one brick twice. Then once again.

Stone shuddered beneath their feet. A grinding sound groaned through the ground. A rectangular slab rose, dust trembling loose, revealing a narrow staircase descending into dark. Air rushed up—stale, metallic, the smell of clay and long-buried bone. Aadhya stumbled back. “I can’t go down there.” The woman tilted her head. Her cataract eyes gleamed faintly in the smoke. “You already have.” Before Aadhya could ask, the woman limped away, dissolving into mist and shadow. The entrance yawned open. And the whisper returned.

“Aadhrika.” She descended. The steps were slick, uneven, closing in on her shoulders. Darkness pressed like weight. Her phone torch cut a feeble path through air that had not been breathed for centuries. At the bottom, the tunnel widened into a circular chamber. Spiral marks were drawn into the stone in ash and dried blood. In the center, on a carved pedestal, sat the cracked skull—the hummer. Its sockets faced her directly. And then it spoke. Not aloud. Not in words. In memory. She was no longer in the chamber. She stood in fire. A vast stone hall encircled her, its walls burning but never consumed. The floor carved in concentric spirals. At the center: a woman. Her own face. Younger. Wreathed in red and gold. Spirals tattooed across her throat and shoulders. Bone fragments strung as a necklace around her neck.

Priestess. Blood speaker. Aadhrika.

The figure stood above a pit filled with skulls, whispering a chant too old for comprehension. Voices answered—male, broken, desperate. Something was being called. Or returned. The skulls rose, black wings unfurling like crows. One turned toward her. And wore Advait's face. Aadhya gasped and fell back against the pedestal. The vision dissolved. The chamber returned—stone, ash, silence. The skull sat motionless. But from the shadows, another figure emerged. A girl - no older than eight, barefoot; her red kurta hung in tatters, centuries old, her eyes were wholly black, entirely fixed.

"You shouldn't have remembered," the girl whispered. Aadhya froze. The girl lifted one hand, pointing to her wrist. The spiral scar bled again. "The next whisper will not be so kind." And then she vanished. No sound. No footstep. No trace. The chamber pulsed with a sudden heat; above her, the stone slab began to close. Panic surged. Aadhya scrambled, clawing at the steps as the ceiling sank. She shoved her shoulder into the gap, lungs heaving, and rolled through just as the slab sealed shut with a hollow thud. Sunlight blinded her. The city carried on, oblivious—chanting priests, the churn of boats, children chasing kites. But the whisper hadn't left. It followed her back to the guesthouse, curling beneath her skin, muttering in her reflection. And that night, when she washed the blood from her wrist, she saw it. Behind her, in the mirror—

The cracked skull perched on her bed, smiling. The skull was still there in the morning. It sat on her pillow like a sleeping crow - cracked, grinning, tilted toward her as though it had spent the night watching her dream. The sockets stared blankly, yet expectantly. The spiraled burn along its temple had blackened, the edges charred like wood pressed too long against flame. Aadhya's throat clenched. She wanted to scream, but the air around her had thickened, suffocating her voice. It was as though the city itself had wrapped gauze around her vocal cords. The silence was heavier than sound. She reached for the skull with trembling fingers. Bone should have been cold, inert, final - but it was warm.

The moment her skin brushed the fracture at its temple, her vision ruptured. Flames surged upward, red-black and hissing. Screams, muffled as if smothered in soil. Seven figures cloaked in saffron and ash circled her - chanting not forward, but in reverse, syllables unraveling like rope pulled against the grain. A mirror shattered inward, shards slicing into her skinless self. Beneath the collapse, something ancient exhaled—a slow, deliberate, hungry breath through the barricade of ash.

She staggered back. Blinked. The skull was gone. Only its impression remained—on the bedsheet, in her lungs, in the itch beneath her skin. Her stomach twisted. She barely made it to the basin before retching bile into the drain. At breakfast, she sat across from the Sens, the old Bengali couple who occupied the room beside hers. Mr. Sen spoke in wheezing half-coughs that turned each sentence into a riddle. Mrs. Sen adjusted her red-framed glasses constantly, peering at Aadhya as though she were a specimen under glass.

"You don't look rested, beti," Mrs. Sen said. "Nightmares?"

"I don't dream," Aadhya lied. Mrs. Sen pursed her lips. "Kashi dreams for you, whether you ask or not." Mr. Sen chuckled low. "Sometimes it even sends you letters." He tapped a folded newspaper with gnarled fingers. "You heard about last night? A rickshaw-puller near Harishchandra Ghat. Dead. Skull cracked open." Aadhya froze mid-bite. "Cracked… how?"

"Like a coconut," Mrs. Sen whispered. "No injury. No blood spilled. Brain intact. Just split." Mr. Sen leaned close, his breath sour with tobacco. "The police call it heat stroke.

Idiots." From behind, the chai-walla boy—barely eleven, hair matted with sweat—murmured under his breath: "Not heat. The Bhairav Path is waking." Everyone at the table turned. The boy stiffened, eyes wide. "I—I heard the priest say so. The one with no tongue. He lives behind Nepali Mandir. They say he speaks in smoke now." Aadhya's stomach sank. This wasn't just her anymore. The whispers were seeping outward.

By afternoon, rain struck the city. Not a drizzle, but a sudden monsoon downpour - as though the heavens themselves had flinched. The ghat stones gleamed, slick as glass. The dogs scattered, tails low. The air smelled of wet soot, grief, and something metallic. Aadhya returned to the ossuary breach Mahadev had once described. Her fingers remembered the stones. She pressed them and found the opening. But this time she wasn't alone. A man stood just within the tunnel - cloaked in saffron, robes far too clean for this part of the ghat, his spine straight as a pillar, hands folded behind his back. When he turned, she noticed his teeth first - too many, filed sharp, predator-white.

"Welcome, *Aadhrika,*" he said, pronouncing her name in a way that made her bones recoil, as though he had reached inside her throat and twisted the syllables. Her breath snagged. "How do you know—" He raised one hand. "Your name remembers you, even if you do not."

"Who are you?" she asked, voice cracking. "I am called Brahmanand Ji," he replied, bowing slightly. "But that name is borrowed. Like yours. Once, I was a priest. Now, I am the guardian of the Vaatika's edge—the silence between burnings." Behind him, the tunnel seemed to breathe. "You're a priest?" she managed. He laughed. The sound was wet, cracked, joyless. "Once. Before my tongue was split for uttering a shloka not meant for this yuga. Since then, I have listened more than I speak." His eyes gleamed, not with reflection, but with absence—voids that seemed older than gods.

"I saw a skull," Aadhya whispered. "On my bed. Marked with the spiral." Brahmanand's teeth flashed. "Then the Vaatika has begun whispering again."

"What is the Vaatika?" "You ask well," he said. "But too soon."

"I need answers."

"You need memory," he corrected, voice low.

"Not the fragile kind stitched to your passport.

The marrow-deep kind, etched in fire and bone." She followed him deeper. The air chilled. Not the cool of stone, but the uncanny cold of entering a mouth just before being swallowed. The passage opened into a chamber unlike any she had seen above ground. Circular. Ritual. Seven stone plinths stood like the petals of a flower; black soot clawed up the walls. The smell of charred bone clung heavy, thick enough to taste. Above each plinth, spirals were etched. Names—not in any script she knew, but curling, ancient, self-consuming.

"These are the Seven Who Remember," Brahmanand said. His voice was almost reverent. "Their bones were never found. Their skulls never split." Aadhya's legs trembled. "Why?"

"Because they were not fully human." Her stomach lurched. "And what am I?"

Brahmanand said nothing. He walked to the central plinth, placed a finger against its blackened stone. It hissed. The air shimmered. And then it appeared. A face above the plinth, wavering like flame. Her face. Younger. Spiral tattoos coiled around her collarbone, ash-rimmed eyes, mouth painted in vermilion. "No," she whispered.

"This," Brahmanand said, "is the shard of memory the city cannot swallow. You walked this chamber once, Aadhrika. You lit the sixth pyre with a chant no Brahmin dared to hear." Her breath came ragged. *"This is hallucination." "It is worse," he said. "It is truth."*

She shook her head. "Why show me this?"

"Because the ghat bleeds again. And that means she is coming."

"Who?"

Brahmanand leaned close. She smelled sandalwood rotting into blood. Between his sharpened teeth, a brownish-red tinge gleamed. "The one whose skull was never burned." His voice fell to a hiss.

"The Whispering Bride."

A sound slithered through the chamber then. Wet. Ragged. Like cloth dragged over stone. A whisper.

"Adhira…"

Aadhya turned. From the shadows, something crawled into the torchlight. Not walked. Crawled. Limbs bent wrong. Head twisted too far. Hair matted with blood. The face a ruin of ash and shattered teeth. Spiral tattoos crawled across her arms. Aadhya's own mark flared. "She remembers you," Brahmanand whispered. "But not fondly." The thing surged forward. Aadhya turned and ran. The chamber dissolved into blur. The tunnel walls scraped her shoulders. Smoke clawed at her throat. Behind her, whispers sharpened into screams. She burst into sunlight, stumbling into the gali. Fruit carts toppled. A child screamed as she collided with him. Somewhere above, a temple bell rang thirteen times. She didn't stop until she reached Assi Ghat, collapsing at the steps, retching into the river. But even then, the whisper clung.

"The sixth name burns last."

Night bled into the walls of the guesthouse. Not metaphor. Reality. The plaster itself darkened, veins of shadow swelling beneath the surface like blood forced through capillaries that should not exist. The air was heavy, damp, saturated with sandalwood smoke laced with something raw—sinew, old marrow, the sourness of bones long denied burial. Aadhya had bolted her door. Wedged towels into the cracks. She hadn't spoken to anyone since staggering back from the Vaatika—not even Mrs. Sen, who had knocked thrice and left a steaming bowl of khichdi on the floor outside like an offering to a reluctant god. Ants had already begun to circle the dish.

Inside, she stood before the mirror. Not to see herself. But to see her. The woman in red. She appeared with unsettling regularity now—first in the basin mirror, then in the silvery reflection of the guesthouse window. Now she stood directly before Aadhya in the bedroom glass. Head tilted. Fingers trailing ash. A hollow silhouette clothed in fire-stained robes, her presence flickering like an old film played on damaged reels. Aadhya's scar burned faintly on her wrist. The ember of something waiting to reignite.

"Say it," the ash-woman whispered. The voice came not from the glass but from the wood behind it, from the wall itself—as though the mirror were only a skin stretched across something deeper. Aadhya's knees buckled. "What do you want from me?" The figure lifted her hand. In her palm glowed a severed tongue, blackened and shriveled, yet marked with a spiral burned into its underside. The glass cracked. Once. Just once. But the shattering rang like thunder, rattling the books from her shelves, making the floor quiver under her bare feet. The bulb above her fizzed, flared, and died.

Darkness. But not silence. Whispers. Dozens. Hundreds. Thousands. They seeped from the ceiling cracks, murmured beneath the floorboards, slid from the hollow of the walls.

Skulls. Speaking. Ash-throated voices reciting names half-swallowed, shlokas unraveled in reverse, funeral chants spat back into breath.

“Aadhya… Aadhrika… Adi-Ra…” Her name split and multiplied, like a serpent shedding skin after skin. Each version heavier. Older. She pressed her palms to her ears, but the voices slipped through, intimate as breath on her neck, fingernails grazing the cartilage. Then one voice cut through. Deeper. Older. Venomous, dripping with the weight of a forgotten throne.

“Speak the name, child of ash. Speak the name that split the sky once before.”

The floor beneath her ignited—not with fire, but with light carved into form. A spiral blazed outward from her feet, lines of flame licking across the bed, walls, and ceiling until the entire room pulsed like a living sigil. Her mouth opened. Not willingly. Her jaw moved as if memory itself had reached inside her skull and pulled the strings. Syllables tumbled forth, guttural, alien. Her body remembered what her mind refused. The mirror didn’t crack this time. It opened. The ash-woman stepped through - no sound as she emerged; no footstep, no breath; only the hiss of fire dying in water. Her face was clearer now - and worse, because it was no face at all. Just bone streaked with soot, two sockets leaking a dark vapor, a mouth sealed yet whispering ceaselessly. Her robes clung heavy, sodden with something too thick to be blood. Her hands moved with the stiffness of a corpse remembering how to mimic the living. She reached out.

Aadhya couldn’t move. Couldn’t run. The spiral on her palm blazed like molten iron, and the woman raised her own hand. They mirrored each other. Scar against scar. Burn against burn. Then the names began. Not spoken aloud, but poured directly into her marrow. Seven. Each syllable was a wound. The first name clawed away her father’s voice from memory.

The second blurred her childhood into haze. The third stole the warmth of her mother's touch. By the fifth, she no longer remembered why she had been afraid. Then the sixth. It cleaved her chest in two. She screamed, though no sound escaped. The voice that uttered it was not the ash-woman's. It was her own. From deep inside. From a place older than her body, older than her birth. The ash-woman smiled with hollow gum, and whispered the last name.

"Daityagarh."

The lights came back. The mirror was intact. The room, untouched. Her scar had vanished - skin smooth where it had burned for years. And she was alone. Utterly. Terrifyingly. Alone. Except— On the floor, where the spiral of fire had burned, a skull remained. Small. Child-sized. Carved with seven spirals etched into its crown. One for each name. Its mouth opened. Something fluttered out. A scrap of cloth, brittle and brown with age. Aadhya bent to pick it up, fingers shaking. She unfolded it slowly. A name written in vermilion. Not Aadhya Roy.

Aadhrika Shatrulokini.

Her breath fractured. Memory surged—not whole, not complete, but enough. The sixth pyre had never lit. Because she had refused to speak the name. Because it had belonged to someone she loved. Someone she betrayed. Someone who was returning. Not as whisper. But as fire. She sat all night with the skull - knees drawn to chest, eyes fixed on the spirals carved into its crown. The whispers had ceased, but the silence was worse. Thick. Expectant. It pressed against her skin like unseen hands. When dawn finally broke, Aadhya rose. The city outside was waking—choked bells, bargaining voices, the splash of oars on gray water. But inside, only one thought burned through her skull like an ember refusing to die: She had to find the seventh name. Before it found her.

Chapter - 7
The Unwritten Shloka

The havan kund had gone cold; only embers remained, pulsing with the hesitant rhythm of wounded hearts. A brass diya beside the pit swayed minutely, though the air in the room was still - as if some invisible hand were testing the balance of things. Aadhya and Advait sat on either side of the empty pit, the silence between them no longer neutral but tactile—thick as damp cloth, clinging, intimate. Outside the alley behind Pandit Mahadev's modest dwelling a fog rolled in, sudden and fetid. It smelled of old incense - yes - but beneath it lay the tang of rotting neem bark and turmeric—and another scent Aadhya could not name: coppery and wet, like a wound left to dull itself. She watched Advait bend forward, eyes following the faint burn-marks cut into the stone floor—an unfamiliar *glyph*: a curve interrupted by three downward strokes.

"That's new," he murmured.

"No," Pandit Mahadev replied from the dim end of the room. His voice was the rasp of wind through dry leaves. "It is very old - newly awakened, perhaps." Mahadev did not lean in to inspect the mark. His milky white eyes were fixed beyond them, seeing something else. "What does it mean?" Advait asked, hoarse from hours of chanting and inhaling smoke. "The syllables you spoke are not of the Vedas," the old man said. "They belong to a tongue older than Rigveda. You did not chant them—something used your mouth." Aadhya's fingers tightened on her shawl. She remembered the fire that had leapt—impatient, upright—when the sound had escaped her. She had not chosen the words. A phrase had torn itself from her lips: jagged, sudden, as if stolen from the memory of a body that no longer belonged to her. "I didn't know what I was saying," she confessed. "But the fire did," Mahadev answered. "So it answered."

Advait traced the glyph with a gloved fingertip. "You said these were Daitya words," he said. "Pre-Vedic. Why now? Why her?" He looked up. The old priest made no reply. The stone beneath the diya creaked; and then, with the small, obscene decisiveness of a door locking, it gave a dull crack. The diya toppled and its tiny flame winked out in a puff of black smoke. The lamp did not shatter. It lay on its side, warm. Where the wick had danced, a dark circle remained on the stone—letters scorched thin into the floor. Advait read them aloud, uneasily.

"Na…ama…stra…" he faltered. "What does it say?" Aadhya asked. He only shook his head. "It breaks off. Mid-word—as if some hand stopped writing." Pandit Mahadev exhaled so slowly that the breath seemed to belong to the walls. *"The Unwritten Shloka,"* he said. "The hymn that was not permitted an ending—the line the world refused to complete."

"Why would that matter?" Aadhya asked."Because if the remainder were spoken," Mahadev said, and his voice dropped so low it was barely the friction of a reed against stone, "reality would wobble. The balance the seals keep would tilt." Outside, the fog drew in like a held breath. It crept around the low parapet of Manikarnika, threaded between boats moored at the ghat, slid under doors and pooled beneath the threshold.

Although the pyres continued—the doms were stubborn in their work tonight—the wood cracked with a different music. Several doms halted mid-stroke and listened at the shrouds as if something below the cloth were whispering back.

Aadhya lay awake in her small guestroom upstairs, the unfinished shloka looping in her skull. Sleep came in shallow tides; she would hitch toward oblivion only to jerk awake with the ghost of a syllable lodged behind her teeth. When her phone buzzed—Advait's name flashing—she hesitated, then answered: "Still awake". She typed back: "Me too". Meet at the mirror. They met on the third floor, before the old wall mirror where - months ago - she'd glimpsed the woman in red for the first time. This time the frame had a film of fog pooling fatly at its base; a slit where rain had leaked through the window, staining the wood. The glass itself shimmered as if it were water just barely held in place.

"You see this?" Advait asked. He moved to photograph it; the camera refused to recognize its own reflection, calling the image a void. "My phone calls it a black field." Aadhya pressed her palm once to the mirror's cool edge. When Advait wiped the glass with his sleeve, it did not come clean - the cloth left streaks thick and sluggish, like oil. Beneath the sheen, a corridor appeared: stone walls lit by dim lanterns and, at its far end, a lone figure with her back turned.

"She's back," Aadhya whispered. They said little. In the morning the mirror would have resumed its ordinary life. At night, however, it gave up its silence and showed what the house remembered. They did not speak of the corridor's length, nor of the patient way the figure waited. Pandit Mahadev called them into the courtyard beneath an ancient peepal tree. Its bark was webbed with red threads—some fresh, some grey and stiff like old scabs. "This was *tied* the day you were born," he told Aadhya quietly. "Your mother came here to pray. She was warned not to tell you." His voice scraped like a knife. "If your soul remembered, the seals would begin to crack."

Aadhya blinked. ***"Seals?"***

"There were five," Mahadev said. "Seals to bind Daitya knowledge, to keep it from drowning our present age. One of them - the *Kalkini* seal - lies far off in *Kuldhara*. But the first lies buried here in *Varanasi*. You were drawn to it."

She objected before she could stop herself: "We didn't break anything. We merely—"

"The syllable you gave voice to was an old latch," Mahadev interrupted. "You did not start the sound. You only finished the motion of returning it." A knot of guilt tightened in her chest she did not have words for. Later that evening, while the fog still writhed at the street corners, a bent woman arrived at the guesthouse. Her back was a sickle; a cloudy white film clouded one eye, but her voice cut like glass.

"I was told the bloodline has returned," she said to Mahadev without preface. He made no denial. The woman peered past him, at Aadhya. "I saw you as a child," she said. "Crying near Harishchandra. You had a burn on your palm—like a flame." Aadhya felt the old scar at once, a phantom heat along her skin. The woman drew a folded scrap of cloth from her shawl and handed it to Advait. It was a corner torn from some ancient scroll. When he unfolded it, tendrils of a script crawled across the weave — letters that twined like smoke. "There are names here," the woman said. "Seven names. Some are whole, some are eaten by flame. Find the ones that remain. They will tell you what is still sealed."

Advait tilted the cloth to the candlelight. Some characters shimmered faintly; others lay black as cinders. "What language is this?" he asked. "No one living speaks it," she murmured. ***"But those who listen in the dark will learn its***

rhythm." That night Aadhya dreamed of white flame—cool, spectral fire that did not consume but remembered. Her father's voice, thin with age, called a line before he vanished: The shloka ends with your name. She woke with the words burning a hollow in her mouth. The city felt wound and raw. They moved through a gully after midnight that smelled of damp marigold and cow dung - the usual scents of Kashi - undercut by a metallic note. At Thatheri Bazaar a barefoot boy under a crumbling arch hummed a tune like a nursery rhyme pitched wrong. His ash-smudged lips moved; the rhythm carried the geometry of a ritual.

"Can you hear it?" he asked Aadhya, cocking his head unnaturally. He pointed at the hollow of her lower back. "It's written on your spine." His grin revealed blackened teeth. Before they could step forward, the boy vanished into an alley like breath drawn into a crack. Advait's face was pale when he found her. "What did he say?"

"Where the flame forgot to die, the shloka still burns," she repeated, the boy's cadence still in her ears. ***"It cannot be spoken; it needs to be bled."*** The sentence lodged there like a splinter. They made no attempt to sleep. Instead, they sat with Pandit Mahadev at dawn by the Ganges while the first aarti bells began to call. He stood with his toes in the water, chanting softly to the river as if it were a patient he could soothe. When he turned to them, his face was a map of careworn lines.

"The unwritten shloka remembers itself," he said. "Remember—blood before ink. Breath before fire."

Advait leafed through his scattered notes later that morning. Among them was a brittle book he'd extracted from the ruins of a shrine: pages eaten at the edges, the center ringed by black soot. "It's as if the words erased themselves," he muttered. "Or refused to be marked."

"Perhaps they were never meant to be written," Aadhya said. "Then how did they exist?" he asked, eyes narrowing. "How does the dust step aside when the syllable wants a mouth?" That afternoon Aadhya returned to Manikarnika alone. The ledge where the ghat had bled days ago was now dry and dark—stone that absorbed light like a mouth. A young dom caught sight of her and warned softly, "You shouldn't stand there. That's where her name bled."

"Whose?" she asked. "The one who was never born, yet burned," he said, and disappeared into the smoke. She crouched at the edge where the blood had been, pulled out a pen, and tried to mark the stone. The nib would not move; ink slid across the grain as though it were repelled. Behind her, a whisper threaded itself through the air: Aadhya… Aadhrika… She had the strange sense that the city was addressing her in a voice she had once known. Before she could make sense of that, Advait called her urgently. "Come. Now."

He led her to a crumbling haveli near Chaukhamba, where charcoal scrawls crawled up walls in an indecipherable script. An old woman emerged from the inner courtyard—not frail but keening with clarity. "They come when they cannot stay buried," she said. "They seek mouths." Advait drew back at the sight. "Who are you?"

"A failed priestess," she replied. "A failed mirror. Once the verses used me. Then they left." She revealed a mirror from beneath a cloth. The glass fogged, then bled across its surface; a name began to form – AADH - and then the mirror split.

The old woman screamed and collapsed. By the time the medic took her away she could no longer speak coherently. Outside, the evening dust curled like thread. Advait and Aadhya stood silent while an ambulance vanished into the lane. He said, "She said the verses are hunting for a mouth." "What if that mouth is you?" Aadhya asked, voice small.

Advait said nothing. He watched the road as if it might vomit an answer.

At 2:09 a.m., Aadhya woke to humming—low, layered-a chorus that thrummed inside her skull. She walked the corridor and found Advait before a mirror: the same mirror from the haveli, impossibly transported. He was mouthing syllables; behind his reflection, a cinder-skinned figure stood. The glass shattered without sound—no shards, no echo—only the abrupt end of the hum. Advait slumped to the bed and whispered, "I wasn't asleep. I was… used."

From papers on the desk, an ash-ringed page showed new marks: lines that had been burn scars were now forming letters in a red that did not stain white. Aadhya lifted the sheet and felt the word thrumming in her throat. When she tried to form it, her tongue flamed. The page burst into flame and became ash; the echo of the word remained, lodged like a splinter. Silence settled like fresh dust, but both of them had seen the same burning woman, and recognition passed between them like a fever. They stayed until dawn, until the first aarti bell cut the air and the city exhaled into light. Somewhere a child laughed—a high, brittle sound that ended too quickly—as if someone had remembered something they ought not have.

The unwritten shloka had begun to un-write itself into the world. And in its margins, Aadhya felt a single, terrible certainty: the shloka finished with her name.

The Unwritten Shloka

By dusk, the fog along the ghats seemed to coil tighter, as though listening. The guesthouse lamps flickered, and the smell of incense could not smother the rawer stench beneath: char, copper, and something damp and fungal, as if the very air had begun to rot. When Pandit Mahadev spoke, his voice carried a finality that brooked no argument. "If you wish to survive the syllables, you must return to the source—the well where the shloka was first silenced. Vatnash Kund. Go before the moon sheds again. Go before the seventh mark is carved." The name alone was enough to blanch Aadhya's face. *Vatnash Kund*: a ruin by the river, abandoned decades ago after drownings and whispers. Locals spoke of it only in passing, and even then, as a place to avoid, a wound in the landscape.

That night, as bells from distant shrines tolled the first hour past sunset, she and Advait slipped from the guesthouse. The lanes were empty, but the silence was not reassuring. Every shuttered window seemed to watch. Every dog curled in an alley flinched as if in the grip of a dream. They walked without speaking until the last shops thinned and a broken iron gate appeared, strangled by vines. Behind it sprawled the black ruin of the old stepwell temple. No priest had lit an aarti there for years. The air was heavy with the damp of weeds and stone, yet beneath it hung something metallic. Blood, though none was visible.

They passed beneath the gate, the crunch of gravel startlingly loud in the absence of birdsong. The kund's mouth yawned below—a square throat lined with slick steps that disappeared into shadow. Vines dangled like veins. "Stay close," Advait murmured. Their torches bobbed in tandem as they descended. The deeper they went, the colder it became. Not the chill of ordinary stone, but something drawn from another scale of existence, a temperature that settled in marrow and thinned breath. Halfway down, the light caught something glistening on the steps. Aadhya froze: her boot had smeared through a sheen of liquid – red, too bright to be rust. She touched it with the edge of her scarf. Still warm.

"Blood," she whispered. The stairs led to a flat landing. At its center stood an altar—stone scarred by centuries, but strangely intact. Upon it rested a mirror. It was cracked, yes, but unlike the others, this one pulsed faintly. Not reflecting, not waiting.

It seemed to breathe a slow, patient breath that kept time with something very old. A slow, deliberate rhythm that seemed to keep time with her own pulse until she could no longer tell which was which. Advait's torch sputtered once and died. The darkness that fell was not ordinary night. It was total. Consuming.

And in that blackness, the voices began. Not aloud. Inside them. A chant layered on itself, each syllable rasping as if through dry throats, yet vast, intimate, undeniable: Not of ink. Not of tongue. Not of death. But of the name that burns before breath. The altar blazed suddenly with blue fire - cold, soundless flame. Advait staggered, his face drawn into a grimace of recognition, not pain. His body arched as though strings pulled his spine from above. His eyes rolled back, mouth working.

"Advait!" Aadhya ran forward, gripping his shoulders. "Stay with me!" His lips moved. One syllable slid free, ancient and wrong, the first sound of the unwritten shloka. The fire shuddered, then died. The mirror cracked again—not with the brittle sound of glass breaking, but with the wet split of flesh opening. And through it, a hand emerged. Grey. Desiccated. Fingers knotted like roots. The rest followed. A figure pulling itself from the mirror, as if glass were water. Its limbs were stitched from funeral garlands, flowers blackened and fused into sinew. Its torso was scorched wood wrapped in ash. Its eyes were two empty lamp bowls, still rimmed in oil.

And its mouth— Its mouth was hers. Her lips. Her jaw. The scar etched into her wrist curled faintly across its skin. Aadhya screamed. The creature smiled. And then it chanted. Not words. Not language. But the shloka in its entirety. The sound did not fill the chamber. It filled her bones. It was not loud; it was invasive, a resonance that slotted itself into the spaces between heartbeat and breath. She felt her own ribs vibrate with the cadence. The stone walls wept. Water poured upward from the cracks, defying gravity, laced with ash. The steps convulsed, melting into sludge. Advait convulsed too, clawing at his chest as though the sound were carving him open from the inside. His eyes brimmed with blood.

Aadhya stumbled back, hands over her ears - but it was useless. The chant was inside. Inside her lungs, her skull, her scar. The creature walked toward her, its movements stiff and deliberate, like a corpse rehearsing the imitation of life. It raised one charred hand, touched her forehead. And time broke. She saw herself—small, childlike—standing at a ghat whispering to shadows. She saw her mother, lips moving in sleep, mouthing something no one had taught her. She saw a temple made of skulls, torches blazing in sockets, chants ricocheting off bone. She saw a woman aflame, her body giving birth not to flesh but to ash. She saw spirals tattooed into the inside of her skin. She saw her name being rewritten. Not Aadhya. Never Aadhya.

The world convulsed, and then—silence. When she woke, she was sprawled on the slick stone steps of the kund. Advait lay nearby, his chest heaving shallowly, unconscious but alive. The torch lay broken. The altar was bare. The mirror was gone. Only one thing remained: on the altar, carved deep into the stone as if by a blade hotter than any fire, was a word - not written, carved.

Aadhya.

Her breath stuttered. It was not a gift. It was a claim. When Aadhya's eyes opened again, morning had not yet arrived. The air above Vatnash Kund clung to her skin like congealed breath. She pushed herself upright, every joint aching, as though her body had been used as a vessel for something too heavy to carry. Advait lay on the steps beside her, his shirt damp with sweat, chest rising in shallow jerks. His lips were cracked, and blood stained his collar where he had bitten his tongue.

"Advait," she whispered, shaking his shoulder. His eyes fluttered open, but they were unfocused—like he was staring through her into a horizon no one else could see. "Did you… hear it?" His voice was hoarse, as if scraped raw by invisible blades. She nodded, though the word hear was inadequate. They had been heard. Their bodies had been borrowed, pulled like instruments into resonance with a hymn older than scripture. The altar stood bare now. The mirror gone. Only the word remained—AADHYA, carved into stone as though the syllables themselves had teeth.

Advait tried to sit, swayed, and Aadhya caught him. His skin was cold, yet his temples burned with fever. "We can't stay here," she said. Her own voice trembled. The air around them was heavy with silence—not empty silence, but something listening. They climbed the steps together, Advait leaning on her arm. The vines seemed to reach toward them, brushing their ankles, whispering in the rustle of leaves. By the time they stumbled out of the kund and into the open, the night sky above the river was thick with fog. Not mist. Fog that breathed.

She did not remember walking back through the lanes. Only the sense of weight on her shoulders, the word carved into her mind like a brand. When they finally returned to the guesthouse, the lamps outside were all extinguished. No smoke from the kitchen. No sound of the landlady's coughing. Only stillness. Inside, the hallway walls bore stains darker than damp. Lines of soot trailed upward like writing. Spirals. Advait collapsed onto his cot without undressing. His eyes rolled back into a fevered half-sleep. She sat beside him, brushing damp hair from his forehead. His hand twitched, gripping hers suddenly. "Don't let me dream," he whispered.

But dreams came anyway. At some hour between night and dawn, Aadhya woke to the sound of bells. Not the metallic peal of temples, but something deeper—bones clattering in rhythm. She sat up, heart stuttering, and realized the sound was inside the room. On the floor lay the child's skull - the same one from the mirror. Its spirals glowed faintly, one after another, as though each name was kindling a wick. Smoke leaked from its hollow sockets, curling toward the ceiling in thin threads. And from the smoke, shapes tried to form.

Faces: dozens. Each one fragmentary - eyes without mouths, mouths without cheeks, brows carved with spirals. They dissolved before completing, as though the act of memory itself had been forbidden. Her scar throbbed. The syllables of the shloka pressed against her tongue like children begging to be born. She clutched her jaw, biting down until the metallic taste of blood filled her mouth. "Not mine," she whispered. "Not again." The skull exhaled. A hiss. And then silence. When dawn finally came, Advait's fever had broken, but his voice was ragged. He refused to speak of the night. Instead, he began scribbling in his journal—lines of half-translated mantras, sketches of the spirals, desperate notes that looked more like confessions than research.

Aadhya left him and went to the riverside. The ghats were already alive with the day's first cremations. Smoke rose lazily, indifferent. Yet she felt the difference. The air no longer carried only fire and ash. Beneath it was another smell—thick, metallic, like the kund had bled into the river. Pandit Mahadev was waiting. Barefoot on the stone steps, his frail figure silhouetted against the burning pyres, he seemed to have been there for hours, muttering to the river as though it would answer. Without turning, he said, "You let it speak."

"I didn't—" she began. "You think your will matters? Words are doors, child. Some open from the other side." Her throat constricted. "Then why me?" Mahadev turned then, his blind eyes glimmering faintly in the firelight. "Because your tongue is not yours. It remembers syllables carved into another body. Another time. You carry the final sound of the shloka." She stared at him, shaking her head. "What if I refuse to use it?" He gave a cracked laugh. "You already have."

Advait appeared then, pale but upright, journal clutched in his hand. "Pandit-ji," he said quietly, "if the shloka was silenced once, it can be silenced again." The old man's smile vanished. "You think silence is safety. But silence is hunger. It waits. It listens. You cannot end it. You can only survive it."

"And how do we survive?" Aadhya asked. Mahadev pointed to the opposite bank, where the fog hung like a curtain over the river. "Where the kund remembers. Where blood was given instead of ink. You must go back." Her breath caught. "We already went." He shook his head. "You only descended. You did not listen. The shloka was never unwritten. It was bled. And blood demands return." That evening, as dusk bled into the sky, the guesthouse began to change.

The walls hummed with low vibrations, like conches blown underwater. Shadows elongated beyond the lamps, moving against the direction of light. Mrs. Sen no longer emerged from her room; when Aadhya knocked, there was only the sound of someone scratching on wood. In the corridor, she found the boy who had once carried the mirror to her room. His eyes were sunken, lips cracked. He held a strip of cloth—old linen, burnt at the edges.

"This is for you," he said softly. She took it. A spiral inked in blood sprawled across the fabric. Beneath it, one word in jagged script:

"Breathe." Before she could question him, the boy turned and vanished into the stairwell. She unfolded the cloth further, her hands trembling. For the first time since childhood, she felt the shape of the missing syllable pressing fully against her tongue.

The syllable she had nearly spoken in the kund. She clamped her jaw shut. Advait's voice startled her. "What does it say?" "Nothing you want to hear." She stuffed the cloth into her satchel.

That night, they did not sleep. The whispers rose again—not inside the mirrors, but inside the walls of the house itself, seeping through brick and timber. They were no longer fragmented syllables. They were verses, half-sung, half-screamed. The unwritten shloka was no longer unwritten. It had found mouths again. In the dark, Aadhya pressed her palms to her ears, rocking slightly, whispering to herself: "Not mine. Not mine." But the voices answered in unison.

"Yours."

By dawn, her resolve had curdled into a grim clarity. She could not keep running from the syllables. She could not pretend silence would protect her. Standing at the balcony, she watched the river roil with a turbulence no one else seemed to notice. Advait joined her, his face gaunt, his eyes raw but steady. "What now?" he asked. She did not look at him.

Her scar glowed faintly again, as though remembering itself. "We go back," she said. "To Vatnash?" She nodded. "To finish what was left unsaid." Advait said nothing for a long time. Then he exhaled, closing his journal. "Then we do it together."

She finally turned to him. For a moment, they simply held each other's gaze - not as scholar and skeptic, not as priestess and vessel, but as two bodies marked by the same curse, the same song. And somewhere, in the river fog, something laughed - not with joy, but with recognition.

Chapter - 8

A Name Carved in Flame

The air changed the moment she stepped into the vault.

For hours, the night had been stagnant with the monsoon's breath—the sour perfume of incense, smoke, and rot pressed into every corner of Varanasi's ribs. It was the kind of air that clung to the skin like damp linen, that seeped into thoughts until one could taste grief. But beneath the ghat, where the half-burned chamber opened like a wound, the wind altered—cold, metallic, and edged with the memory of old blood across a blade. It tasted of rust and ritual, like something sharpening itself in the dark—neither fresh nor dead, only waiting. Aadhya hesitated on the stairwell. These steps were not supposed to exist - not in any municipal plan, not in any archaeological survey. Pandit Mahadev had warned her, his voice rasping as if torn between caution and inevitability: "Do not go beneath the plinth unless you are ready. The stone remembers." But she was here now, feet moving before thought could catch them. Advait followed, his flashlight beam stuttering against soot-caked walls. The narrow passage was carved not by human hands seeking permanence, but by hands that wanted to hide. “This isn’t on any archaeological record,” he muttered, his voice taut with awe and unease. “Not even in the *1873 city restoration maps*.”

“Because it wasn’t built by people who wanted to be recorded,” she whispered back. The phrasing felt less like her own and more like a memory exhaled through a mouth that had once said it. Seven marks adorned the wall—spirals and slashes burned into stone like wounds. Six of them glowed faintly, ember-burnt scars that pulsed with a rhythm older than the chamber. The seventh mark, which had lain cold, stirred as she approached and began to hiss and fume. It hissed. Fumed. And then flared with a breath that wasn’t breath at all. A single character burned there, alive with fire that remembered its own age: *Aadhrika.*

The flames licked upward - not spreading but coiling, as if inhaling after centuries of suffocation; the name pulsed once, then again—like a heart remembering it had once beaten. Aadhya froze, every muscle in her body seized, and yet inside, something unraveled. A thread from a past she had never lived tugged itself forward, violent and undeniable. Her knees weakened. Advait caught her before she collapsed fully.

“You alright?” his voice was steady, but she felt the tension in his grip. “I know this place,” she whispered, shivering though the air was not cold. “But I shouldn’t.” Advait did not answer. He was staring at her now—not like a skeptic, not even like an archaeologist studying evidence, but like a man who had stumbled onto a truth too sharp to name. Confused. Frightened. Fascinated. And beneath those reactions, something like recognition simmered in his silence. The chamber deepened into a tunnel, narrow as a throat. Ash - patterned urns lined its length, their clay cracked and blistered by heat that no longer burned. Shreds of silk clung to the stone like molted skin.

One urn bore markings that caught Advait's eye. He crouched, sweeping dust away. "This script..." He traced the fading lines with a reverent finger. "It's Kalibhoomi dialect. Ancient tribal text. Pre-Aryan. I've only seen fragments in burial cairns." Aadhya reached out without hesitation. Her fingertip followed the same grooves, and words she had never learned fell from her lips. "Do not wake the seventh fire. For it does not forget. It only waits." Her voice quivered at the end. The chamber answered. The stone groaned, trembling beneath their feet. Behind them, the entrance slammed shut with a force that rattled bone.

A rumbling sound echoed from the tunnel, slow at first, then rhythmic. Not footsteps. Not drums. It was the sound of a remembered fire—the echo of flame without heat. At the end of the passage, the wall shifted. Stone peeled away like skin from bone. From the darkness, a shape emerged a sculpture — no: an effigy fused into the living rock. It towered above them, its hollow eyes gouged into voids, its mouth carved wide in a silent scream. The stone face twisted as if it had once been human and had frozen mid-suffering, mid-betrayal.

But it wasn't the face that rooted Aadhya in dread. It was the mirror carved into its chest. A reflective plate of metal, liquid and solid at once, rippled as if breathing. It had not been inset by human hands; the metal rose up from the stone like a membrane grown over bone. Advait's voice cracked through the stillness. "Aadhya... is it just me, or is that reflecting a different room?" Her throat went dry. She stepped closer, unable to resist. The reflection showed not the chamber they stood in, but another.

A procession. Hooded figures in ash-colored robes, each holding vessels of fire and bone. They circled a woman kneeling at the center. The woman's face was her own.

Aadhrika.

The woman raised her hands. Her eyes glowed with an orange light that was not flame, not human. The hooded figures chanted her name in unison, their voices vibrating through the glass like a dirge. Then —

One figure broke the circle. A knife glinted. A slash.

The woman's throat opened in silence, and blood sprayed not into the air, but across the glass itself. The mirror screamed - not sound but vibration, memory, anguish. The chamber did not echo it. But Aadhya did. She clutched her throat and fell, choking as though the blade had found her. The taste of iron flooded her mouth. The world tilted. Advait lunged to catch her, arms locking around her trembling frame. His own face was ghost-pale, jaw clenched in terror.

"What the hell was that?"

She couldn't answer. She was drowning in the vision—the betrayal, the circle, the blood that should have been centuries old but felt wet on her neck even now. And then the whisper came. Not from the mirror. Not from the walls. From the stone itself. From the city. A voice neither hers nor Advait's:

"The first seal stirs. Rajasthan listens."

Outside, Varanasi shifted. The chamber may have been buried, sealed, forgotten by men who mapped and measured stone, but the citOutside, Varanasi shifted. The chamber may have beeny had always remembered. Now, with Aadhrika's name rekindled in flame, the memory moved through its streets like a muscle waking. The wind went still. On Tulsi Ghat, Pandit Mahadev sat barefoot in his darkened sanctum. His blind eyes, milk-white and unblinking, turned instinctively toward the Ganga though he could not see its surface. His hand hovered above the wooden board of engraved braille he used for his scriptures. Tonight, the carvings were restless—the grooves shifting beneath his touch as if the wood itself had begun to breathe.

"She has touched her name," he whispered into the silence. "And the mirror has remembered." Behind him, a curtain stirred though there was no wind. Somewhere in the corner of the sanctum, the flame of a single brass diya bent sideways, bowing toward the earth, then righted itself again. Mahadev's mouth tightened. "She must leave soon. The desert calls." But even he knew: Aadhrika's return was not hers alone. Memory was not impartial. Those still loyal would stir… but so would those still be hunting.

At the guesthouse, Aadhya and Advait sat across a small wooden table, a candle guttering between them. Neither had touched the tea cooling at their elbows. The name still smoldered in her mind. Not just Aadhya Roy—Aadhrika. The syllables burned like embers trapped under skin. Not a word. An identity. A wound that refused to scar. "I don't know if I believe in reincarnation," Advait said finally. His voice was subdued, as if admitting treason. "But I saw what I saw. That wasn't trickery. And it wasn't just your imagination." Aadhya raised her eyes, searching his. "Do you think I'm going mad?"

He hesitated, weighing truth against comfort. "I think," he said carefully, "that you're on the edge of something ancient. Something that doesn't care whether we believe or not." Silence stretched between them, filled only by the soft hiss of the candle. Then he reached into his satchel. "There's more." From within protective parchment, he drew out a small scroll. Its edges were brittle, its surface darkened by centuries of soot. He spread it gently across the table.

"I found this wedged behind the effigy's ribs. The stone had loosened." The parchment revealed a diagram—not a map of earth, but a map of memory. Seven flames arranged in a spiral around a central, black sun. Each flame was marked by a glyph, inked in ochre that had not faded. And at the spiral's heart, one symbol pulsed even now, as if remembering fire. A desert glyph - etched in red. Aadhya's stomach knotted. "Where does it point?"

His voice dropped, almost reverent. "Rajasthan." The word hung like an omen. As if to answer, the candle's wax climbed upward in thick tendrils: gravity itself reluctant to remain true. The blue flame that shivered into being did not burn the wick; instead it held a shape, and inside that shape a whisper rose:

"The name has returned. And so must the guardian."

The flame warped into a face - obsidian features, jagged as if chipped from stone. A warrior's visage, but inhuman—its sockets filled with ash, its mouth twisted in silence.

Agnivrat.

The apparition lingered only a breath before the flame imploded. Smoke coiled once and vanished. The room was left dark, the candle a mere stub. Aadhya pressed her palm to the table to steady herself. "What the hell was that?" Advait's jaw was tight. "Whatever it was, it wasn't metaphor." She looked at him sharply. He exhaled, low. "The seal is broken." Neither of them slept that night. At dawn, the bells of Manikarnika rang strangely—slower, each note dragging like a warning stretched on a string. The ghat was hushed. Even the doms who tended the pyres moved quietly, as though the air itself demanded reverence. Advait went early to meet a local historian, chasing fragments of Daitya lore in temple records. Aadhya stayed at Pandit Mahadev's dwelling, her gaze fixed on the mirror he had covered with sandalwood paste and wrapped in old cloth. She could feel it breath behind the silk.

The Pandit sat at his incense table, unmoving. His face was gaunt, his beard unkempt, but his presence was heavy, like a stone anchored in riverbed currents. “Panditji,” Aadhya said softly. “The name. What does it mean that it was mine?” For a long moment, he did not answer. Then: “Names are vessels. Yours has been locked for centuries. Now the lock is cracking.” Her voice trembled. “And the flame?”

“That was no ordinary fire,” he said. His blind eyes blinked once, slowly. “That was Chhaya Agni. Shadow fire. Fire that remembers. It lives where stories refuse to die.” Her stomach clenched. “Then why me?”

“You ask that again and again,” Mahadev said gently. “But sometimes the flame does not choose. It returns to the hand it once knew.” Her breath faltered. “What if I don’t want it?” The Pandit smiled, sad and unyielding. “You don’t have the choice anymore, Aadhrika.” The name struck her harder than his words. She froze. “What did you call me?”

“Aadhrika,” he repeated, his expression unreadable. “The name carved in flame.” The silence that followed felt enormous, like the pause between a drum’s strike and its echo. Finally, he turned his blind eyes toward the mirror. “Cover it completely. Burn the cloth after. Do not look again.” Aadhya nodded numbly. She lifted the silk wrap and laid it carefully across the glass. The moment her fingers brushed its surface, a chill leapt through her veins. For the briefest second she thought she felt fingernails knocking from the other side. She let go quickly, heart pounding.

By mid-morning, she met Advait again near the half-submerged stepwell at Harishchandra Ghat. His face was taut, his satchel bulging with papers. “I found something,” he said without preamble. “*A mention in the Avandia Manuscripts.* There was a priesthood here three thousand years ago; they were called the Dairymen.” Her throat tightened at the word. “Daitya. As in…?”

"Not demons," he interrupted. "Not exactly. They believed in blood memory. That names could be preserved in fire, carried across lifetimes." Her palm burned faintly, recalling the spiral scar that seemed to deepen with each night. "One of those names is mine?" Advait hesitated. "I don't know yet. But Pandit Mahadev might." She turned away, staring at the river. Its surface was too still. No ripples, no current. Only sky mirrored back. Behind her, Advait spoke again. "Why now? Why is all this resurfacing?"

Her lips moved before she knew what she was saying. "Because the seals are breaking." Advait stiffened. "What seals?" She blinked, disoriented. "I… I don't know." The words felt pulled from her, like an echo that belonged to someone else. That night, the city trembled.

At Tulsi Acara, an old sage was found balanced on one leg, muttering in a dialect no one recognized. His tongue had turned black. His feet were burned, though no fire had touched them.

At Dashashwamedh Ghat, the evening aarti brought hundreds of Diya's to the river, but none drifted downstream. Instead, they circled slowly mid-current, then dimmed one by one until the water went dark.

At Kashi Vishwanath temple, the great Nandi statue began to cry. Not tears. Saltwater.

And at Panchganga Ghat, a little girl pointed to the sky and asked her mother, "Who's watching from behind the moon?"

In her guesthouse, Aadhya shivered without cause. She could feel Varanasi tightening around her. The city itself had begun to breathe differently. And the name—Aadhrika—kept burning behind her teeth, refusing to sleep. By the following dusk, Pandit Mahadev had summoned them both. His sanctum smelled of ghee lamps and dried basil, but the air carried something heavier—inevitability. He stood, frail yet rooted, his blind eyes raised toward the Ganga as though he were listening to its hidden current.

"There is no more time," he said without greeting. "You must leave for Rajasthan." Aadhya flinched. "But you said—"

"I said you could not leave before," Mahadev interrupted, his voice sharp. "Now you must. The mirror has spoken. The first name has awakened. And the fire will follow you unless you find what waits in the desert." Advait's jaw tightened. "Find what?" The old man exhaled, shoulders heavy as if bearing centuries. "A woman with a white peacock tattooed on her tongue. Her name is Kalkini." The word itself seemed to ripple through the air. Aadhya's skin prickled. He reached into a cedar box and handed her a small scroll, no larger than her palm, bound in brittle black thread. "Do not open until the fire reaches you. It will know when."

She accepted it reluctantly, the weight of the parchment far greater than paper should allow. **"The ones who walk together now were once together then,"** Mahadev added, his voice lowering to a whisper. "You are bound. Not by choice. By memory." Advait turned away, muttering, "I don't believe in destiny." Mahadev's blind gaze sharpened. "Destiny does not need your belief. It remembers you regardless." The words hung in the air like embers refusing to fade.

They began their departure at dusk. The streets of Varanasi seemed to resist them, as though the city itself had grown possessive. The lanes were unusually choked—cows standing stubbornly in narrow galis, funeral processions weaving across their path, vendors calling out names that weren't theirs but made Aadhya glance anyway. As they neared Nepali Temple, a bent figure stumbled into their way. A beggar, muttering under his breath. His hair was matted, his eyes veiled with cataracts, yet when he looked at Aadhya, his voice rose clear as iron.

"You are fire," he said. "You are the name they buried in glass." Aadhya froze. Advait stepped instinctively in front of her. "Sir, please—" The beggar ignored him. From the folds of his rags he drew a shard of blackened mirror, edges sharp, surface soot-dark. He pressed it into Aadhya's palm. "She'll need this in the desert," he whispered. Before they could reply, he slipped into a side alley and vanished, as though the city had swallowed him whole. Aadhya stared at the shard. In its reflection, her face was not her own but blurred with soot, like a memory trying to forget itself.

The train clattered out of Varanasi that night. The city's lights receded behind them, orange pinpricks against the dark, until only the sound of rails remained. Aadhya pressed her palm to the glass of their compartment window. It burned faintly, though no heat rose from the pane.

"Still think this is myth?" she asked quietly. Advait didn't answer immediately. Instead, he reached into his satchel and pulled out a folded sketch. The paper was yellowed, edges brittle with age. "My father drew this years before he disappeared." He unfolded it. A woman stood in a circle of fire, spiral tattoos snaking up her arms, her face caught between beauty and terror. Below, in his father's slanting hand, was a single name: Aadhrika.

Aadhya's breath hitched. "Maybe," Advait murmured, "I've believed this longer than I wanted to admit." The train thundered over the Ganga's bridge. For a moment, the wheels shrieked against iron, metal screaming like an omen. Outside, a single diya floated beside their carriage. It burned steadily, even against the wind. It stayed with them for a full minute—keeping pace with the train—before vanishing into the dark river below.

Neither spoke after that. At some point, Advait drifted into a shallow sleep, arms crossed, brows furrowed even in rest. Aadhya sat awake, sketchbook balanced on her knees. Her hand moved without her permission, lines looping feverishly across the page. When she finally looked down, her stomach twisted.

The face she had drawn wasn't hers, yet it was. Hollow eyes ringed in spirals. Teeth like arrowheads. A symbol across the forehead she had seen once before—carved into stone near Manikarnika, just before the ashes had shifted. The train lurched violently. Aadhya slammed against the wooden berth, pen scratching an ugly line across the page. The whistle screamed once. Twice. Then three times.

The train slowed. She jolted upright. "Wake up," she hissed, shaking Advait's shoulder. "We're stopping." He blinked groggily. "What? We're not scheduled to stop until—" "I know. But look." Mist pressed against the windows, thick as cotton. Through it, a faint yellow glow swayed like an old lantern caught in the wind. The wheels ground to a halt. Aadhya wiped condensation from the glass. A station board swam into view, its paint faded, its letters almost eaten by time.

Khari Baisa – 7 Minutes Halt

She frowned. "Khari Baisa? That isn't on the schedule." Advait's face drained. "I checked the entire list. There's no Khari Baisa anywhere on this line." The platform was narrow, cracked in places, weeds splitting through old stone. No vendors. No passengers. Just mist curling like breath over the ground. And someone was standing there. Tall. Too thin, limbs taut as rope. A saffron kurta hung from his frame, frayed at the hem. His hair was wild, eyes glowing faintly yellow beneath the tangle. He did not move, he only stared directly at their window. “I don’t like this,” Advait muttered, clutching his satchel. “We should stay in.”

But Aadhya had already risen, compelled by something deeper than choice. She stepped into the corridor. Advait cursed under his breath and followed. The exit door was open. Mist curled inside, dampening the metal railings. The figure on the platform spoke before they could. His voice was low, brittle, like dry leaves scraping against stone.

“You shouldn’t be here.” “We didn’t mean to—” Aadhya began. “You didn’t,” he interrupted. “The train stopped for you. Only seven minutes. Then it forgets.” Advait’s shoulders stiffened. “Who are you?” The man tilted his head. “I am called Anang. Once, I spoke to birds. Now I speak to what comes after.” The mist seemed to coil tighter around them. Aadhya swallowed. “Is this a village?”

“No,” Anang said, voice thin. “Not anymore.” He turned slowly and gestured toward the fields beyond the platform. Barren earth stretched into nothingness, but at the far edge stood an archway. Made not of stone. Not of wood. Of bones. Human bones, arranged into a gate.

“No one passes unless they have seen their name in ash,” Anang whispered. “You have. Both of you. And the one who waits beyond is listening.”

The ground shivered. The train’s horn blew once. Long. Warning. Anang’s yellow eyes flicked toward the sound. “It remembers. You must leave.”

Aadhya took a step back. Advait caught her hand instinctively, as if afraid she might cross the bone-arch herself. “What is this place?” he demanded. But Anang only reached into his kurta and drew out a folded strip of silk. He pressed it into Aadhya’s palm. She’ll need this in the desert,’ he whispered. The fabric was impossibly cold, as though it had been soaked in something older than water. "You'll need this in the next fire," he said softly. *"It remembers screams."*

The horn blew again. Louder. Anang stepped back into the mist. His body dissolved, piece by piece, until only the faint shimmer of his eyes remained. Then nothing. The third horn split the silence. The wheels shuddered. The train lurched forward. They scrambled inside, hearts racing. By the time the platform slipped from view, it was gone—not receding, not hidden by mist, simply erased, as if it had never existed. Advait clutched the railing, chest heaving. "Did we just dream that?" Aadhya slowly opened her palm. The silk gleamed faintly. Stitched into it with golden thread were three words.

Daitya. Vatnash. Aadhrika.

Her breath caught. She folded the cloth tightly, as though concealing it from the dark itself. By dawn, the sky was bleeding rust. Stations gave way to red sandstone ridges, desert winds carrying cumin, dust, and a faint sting of fire. The train hissed to a stop at a small forgotten halt. A hand-painted sign read: ***Kuldhara***.

Silence pressed down like centuries. No vendors. No porters. Only wind whispering through abandoned ridges. A man waited on the platform - broad-shouldered, clad in a deep indigo angarkha, a crescent-shaped scar carving down his cheek. His eyes were black, steady, almost animal.

Aadhya stepped forward cautiously. "Bhairav Singh?" The man inclined his head once. His gaze lingered on each of them, measuring, heavy as judgment. Then he spoke. "Many have come," he said slowly. His voice was thunder wrapped in velvet. "But you are the last." The desert wind rose behind him, carrying with it the faint, brittle sound of laughter. Not human. Not entirely.

And so Rajasthan began.

Part – 2
Rajasthan
The First Seal

Chapter - 9
The Dance of Kalkini

"Many have come," Bhairav Singh repeated, his voice like gravel dragged over stone - "but you're the last." Aadhya said nothing. Her legs still trembled from the halt that should not have existed—the *phantom platform*, the seven minutes of someone watching from beyond the tracks. Advait's fingers hovered near his satchel; his knuckles were white. Outside the carriage, the tiny diya that had accompanied them vanished as if a hand had pinched it out of the night. The station itself was more suggestion than place: a strip of cracked concrete half-sunk into dust, a single rusted bench, a scrubby neem. Bhairav stood waiting beneath a red turban wound about his head like a coiled flame. For a breath, his irises flashed gold, an absurd, animal gleam that skated across his face and was gone.

"Are you Bhairav Singh?" Advait finally asked. Bhairav's mouth twitched into something like a smile. "Depends on who's asking."

"We're Advait — and Aadhya Roy," Advait said. "We were told to meet you here."

"I know who you are," Bhairav replied simply, and without further parley he turned and beckoned them to follow. The path from the platform was a narrow cut through thorn scrub and bleached stones. Night in the desert was colder, thinner than Aadhya had expected - a sharpness that bit through shawls and resolve. For ten minutes they walked in a brittle silence until a ruined arch rose low against the black sky. Beyond it lay Kuldhara. The village had the look of a thing paused mid-life: low sandstone houses half-buried in wind-driven sand, doorways yawning into shadow, staircases that led to nothing. A banyan had grown where no tree should, its roots braided into the broken masonry. A faceless stone goddess lay half-swallowed by dust, her chest stained with old vermilion. The wind sighed through the gaps like a held breath being released.

"It's abandoned," Aadhya said. "It is," Bhairav answered. "But not empty." They reached a relatively intact haveli on the village's edge. Inside, oil lamps guttered, throwing the walls into a weathered tapestry of salt and rot. A woman in white—Maya—moved without sound, setting brass bowls on a low table. She was mute, Bhairav explained when she vanished behind a curtain without greeting. Her presence in the house felt ceremonial, as though the place itself required her caretaking.

Bhairav watched them eat with a patient, predator's hunger. "You must eat while you still can," he said. When Aadhya opened her mouth to refuse, he only shrugged. "Eat. Kuldhara notices when you grow too hungry. Hunger is an invitation here." They ate bland lentils and bajra rotis, with a bitter green chutney that seemed to clear the city's residue from the mouth. Outside, the desert wind rose and rose, a low animal sound that threaded through the shutters. After the meal Bhairav unrolled a brittle map on the floor. The parchment was ochre and cracked; the ink shimmered faintly in the lamplight. At the center of the map lay a spiral, concentric rings radiating outward; between jagged symbols of dunes someone had scrawled a single name in an older hand:

Kalkini.

"She was the guardian of the first seal," Bhairav said. "A Daitya sorceress—called the flame dancer. They bound her with fire and silence. They thought that would be enough."

"Is she a legend?" Advait asked. "No legend leaves footprints," Bhairav replied. "And no legend eats jackals under the red moon." Outside the house something howled—long and wrong. Aadhya's scar pulsed against the inside of her wrist, a steady, sickening drumbeat. When Bhairav rolled the scroll away, he spoke again, quietly. "We will walk to the old well beyond the temple ruins before dawn. That is where she danced last. Where the fire swallowed the living. Where the seal was cast." He looked at her. "Do not leave the haveli tonight. If you hear the rhythm — do not follow it."

Maya reappeared with keys and motioned them upstairs. Advait went first; Aadhya lingered. "Bhairav?" she asked. He turned from the doorway in the half-dark. For a second his eyes gleamed gold. *"She never forgot you, Aadhrika,"* he said. The name tumbled out of him like a verdict. Aadhya felt something inside her unhook and slide toward it. The night swallowed their rest. Kuldhara did not sleep; it only quieted, its silence thick and watchful. When they left the haveli after midnight, the village seemed more a skeletal theatre than ruin: jali carvings like ribs, columns like joints, the air mica-sparkled with drifting sand. Murals peeked through flaking plaster—dancers, serpents, women with spirals tattooed along their cheeks. One painted woman wore the same red sari Aadhya had seen in the mirror.

Bhairav led them to the village square. At its center, an obsidian dais lay ringed with charred bones—the only thing that did not crumble. The sand around it was blackened as if struck by lightning. A wind rose from the north and the hair along Aadhya's arms lifted.

"She danced here," Bhairav said. "Kalkini?" Advait whispered. "She was fire," Bhairav said. "Not a queen. Not demon by our names. A keeper of flame. Her last dance ended when five seals were invoked—placed into stone and silence. One of those seals sleeps beneath this platform." Aadhya knelt and pressed her palm to the stone. It responded with a dull thud, like a heartbeat. A fissure spidered across the surface. From it bled a thin thread of red light. Sand eddied; the air changed. A low sound—no music and not quite wind—began: a rhythm so old it felt like a memory surfacing.

From somewhere distant came the cadence of anklets, slow and unsteady. Advait stepped back as if struck. "What is that?" he breathed. "The sign," Bhairav murmured. "When the seal stirs, the dance begins." Above them, the sky seemed to shift; stars slid, unfamiliar constellations winked into being. A shape of flame lifted from the crack and formed a silhouette—limn at first, then clearer: a woman wreathed in fire, anklets chiming though there was no sound. *Kalkini* manifested not as flesh but as memory: the precise arc of a shoulder, a hip's calculation, hands poised in a *mudra* that could unmake vows.

Aadhya's throat closed. The figure looked into her as if into an old mirror. "You still remember the rhythm, Aadhrika," the apparition said, its voice like silk and grinding stone. "Even if your name denies it." Advait lunged forward. "Don't speak to her," he snapped. Kalkini's amusement was a cold thing. "A protector," she said. "So like the last one... Advaita." The name grazed Advait and landed as recognition—his face blanched. Bhairav cursed softly. "She remembers everything."

Bhairav flung ash at the flame, chanting words older than Hindi. The smoke coiled and the fire did not extinguish; instead, Kalkini's lower body began to snake, coal and heat spiralling into a serpentine torso, her arms held in strange, beautiful geometry. "You cannot stop a dance once the first note has been struck," she whispered. Then she vanished into a flare of red and the fissure sealed as though nothing had happened. The platform was whole again, and the night resumed its watch - but something fundamental had changed: the village no longer felt merely abandoned; it felt awake, waiting.

Aadhya fell to her knees, the stone was hot where she had touched it. "I saw it," she said. "I saw her sealed. I—" Her voice splintered. "I helped lock her away." Bhairav exhaled like someone who had been holding a breath hoarded for centuries. "Then you are not only the key," he said. "You are the hinge." They did not rest that night. All around them, *Kuldhara* breathed and remembered. In the distance, a woman danced beneath a black temple—some shadow of Kalkini twining through heat-thinned air. From rooftops figures watched with mouths stitched shut; children with sunken eyes clung to parapets as if remembering being remembered.

As dawn bled a rusty grey, they left the village, moving like trespassers in a memory that wanted its due. The obsidian platform hummed somewhere beneath their feet. Far below, under ten thousand grains of sand and the bones of watchers, the first seal had cracked. Kalkini's voice followed them as they left: a soft benediction or a vow. "Dance, Aadhrika," she said. "Dance and remember me." Aadhya felt the syllables root themselves under her ribs. The scar on her wrist burned in time with the pulse beneath the stone. She had thought she could bear being called a name out of time. Now she realized names could call back—they could become bones, they could become weather, they could become hunger.

Bhairav's lantern swung ahead, throwing long, gnarled shadows. The desert closed behind them like a lid. And far beneath Kuldhara's dunes, something ancient flexed, as if testing a limb that had not moved in an age.

The dance had begun

They did not sleep. The wind that night in Kuldhara carried ash rather than sand; it smelled of old rites and half-remembered prayers. Aadhya lay awake on the roof of the haveli while below, in the square, the obsidian platform sat like a held breath. Her hands twined and untwined in the thin blanket, fingers finding the spiral scar on her wrist as if looking for a pulse. Each time she closed her eyes the image returned—Kalkini in mid-dance, her throat opened to a song no tongue should carry, the crowd's shapes like warped mirrors. The last moment before the fissure sealed pressed itself into her mind: the dancer's smile, a cut both intimate and terrible, as if someone had smiled with a blade.

Advait paced room to room, restless as a caged animal. He had been quiet since they'd left the platform—silent in a way that felt dangerous. Once, he slipped handfuls of sand into a small tin and tossed it into the inner courtyard. "So if the seal wakes, it stirs like a furnace," he said. "Heat, light, sound. We know this. But there is also scent. Something old and metallic. It isn't flame alone that wakes it—it's memory."

"Memory makes designs," Aadhya said without looking up. "Patterns that the world obeys." She thought of the scrolls, of families who had vanished for whispering the wrong syllable into earth. "If I was the hinge—if I helped seal her before—then what binds me now?" Advait stopped with the metal tin in his hand. For a minute his mouth formed words that dissolved before he could speak them. Finally he said, "We bind her again. We find the second seal. We do what they did before—only this time we make sure the locking isn't left to chance." His voice did not sound like certainty; it sounded like resolve laced with fear.

Bhairav returned before dawn, his face older in the blue light. He carried a small wooden box. "We go now," he said. "The ritual site is near the well you found last night. There are chants preserved in old Bhavdiya fragments. They are crude, protective. Not to bind a goddess—but to tuck a memory back into sleep." They walked under a sky that refused the softness of dawn, the stars still sharp as pins. The path to the well followed a line where the sand had not stolen steps; it felt like a seam in the land. On the way, Bhairav told them what he could: stories of the Daityavansh priesthood, a lineage of flame-bearers who kept names like bones; of a last, terrible bargain made when the fires went angry and the earth cracked. He kept his voice low; words felt like tinder in that place.

When they reached the well, the village was still; the rim of the stone was rimed with scorched handprints. As they approached, a sound rose: a faint rhythm like anklets striking the inside of a buried urn. "There," Bhairav whispered. "She echoes there." A cross of white salt had been drawn across the well's rim—an old protective mark Bhairav had sketched before their arrival. He placed the wooden box on the ledge and opened it. Inside lay a length of rope woven from human hair and something that looked like silver wire coiled with ash, a bowl of powdered turmeric mixed with ground bone, a scroll tied with black thread. They were relics salvaged not by archaeologists but by those who still honoured older vows.

"Listen," Bhairav said, the tremor in his voice making the words brittle. "The chant must be sung as half-supplication, half-damnation. Not to praise. Not to hate. To put the dance back inside its mirror." Advait unrolled the scroll and traced the syllables with a tentative finger. The script was like fingers arranged in a knot; though he had studied syllabary systems, these marks resisted taxonomy. Yet when Advait's lips moved to form the first sound, the air around them thickened. It wasn't the chant that frightened him, but the knowledge that sound would have purchase here; that language could become a lever.

Aadhya hesitated. The last time she had vocalized a shloka she had woken with blood on her throat and a river of names tattooing themselves across her skin. She thought of the masque they'd found at the ruins, of the woman in red whose laugh had the taste of rust. "We will do it together," she said finally. "If this is to be done, then let it be done with both hands." They began. Advait hummed the drone, low and steady; Bhairav intoned the older syllables; Aadhya found herself speaking lines that were not wholly her own, each syllable shaping the air as if it were clay. At first, the words were brittle and uncertain. Then they fell into each other—one voice completing another's thought. The well listened.

From the darkness below rose a sound like a throat clearing. Not dissenting, not compliant—just the sound of something acknowledging it had been named again. The rim of the well warmed beneath Aadhya's palm; the salt at her feet tingled. When she cupped the bowl of turmeric-bone and let the powder slough between her fingers the grains seemed to vibrate, releasing a faint ozone tang.

They completed the chant in a breath held too long. For a second, nothing happened. Then a wind rose not from outside but from the earth—small at first, then swelling into a keening that pressed on the chest. Shapes of memory unfurled: a ring of dancers drawn in dust; hands lifted to the sky; a woman stepping away from the whirl into a fissure that swallowed her feet. It was the echo of the original rite, not the act itself.

Something rose from the well - not the full-bodied Kalkini but a fog of heat, an afterimage. It swirled, and for a breath Aadhya saw herself there—larger, flayed of time, anklets chiming like distant thunder. The apparition's face, for a heartbeat, matched her own. Aadhya's knees gave; she felt the seam in her history tug hard enough to bruise. Then the fog receded. The well inhaled. The anklet-rhythm faded into the sand. The fissure beneath the obsidian dais stalled, a hair's breadth away from opening. The first seal—already cracked—ceased to widen. For now, the dance had been interrupted.

"You did well," Bhairav said, his voice a tired blade. "You anchored it," Advait added. "For a little while." But none of them pretended the victory was permanent. The charm of that morning had been short-lived: as if the world itself granted reprieve only until the next breath. They had pushed the tide back; they had not removed the ocean. After the chant, as they walked back through Kuldhara's silent apertures, the village seemed to watch them differently. Doorways felt like mouths. Murals had shifted subtly—spiral tattoos had moved an inch higher on foreheads, an anklet catch now suggested in shadow. Aadhya felt a tightening beneath her ribs, a memory trying to clot.

That night a figure appeared at the haveli door: a man wrapped head to toe in an indigo angarkha with a crescent scar on his cheek—Bhairav's contact. He introduced himself as Raghav, though he answered to many names in desert languages. He had been sent by those who still kept watch beyond the dunes—people whose lineage had always minded the Daitya marks. He spoke to Bhairav alone, in a cadence that was both deferential and urgent.

"You were not meant to hear the dancer's voice and return unmarked," Raghav said finally, to Aadhya and Advait's confusion. "She leaves traces. They root. You must learn to read them. Kuldhara offers heat, but the desert offers hunger. Kalkini will not sleep because you asked her to; she will sleep if the world forgets her name. She cannot mind memory where there is no witness." Aadhya thought of the mask, of the carved skull, of the small scrap of cloth with her old name inked in vermilion. “Then we must make the world forget.”

Raghav’s eyes hardened. “Forget is a crueller verb than you think. To forget the wrong thing is to empty a wound. But this forgetting must be enforced by more than song. It must be sealed by stone or by blood that remembers a different rhythm. The desert keeps certain secrets; you will find one.” And so, with the first of the village’s pale dawns touch-ing the sandstone, they planned to push further: to a black temple half-swallowed by dunes where, Raghav whispered, the exact form of the first seal might be buried.

Yet in the stillness before the dawn, Aadhya stood on the haveli’s roof and watched the obsidian dais like an old wound. In her chest something had become heavier: a new responsibility or an old guilt—she could not tell. The name Aadhrika coiled there like a seed. The more she resisted it, the more tenacious it became. When the sun finally rose, it did so over a world that had not returned to its ordinary habits. Distant drums sounded as if played by the wind in some ruined theater. Above Kuldhara, an uncertain heat shimmered; it looked like the world had been put through a lens.

They readied themselves to leave. The black temple crouched beyond the last row of collapsed houses, half-buried and yawning, its doorway like the open mouth of a thing that had swallowed language whole. As they approached, the air rippled with a heat that had nothing to do with the sun. Stones near the entrance exhaled a faint smoky breath. Bhairav’s lantern threw angles of light that trembled as if hands had brushed them. Raghav moved first, as if clearing the way. “This is where the seal was wound tightest,” he said. “If there is a core here, this temple keeps it.”

They crossed the threshold into near-dark. The interior smelled of burnt sandalwood and something sweeter that made Aadhya's mouth water—an old, impossible hunger. The walls were carved with spirals, each one overlain by others until the stone read like a palimpsest of ritual. At the center, a pit opened like a throat. In the pit, bones lay arranged in careful geometry; in the bone-work a hollow had been shaped and filled with a slag-black glass that pulse-lit faintly like lung tissue.

"The original sealing," Bhairav whispered. Advait moved into the pit and unrolled a cloth. "We need to bind it with something that remembers differently," he said. "Stone remembers shape; water remembers flow; but blood remembers lineage. The first seal was woven with blood-song—names that carried other names. We must counter-weave."

"How?" Aadhya asked. "By offering what the seal wants—but redirecting its hunger." Raghav reached into his satchel and produced a small mirror—a thin shard of silvered glass edged in bone. "It will lure the echo. Mirrors were used before to reflect memory back into memory." He set the shard into the black glass and, following the old rites, smeared the edges with turmeric-and-bone so the mirror might not crack under the pressure of history. They began a ritual of containment: Bhairav drumming a slow, skeletal cadence on an iron bowl, Advait humming low frequencies that matched the partial harmonics carved into the stone, and Raghav chanting in a guttural tongue that seemed to scrape the inner rims of their skulls. Aadhya placed her palm on the black glass and felt a vibration like a hand answering a knock.

For a long stretch, time elongated. The chamber asked itself questions and found them answered in muscle memory. Then, as if in response to a puzzle solved, a sound—a soft shiver—ran through the black glass. The mirror glowed; inside it a flicker shaped into the remembered outline of Kalkini—only this time she did not dance. She watched. Her gaze was an ache. "You do this well," the image said, and the voice threaded through the chamber like a chord. "You tie knots and call them binding."

"Then sleep," Bhairav said aloud. The words felt inadequate against that gaze. Kalkini's lips curved. "Once, you and I were part of the same cycle, Aadhrika. The dance was both healing and hunger. You helped learn how to feed it—then you left." The mirror shifted, and for a paralyzing second Aadhya saw flashes of memory that were not hers and could not be foreign: a woman wrapping bone-threads about a new-born's wrists; a circle of watchers chanting at a new moon; a child's cry swallowed and blessed into silence.

Aadhya felt the floor tilt under her. "I—" Her mouth failed her. This was not the first time she had been told her past as if it were a book she had merely misplaced. She had watched the claim made before, in other mirrors, other wells. Reality kept trying to reassert itself: names, deeds, debts. "You offered your name to stop a greater wound," the image said, gentle then sharp. "You chose one body to hold the fire for many. That was the bargain. Do you remember?"

"You tell me the truth," Advait said then, his voice cut with something like sorrow. "If she was once the fire and you the hinge—then why did you leave?" Aadhya tried to see herself in the memory, to take its contours and fit them to waking life. "I remembered," she said, "and the remembering burned me. I thought distance would damp the flame." Kalkini smiled the way a brand smiles. "Distance is an ash. It can be blown into a new altar." The mirror's face blurred, drawing in light like a mouth. For an instant Kalkini's expression shifted to something almost like pity. "You want to sleep again without wounds. But memory does not grant you clemency."

The mirror's light seared inward. The black glass caught the flash and seemed to store it, like a wound cupping the salt of the water. The rhythm in the chamber grew tauter. A figure materialized beyond the mirror: not Kalkini herself but a crowd—faces of watchers and dancers—each mouth sewn, each eye pendulous with expectation. They leaned forward as if to listen. Bhairav's chant rose in steadiness until it was a roar folded into itself. The mirror began to vibrate. The black glass took the reflection of the dancers and, for one harrowing moment the black glass refracted dancers into keylike shape. A small sliver of seal uncoiled and sank into the mirror's silvered seam, where it sizzled and dulled. The pit in the floor swallowed its breath.

Then, like an exhausted animal, the chamber exhaled. The black glass cooled and went still; the mirror lay placid in the center, catching their breaths and reflecting their faces as face after face, each with a flicker of spirals tattooed on the temples like a watermark. They had not destroyed the seal. No god-sized excision had occurred. But they had bought another day. In that small victory was terror: each reprieve tightened the conscience around the thing they had bound; each binding made the seal cleverer.

When they left the temple, the desert sky was a hard, white blue. Kuldhara's ruins spread outward like an admonition. As they walked back to the haveli, Aadhya felt the spiral on her wrist throb steadily—no longer a secret, but a map pulsing under skin. Bhairav brought them before an old stone at the village edge that bore a carved glyph Aadhya hadn't seen before: a wheel crossed by three lines. "That mark," he said, "is a traveller's sign. It tells the world where to find what was lost. Someone has re-marked the map. You will not be safe in Kuldhara long."

Advait looked at the sky - threads of cloud that had gathered too quickly. "We go back to Varanasi," he said. "We return to Mahadev, to the records, to the places where the other seals might be—where their names were folded in cloth and sung into sleep." Raghav nodded. "And then?" he asked. "You keep watch," Bhairav said. "We move. The desert loosens what it keeps close. When you pass beyond this village, the trail will narrow. Remember—names like these are contagious. They are carried like contagion on breath and cloth."

Aadhya felt a fierce, exhausted softness fall over her. The baby's name Aadhrika, once felt like a blade at the throat, now glowed faintly as an ember within her—something she might yet lift or throw. She had bound a fissure, trapped an echo inside a mirror, and bought herself time. Time was necessary currency in the game of returning things to sleep. On the walk back to the station—if station was the right word—they passed a well where a child scrubbed the rims with a rag. He looked up as they passed and pointed at Aadhya with a small, ash-stained hand.

"She will be the last to dance," he said simply. The words were neither prophecy nor idle chatter. They were a reckoning. As the train took them back toward the river, the desert sped away into a smear of beige and ochre. Kuldhara receded, not as ruin but as a place that had been waiting until its dancers could once again step. Aadhya thought of the masks, the skulls, the mirror that now held a fragment of black glass like a secret pulse. Kalkini had not been banished—she had been shelved. And somewhere, perhaps not in Kuldhara but under other stones and currents, other seals were loose and listening.

Advait sat across from her, his notebook open but untouched. For the first time in days his face looked like someone caught between inevitability and stubborn, small hope. "What now?" he asked, but the question was more a way to steady himself. "We keep moving," Aadhya said. "We find the second seal the seals' makers never thought to hide from themselves. We make new bindings. We learn the names the world forgot." Bhairav reached into his coat and handed her a strip of cloth, printed with the spiral motif they had all seen since the beginning—the same symbol sewn into the skulls, into the mask, into the margins of the ledgers.

"Wrap it," he said. "When you sleep, when you chant, when you cannot keep the name from spilling, bind this to your mouth. It is not a ward. It is a promise." Aadhya took the cloth in her palms; it smelled faintly of ash, turmeric, and the salt of old tears. She tied it around her wrist because she could not bring herself to bind her mouth. The strip hummed faintly, a single, perfect note stretched thin. Outside, the train chugged forward. The desert receded. Behind them, Kuldhara's sands rearranged themselves like an animal licking a wound. Ahead, the river waited, and with it, the rest of the city—its ghats, its wells, its mirrors—that would have to be read, rung, and sealed all over again.

The dance had begun. They would learn the steps.

Chapter - 10

Bones That Weep

The fire would not go out. No matter how many times Bhairav poured sand over the ring of embers that gathered around *Aadhya's* prone body, the flame pushed back—first red, then orange, then a pale, waxy gold that seemed to illuminate her from within. She lay in the center of the haveli courtyard, limbs rigid, lips forming syllables that did not belong to any living tongue. Her murmurs threaded through the night like smoke – thin, insistent.

Advait stood over her like a man caught between prayer and panic. The mark on her palm - once little more than a scar - now crawled. It moved beneath the skin as though something impatient had taken root - veins of heat coiling toward her wrist with the patient, deliberate intent of a plant seeking light.

"She's not safe here," Advait said, voice raw. "We need help - a hospital, an exorcist, a priest" Bhairav cut him off without turning. His voice was flat, as if carved from iron. "She won't survive outside Kuldhara. The seal is bound to this land. If you cross its boundary, the lock will shatter." Advait's reply was splintered with disbelief. “What does that even mean? She’s burning from inside!” Bhairav stared into the impossible flames. “It means her body is the lock now, and the seal is the key trying to twist itself loose.” Then Aadhya screamed.

It wasn’t human. High and ancient, the cry tore outward and hung over the sand like broken glass. It sank into the ruins, into the buried bones under the floorboards, and for a terrified moment the whole village answered: a chorus of something that had been sleeping. Silence fell. Her eyes opened, and she sat up - but it was not wholly Aadhya who blinked at them. Something older peered through her lashes, an awareness that slowed its blink as if it had forgotten the tempo of being flesh.

“Do you smell it?” she whispered, her voice thin. Advait stepped forward. “Smell what?” She turned her head toward the haveli’s eastern wing, unfocused. “The bones-they’re weeping again.” She collapsed without warning.

That night the desert lost its generosity; the cooling air refused to come. Bhairav led Advait through the eastern wing’s ruined corridor, following a path Aadhya had always avoided with a flare of unease she could never explain. Here the masonry changed: where the rest of the haveli leaned on sandstone, this passage was hewn from dark granite, etched in faded Daitya glyphs that swallowed light like mouths. Moisture clung to the stone as if the crypt exhaled, and a rope, wound in a careful spiral, sealed the heavy door. Thick as a snake, it kept the darkness pressed in.

“What’s in there?” Advait asked. Bhairav’s jaw hardened. “I hoped I’d never have to find out.” He drew a curved blade, its hilt wrapped in strips of faded marigold garlands, and cut the rope. The door complained and opened downward into a stair which exhaled the smell of grief. The murals were painted in a red that might have once been blood: women dancing with their spines folded back, men without mouths dragging themselves toward a suspended blaze, children bound with thorny vines. Always, at the edge of every tableau, a single veiled figure—fire where hair should be, ash where eyes should be—repeated throughout the panels like a refrain.

Kalkini. At the crypt's floor, bones arranged itself with near-manic precision. Skull after skull faced outwards, jaws agape as if mid-scream; the circles of ribs and femora made concentric rings. In the center a stone basin stood filled—not with water, but with clear, slow tears that seemed to rise from the bones below. They bubbled up as if the cadavers beneath were weeping from inside the earth.

"Every time Kalkini stirs," Bhairav said quietly, "the bones weep. The dead remember her."

Advait peered into the basin. The tears shimmered with a film of something ancient. "Whose bones are these?" he asked. Bhairav crouched by a skull, turning it with respect. "The dancers who failed for her before Aadhya." "Failed?" The word hung wrong in Advait's mouth. "The seal requires a vessel," Bhairav explained.

"The dance is not merely ritual—it demands a body to carry the flaw. Kalkini's fire passes through a chosen host. If the vessel cannot bear it, the body burns from within." Advait swallowed bile. "So Aadhya—" Bhairav's voice cut across. "She might survive. Or she might not. We have to bind it. Tonight." He pointed to a pedestal by the basin. On it lay a broken mask, wood cracked with age and painted with three soot-black eyes.

The Ardhanritva mask, he said – *half truth, half lie. It was used once to bind the madness.* The air tightened when he lifted it. The bones shivered; the basin's tears rippled. A hush - like the intake of breath in a body about to speak. A voice came from within the stone: "Aadhya...come." They spun. The steps behind them had sealed – a wall where the stair had been. Below, the crypt darkened. Above, the haveli's upper room stirred. Aadhya woke. She rose to her feet with the slow precision of a marionette. The mirror at her bedside was fogged from within, and in it stood a woman in black - veil woven of smoke, mouth stitched with ash, hollow sockets leaking dust: ***Kalkini.***

The figure's hand pressed to the glass. Aadhya moved toward it, palms trembling. "Dance… and you shall remember," the voice instructed, honeyed and inevitable. The small flame in Aadhya's palm leapt. Her body obeyed like a thing remembering a choreography. Her feet found a rhythm; her hips rotated; her arms formed strange, practiced mudras. The syllables had not been taught to her in any classroom; they were bone-deep. Below them, in the crypt, the bones answered: one skull rolled, then another, as if the dead had been startled awake.

Click. Click. Click.

Skulls rolled into one another, jaws clattering a brittle counterpoint. Then—and with it—the basin overflowed. What had been crystalline tears thickened into black oil - slick and rotten. By the time the oil trickled toward the bone circles, something in the air had changed: it sounded as if a thousand women had been crowned with silence were now they were screaming into one another. Bhairav made a decision that tasted of rust. *"The mask,"* he said. *"It needs blood and a mirror."* He sliced his palm. Blood fountained and hissed when it touched the oily surface. The skulls howled, the sound human and not at all human, and Advait fell back over the bone-rings, covering his ears. Above, Aadhya's dance accelerated. Her movements became too fast, her joints bending past what the living consider possible. The mirror fog burst—glass exploded inward in a soundless bloom.

Shards rained like a frozen storm; one lodged in Aadhya's cheek. She did not flinch. Out stepped the woman in black. *Kalkini.* She was taller than flesh should permit, her limbs a choreography of twig-thin violence. Skin translucent enough for veins to read like script; her veil fluttered but revealed no face—only an oval of featureless skin split by a mouth that tore vertically to reveal serrated rows of teeth. When she smiled, it was as if a cathedral door opened. "You," she rasped, "you will burn better." She laid one skeletal hand to Aadhya's chest; the flames snapped upward, encasing Aadhya like a second skin. Aadhya levitated, convulsing in suspended terror.

Downstairs, Bhairav whispered, "There is one way." Advait looked up, breath gone. "Tell me."

"You," Bhairav said, pointing at him. "You step into the basin. Trade your mind. It will end you—but it will buy her life." Advait's face went still as stone. The basin seethed. Above, Kalkini's laugh spread like wildfire. The haveli trembled; plaster flaked like old skin. The sand outside corkscrewed skyward. Advait moved before thought: he snatched the Ardhanritva mask, thrust it to his face, and ran upward through collapsing halls - past hands that rose from the earth to claw at his legs. In the room, with flame frozen like a grotesque ornament, Advait placed the mask over his face. The world condensed to a single pinhole of sound. He felt his tongue become a rope; words not his own filled his mouth. He offered himself.

"I offer my mind," he breathed, not fully understanding the syllables. *"Take it. Leave her."* Kalkini considered him as one might appraise a new instrument. Then, with a motion like a curtain falling, she vanished. The fire sloughed from Aadhya; she collapsed into Advait's arms. The eastern wing collapsed into itself, a slow exhale of dust and ruin. The sandstorm scattered and the night settled into an exhausted hush. When

Advait peeled off the mask; his skin burned where metal had pressed. A faint spiral of three dots - now branded into his wrist and throat - glowed with an inner heat. He clutched Aadhya to him as Bhairav murmured that a shift had occurred: the seal had not been broken, only circumscribed. They had traded a life for a postponement.

Outside the ruin, Kuldhara slept as if drugged. Yet underfoot, something ticked and turned in the dark—an old mechanism reawakening in stages. The desert would not forget them. When dawn came it was thin and metallic. Advait lay on his back in the sand, tasting copper. His lungs ached from smoke, and the desert's breath had the scent of old sacrifices. Aadhya's breathing was shallow but steady; her eyelids fluttered as if trying to remember which century belonged to her body. The Ardhanritva mask lay half-buried nearby, its soot-streaked wooden face dull where fire had licked it. Bhairav crouched beside them, eyes narrowed. "You took the madness into yourself," he said to Advait without accusation. "You are marked." Advait rolled his wrist. The spiral of three burned faintly. It throbbed when he moved. "Is it—permanent?"

Bhairav's expression did not permit hope. "It survives like an echo. It will show. It will remind." They carried Aadhya to a squat shrine at the village edge. Bhairav applied a poultice of turmeric and crushed sandalwood to her burns. Advait insisted on doing it himself, hands clumsy with new ownership of a madness he could not name. He felt watched: something had followed him out of the mask and it lingered behind his shoulder like a moth. That night, sleep refused them. Aadhya murmured in her dream-language, syllables Advait could not parse but that made the sand around the village whisper. Once she opened her eyes and for an instant, they were catlike—vertical pupils narrowing in a sliver of a gaze—and the mark at her collarbone pulsed in rhythm with the spiral on his wrist.

Before dawn, Bhairav presented a letter wedged into his palm—a single sheet sealed with wax and stamped with the same three-dot spiral. Inside: a crude map of the Thar's western lip, and a note inked in blood-dark pigment.

"She stirs again. Her dance is not complete. You halted a memory, not the thing itself. The real fire sleeps beneath the Ghungroo Dunes. Go before the seal dreams fully." No signature, only a fingerprint the color of old dried blood. Bhairav read it twice and then folded it away. **"Ghungroo Dunes,"** he said. **"A place where the sand remembers anklets. The caravan dancers were exiled there; their bones are not at rest. If Kalkini's echo reaches those dunes, the seal will find other hearths to burn."** Advait stared at the map. "How far?"

"Three days by foot to the dunes," Bhairav said. "We cannot take vehicles past the salt flats; the earth rejects wheels. You will travel on foot and by night." Aadhya woke to their packing. She looked thin, like a coin pushed through time. Her voice was a dry river. "I saw her," she said once. "In the glass. She whispered the last step." Bhairav folded his satchel with deliberate hands. "We leave at dusk," he said, "when the desert's throat is cooler. We will travel under the new moon and hide from the sun's memory."

As they prepared, the village remained abandoned. No vendors, no ragged children chasing shadows. Even the little well near the center was dry as if suctioned of recollection. The ruins breathed faintly, like a beast asleep with one ear open. At midday a crow circled once and then did not return. They set out when the wind lessened, moving through a landscape that narrowed advantage to a single task. Kuldhara receded like a thought put away. The first night the stars watched them like oblivious gods. The nights were cold enough to make their breath visible and brittle. Bhairav led them down animal tracks no maps could name. Raghav—the man who had come from beyond the dunes with contacts and secrets—walked at their flank, eyes sharp.

At dusk on the second day they camped within reach of a crumbled hamlet, its wells choked with salt. The sand here carried impressions of anklets, faint as fossilized wind. Around the fire, Advait studied the burn on his wrist. It had started to throb nightly with a different rhythm—sometimes a slow pulse like the sea, sometimes a rapid blink like a panic heartbeat. "The mask rewired something," he admitted quietly. "I hear it sometimes—when I close my eyes—women chanting as if plucked from beneath the earth." Bhairav's face was a map of worry. "Masks change the wearer. They are tools not meant for the living. You wore one that was never forged for mortal hands. It took, and it left a trace." Aadhya's voice drifted from where she had wrapped herself in the shawl. "It saved me," she said. "And I am alive. But I remember—bits. The way people closed their mouths. Children tossed into pits. The smell of hair charred into braids. A name. **Daityagarh**."

Advait paled. "You said that once before," he murmured. "The word from the mirror." She nodded faintly. "It is a place and a wound. And the dance was a way to keep it from waking." On the third night, as they approached the Ghungroo lip, the land changed. The wind was thicker, laced with a metallic tang that made their tongues prickle. The dunes rose like a shifting army. For the first time, their lanterns did not throw normal light—the shadows bent wrong, angles contracting where there ought to be none. The sand underfoot hummed like a restless throat.

Near dusk they found the first anklet—half-buried, ringed with rust. It chimed when Bhairav nudged it with his boot. The sound crawled across the dunes, tiny and intimate, and Advait felt a pressure at the base of his skull. At the dune's shoulder, the ground dipped. There, beneath the first thin grasses, lay something that did not belong to the desert.

Bones. Not bleached by heat but blackened and arranged. Ankles bound with copper wire, rib cages stacked like fences. At the center of the arrangement a wooden pole bore a torn dupatta streaked with vermilion, and the air around it breathed a scent of old perfume and ash. The dunes had been piled over a ritual site, like a wound covered and pressed—an attempt to forget. Raghav dropped his pack and bowed his head. "The dancers were buried here," he said in a voice like gravel. *"Not by fate, but by hands that couldn't bear the fire. They tried to smother the memory with sand. But the sand keeps record. It listens."*

That night the anklets chimed from beneath the sand like something trying to memorize the pattern of feet. Aadhya dreamed the dancer's last steps; she woke with the taste of iron in her mouth. Advait cradled his wrist and, as if cued by the earth itself, a low rhythm began to pulse through the sand—a beat like an invisible tambour: anklet, anklet, anklet. They descended into the first gullied hollow at dawn. A scent rose—sour milk and incense, old and clotted. The bones lay arranged in configurations that suggested dance steps: the femur a measure, the clavicle a line, skulls placed like cymbals. Where the dancers had once held space, the sand remembered the impression of skirts. Advait knelt and touched a bone. It was warm. Flesh memory, not decay. When he looked up, the air had thickened. A figure moved at the dune's edge—a woman, but not a woman the world would keep. Her sari trailed in sand like a washed veil, and her anklets did not jingle; they hummed.

"Kalkini's Chhaya," Raghav whispered. "A shadow dance."

The woman did not turn her face. She pirouetted with a grace that made no sense under a sky no one had named. Her steps sank into the sand and the sand took them as if writing. Whatever she walked over sprouted that faint, terrible echo. Aadhya felt the old bond in her bones—the steps pushing back into her like a tide. "We are too close," Bhairav said. "We came for this," Aadhya replied with a thin laugh that had no humor. "We have to finish it." As they more closely approached the place where the dune bowed into a hollow, the wind shifted. A sound rose from the ground itself: a rustling like a mass of skirt hems brushing across bone. The chhaya's figure blurred and then was gone; in its place was a long shallow pit, cut into the earth and ringed with small charred stones. At the pit's center, a raised slab was scorched black, and upon it lay an object that made Advait inhale sharply: a small mirror, black as coal, set in a frame of braided hair.

Advait's throat tightened. "A mirror," he breathed. "Just like the one in the temple." Aadhya stepped forward, bare feet sinking into found memory. "This is where the real seal sleeps," she said, voice like a stone dropped into a well. *"Not buried by stone or steel. Buried by dance and promise."* Bhairav put a hand on her shoulder. "We will not break it," he said. "We will not free it. We will bind it deeper." But the dunes remembered more than the people who had walked them. As the sun slid and shadow shifted, the anklets below them began to chime from under the sand, faint then rising like a chorus. The earth hummed; the hollow exhaled. The black mirror on the slab began to drink the light.

At that moment, the Ghungroo Dunes decided that this matter was no longer secret. The dunes did not wait for permission. Once they acknowledged a name, it replicated. Anklets under the sand began to echo in patterns that matched Aadhya's limp fingers, and the atmosphere tightened as if a mouth had closed around their breaths. Bhairav unrolled the small strip of cloth he'd been given in Kuldhara—the spiral-patterned strip—and tied it around Aadhya's wrist like a tether. It hummed, a single note of rebellion.

They arranged a perimeter around the mirror: Bhairav's salt-and-ash lines; Raghav's hair-rope coiled like a noose; Advait's pragmatic knots; and a bowl of turmeric-and-bone paste. The black glass reflected only the sky at first - empty like a wound. As their incantations threaded into air, the mirror grew hungry with images not the present: dancers frozen mid-leap, an amphitheater collapsing into flame, a woman turning to lock eyes with Aadhya across centuries.

The sand's humming rose. *"Sing,"* Bhairav ordered, voice flat. *"Half-supplication, half-barring. Pull the memory into the glass and close it away."* They began. Advait's voice had changed since he wore the mask: the syllables came smoother, like gravel polished into glass. Aadhya's throat tightened—when she tried to sing, a different rhythm emerged in her mouth, an echo of anklets, the staccato beat of the dance. The mirror responded. The chhaya danced within the glass, a figure made of refusal and ash. Kalkini's echo reached out, not with hands but with choreography—angles designed to undo bone. The sand around the pit rose in miniature eddies, like breath going out to call the tide. "Now," Bhairav hissed, and he let a trickle of blood from his thumb fall into the bowl of turmeric-bone. The dust hissed and shifted—some force accepted the offering.

But the mirror resisted. With a tremor, its surface rippled, and the chhaya inside it smiled in a way that tore something between Aadhya's ribs. The glass did not want to hold the memory—it wanted to include it, to become a gate. The anklets below chimed louder, not as echo but as invitation. Suddenly, the desert answered in a new register. A low drum sounded beneath the dunes, the skin of earth beating in measured time. A column of sand rose like a slow, unwinding thread, and from it materialized a shape that was neither human nor weather: a figure woven of leftover rituals, part-song, part-bone. A chorus of stone voices rose from the pit.

It seemed then that the world had an appetite they could not outpace. Kalkini's chhaya split from the glass and ran along the rim of the sand like a hand tracing a wound. It did not touch flesh; it touched memory. Anyone who looked at it felt childhood names slip away like thread. Aadhya faltered. She could feel the seam between herself and the echo lining up; the dancer inside her lungs was counting steps she had been taught before birth. She stumbled and the strip around her wrist slid down, drawing the spiral like a map. The mirror flashed. The earth opened. Not in a single rupture, but in a yawning split—narrow at first, then widening, a throat dredging up things long meant to be quiet. From within the split came a smell like iron and ash mixed with the sweetness of marigolds. A figure like a memory climbed, followed by others—shapes that had once been dancers, eyes sewn closed, mouths turned inward.

"They're coming out," Advait croaked. "This was never meant to be found again," Bhairav said. "They were buried precisely so they could not remember who they were." But the memory had been woken by song, by the insistence of Aadhya's bones. As the first of the undead figures stood at the split's lip, a sound rose: a thousand anklets struck at once. The dune shimmered. In the mirror, Kalkini smiled wider and stepped free. Her body was wrong. Not because it was monstrous—though it was—but because the human shapes she borrowed were all wrong sizes and ages, patched together like a scavenger's quilt. The chhaya looked at Aadhya, and for the briefest instant, the two shared a look that was not surprise; it was recognition, like two family members glimpsing an ancestor's face in a river.

"You returned," Kalkini said, her voice a scrape of silk on stone. Aadhya's knees buckled. "I didn't mean—" Kalkini's hand brushed her cheek. The touch did not burn; it translated memory into light. "You offered the step," she said. "You were the hinge. Come." The dunes answered with a chorus: **anklet, anklet, anklet.** Raghav thrust forward. *"We must break the circle,"* he barked. He slung a coil of hair-rope and flung it across the opening. The rope's fibers hissed and splintered; the hair burned where it met the sand's mouth. Bhairav moved to the slab and began to chant in a voice that seemed to come from under the throat. His syllables were old and cruel in their accuracy. Advait, heart hammering, found himself echoing the words involuntarily. The black mirror pulsed and then sighed as if someone exhaled into glass.

For a moment, the dune became a battleground of sound and cloth. Kalkini danced along the edge, tempting the figures of memory to step free. The anklets clicked. Human hands, seeking warmth, reached for the surface. But Aadhya's voice rose—not with the dancer's rhythm, nor the mirror's harmonics, but with something rawer: the sound of a woman unwilling to be pulled apart. *"I will not trade my name,"* she said - the statement held like a bell. Kalkini paused. Her smile thinned into an appraisal. "Names are costly," she said. "You will have to pay to keep yours."

The dunes heaved. A hand the color of smoke reached from the split. Another, smaller and child-boned, followed. A silence spread like oil—an anticipatory quiet that suggested a world bracing itself. In the lull, Advait made a choice that wrote itself in actions rather than words: he stepped forward and placed his own palm against the black mirror. "If you were the door," he whispered, "then I will be the hinge." He felt the glass drink him; it did not cut but drew as a mouth draws breath. The spiral brand beneath his wrist flared, and for a second every name he had ever owned flashed across the surface of the mirror. Then *Kalkini* laughed, a sound like dry bones rubbing together, and the mirror cooled. The split closed. Silence returned, heavy and black. The anklets stilled. The dancers' forms slumped and folded back into the sand like ribbons being rewound. Kalkini looked at them both—Aadhya and Advait—her face impossibly distant and personal all at once.

"You bind well," she said. "For now." Then she stepped back into the mirror, and the surface swallowed her whole. The slurry of sand and glass calmed as if it had licked its own wounds. The dunes shuddered, as if settling the bones beneath. Advait sank to his knees, dizzy and empty. The mask had burned a memory into him that tasted of salt and old lullabies. His lips trembled as he tried to form the chants that had kept the split closed. He felt older, hollowed, as if someone had removed prints from his fingers. Bhairav sat opposite them, chest heaving in a manner that looked close to prayer. "You bought time," he said quietly. *"But these seals are clever. They do not sleep for long."* Aadhya reached for Advait's hand and squeezed. He answered the pressure with a weak smile. "You're still here," he mouthed.

She nodded—an acknowledgment, not a promise. The black mirror sat between them like a contained animal, still breathing faintly with captured tides of memory. They left the Ghungroo Dunes as the sky lightened into a brittle blue. The dunes closed behind them, reluctant to give up their secrets but satisfied to have swallowed the fresh heat of disturbance. Kuldhara appeared below the horizon like a bruise: a place that had been touched and changed. Their caravan of three returned to the ruins where the haveli's remains still glowered from the night's conflagration. Bhairav examined the collapsed frame with an old sadness. *"The eastern wing is gone,"* he said simply. *"A sacrifice. The mask took its toll."*

In the days that followed the marks on Advait's skin did not fade: the spiral on his wrist grew a faint silver sheen, and sometimes at midnight he would wake with the taste of smoke and the feeling of anklets ringing just behind his eyes. Aadhya's dreams were quieter, but there were moments when she would stop mid-step as if a phantom rhythm ran through her with the jagged precision of a chain. Each knew that their deed was a reprieve, not an absolution. Far to the west, under the salt-wrinkled sky, five figures stood in a domed chamber and watched the lights flicker in their oil bowls. They wore veils of black and rings carved from bone. On the far wall five seals were etched deep into stone: each oriented to a direction and one oriented downward, into the place below everything. The first seal bore a hairline crack. "She moved," one whispered. "The one in the haveli."

"Use the map," said another. "The caravan route. The woman with the white-peacock tongue. The city remembers." They leaned forward. A candle guttered. A name was traced onto the damp floor with a finger that left no ink, only cold: **AADHRIKA.**

Back in *Kuldhara*, Aadhya sat by the ruined well, tracing the old anklet marks in the sand with a hesitant finger. She felt lighter, somehow, as if a weight had been relocated—moved and parked inside someone else's shadow. Advait sat beside her, his palm over the spiral brand on his wrist. They did not speak of bargains. Bargains unmake speech. Instead they listened: to the distant clink of anklets under dunes, to the wind that no longer howled, and to the low, coiled memory in their bones that would not be quieted for long. **The Ghungroo Dunes had been awakened.** The masks and mirrors had bought them an interval, a fragile lease. But the bones remembered. The anklets would not stop chiming. And in the thin light between dawn and day, in a world that was learning to speak old names again, the next step had already begun.

The next step begins.

Chapter - 11

The Black Peacock Eyes

The desert was not a single colour. At a distance it read as gold—dried, cracked, and endless—but as the sun climbed, the horizon pulsed: fields of violet flared like bruises, mirages washed in a bruised crimson, and underfoot the sand glittered as if remembering a former blaze. Aadhya and Advait moved through that remembered light with Bhairav Singh ahead of them, a dark silhouette against a landscape that felt older than the maps that named it. They walked without words. Ten hours had passed since *Kuldhara's* ruined alleys gave way to the wide plain; the wind, when it came, was capricious and abrasive, tearing sand across their faces like fingers seeking entry. Bhairav's staff tapped an even cadence; his figure remained steady, as if the land listened to him and altered its steps accordingly.

Aadhya had not spoken since dawn. She woke early, packed quietly, and led the small caravan without waiting for instructions. She carried nothing that could be called a weapon—only a small *mirror* wrapped in black cloth and bound with red thread. She avoided looking into it. She avoided looking at Advait.

There was something in her gait now that had not been there before: the economy of someone who knew where to place a foot, who could follow a rhythm the mind refused to name. Advait trailed her with the patient anxiety of someone learning to read unfamiliar gestures. He watched the rise and fall of her shoulders, the way her hands clutched the wrapped mirror. There was a new gravity in her posture - not merely fatigue, but the retained muscle memory of motions learned long ago and forgotten by reason.

By noon the salt flats opened: a broad expanse of pale, cracked crust, its surface blistered into millennia of desiccation. Each step sank in a little deeper than the last, leaving footprints like relics. The sky was a distracted blue; the ground, mute. Even the wind here seemed wary, as if the plain had been asked to hold its breath. No birds, no insect-chorus—only the brittle sound of their own boots on salt. They paused by a half-buried stone shoulder, its face scored with figures that had once been elegant and now were mere scratches of pain: dancers in contorted postures, limbs arced like the bow of a ritual, anklets and tridents and severed heads worked into a frieze of obsession. At the center of the carving, almost lost under encrusted age, was a tiny glyph - a teardrop ringed with filigree and a single small dot: a peacock's eye rendered in the language of stone.

"This is where the exiled walked," Bhairav murmured. "The dancers who refused to end - they became a rite, then a curse."

"Why here?" Advait asked. The salt flats offered no sanctuary, no shade, only an indifferent preservation.

"Salt eats rot and preserves ruin," Bhairav said. "No god watches here; no priest's hand consecrates ashes. That is why the rite took root. Salt keeps memory from decay."

He knelt and let his fingers trace the carved peacock eye. "It is a gate," he said. "The dancers were placed standing, anklets locked. They were not buried so much as suspended. The earth held them upright so the rhythm would never cease." Aadhya pressed the wrapped mirror to her chest and did not speak. She saw the symbol and something old unspooled in her—a memory that was not memory but inheritance: a circle of feet, the clink of ghungroos, a rhythm hammered into bone.

By dusk the Ghungroo Dunes rose like a waiting audience: graceful, merciless waves of sand, each crest a promise of movement. Even from a distance the dunes transmitted a vibration you felt not with your ears but through the soles—the thud of anklets beating under the ground. They made camp on a shallow rise. Aadhya built a small fire while Bhairav sat with his eyes closed and Advait stared west, watching shadows gather like a crowd taking its positions. The night's first sign came as the flames turned a strange blue, as if the fuel were remembering a different chemistry. Then the wind dropped altogether—one instant a restless breath, the next an oppressive stillness that pressed the air taut. The fire bent toward something unseen, as if a gravity of memory tugged at the light.

"He comes," Bhairav said without opening his eyes. Before anyone could answer, a figure stepped out from the dunes, at first indistinct, then whole. He seemed, at a glance, like any traveller - wrapped in a long scarf, robes dusted with sand, bare feet. But when he came closer, they all saw what separated him from ordinary men—the eyes. Not brown, not coal, but shifting iridescence that flashed blue, green, and purple in the uncertain light - the slow, oily sheen of a black peacock's tail. The effect was animal and utterly alien. Aadhya drew back as if struck. Her hand tightened on the mirror's cloth.

"Don't," the stranger said, his voice low and oddly musical, as though he spoke by plucking strings backward. "I mean no harm. I only wish to rest." Bhairav opened one eye and inclined his head. "You're late."

"I'm always late," the man smiled. He sat just beyond the circle of light, neither close enough to touch nor distant enough to ignore. Advait's hand hovered near his satchel, not entirely relaxed.

"Who are you?" Advait asked finally. The stranger smiled wider, and for a moment Advait saw other vistas flicker through his iridescent gaze—flame, a woman dancing, a scream braided into language not yet born. "I am whoever remembers you," the man said. "And whatever you have let go."

A silence settled, heavy and deliberate. Aadhya's look was not of fear so much as recognition. "You were there," she breathed. "I have always been," he answered. "Even before the mirror split." Bhairav's tone sharpened. "Riddles and mirrors will not get you anywhere. Speak plainly." The stranger's tone changed like a wind shifting. "The second seal weakens. The sands remember her steps. And they remember him." He nodded toward Advait. "You carry an imprint - the Ardhanritva mark. You will feel the balance tilt soon." Advait's heart lodged against his ribs. "I don't understand."

"You will," the man said, and stood with the same unhurried grace with which a dancer rises to the last chime of a performance. As he did, he looked at Aadhya and, oddly tender, said, "Be careful with that mirror. Not all who look through glass return the same." Then he walked away, dissolving into the dunes as if he were a memory reclaiming its shape. The heat of his presence lingered, like the afterglow of a bonfire; when he was gone the night seemed emptier, as if a crucial note of song had been removed.

That night Aadhya dreamed in a circle of women whose hair was flame and whose anklets rang without sound. She moved with them, bare feet printing an ancient mandala, blood on her palms, mouth shaping syllables she did not know she remembered. At the center of the spiral the peacock-eyed man stood, smiling with too many voices inside his mouth. *Seven voices spoke to her at once: your name is not yours; your blood is older than the gods; if the seal breaks you will not survive the person you are supposed to be.*

She awoke with the scream lodged raw in her throat. The fire had gone out. The dunes answered only with the faint echo of anklets moving under the surface. The wind picked up again, colder now, and the night stretched long and listening. Aadhya moved in the tent as if called. Advait watched, helpless and bewildered, as she rose, walked without sound, and drifted out into the white hush. Her bare feet left no sound on the packed sand, but when she began to turn in spirals—a dance without music—Advait heard it in his bones: the ghungroo rhythm, soft and irresistible.

She spoke then, in a tongue that pulled at something under his own ribs: **"Aakalritya... Dhritya vakra... Kalkini nartana..."** ("Having invoked... with fierce resolve... the twisted dance of Kalkini.")

The words were neither blessing nor curse but a hinge. Mid-chant she collapsed against Advait's shoulder and, with the dawn, came back to herself—the mirror's muslin strap still clutched in her hand; the salt from the plains crusting the soles of her feet; faint, circular bruises around each ankle as if something invisible had tightened there.

"We must move," Bhairav said when the sun began to harden the sand. "Before the dunes learn to hum more than a warning."

They crossed into a section of desert that began to breathe memory—the air blurred with heat and shadow and mirage.

Bodies, half-seen and ghostly, shimmered across the dunes: women in trailing veils, bowls of fire cupped like hearts, drums that made no sound yet kept perfect time. Then a wind rose and a rift opened, a gorge where none had been before, its mouth revealing steps carved in old stone descending into dark.

"This was not here," Advait said, voice thin. "No," Bhairav admitted. "But now the place remembers it was always meant to be." They threaded the newly born stair into the dark. The air changed from dry to damp, the walls flecked with mica that blinked like watchful eyes. When the corridor opened into a circular chamber, a roof gaping like a rent pupil to the sky - all speech fell out of their mouths. Seven statues stood within—tall, lithe, headless women locked mid-dance; their anklets real and tarnished; piles of charred feathers heaped at their feet. And behind them, as if he had been waiting the whole time, stood the man with the peacock eyes, robe woven from something that drank light.

"You came," he said, and the room received it like the final note of a long song. Aadhya—already trembling, already pulled by things she could not yet name—stepped forward. Aadhya's voice was quiet but certain, like she was speaking to someone she had already met. "Who were they?" Aadhya asked, gesturing toward the statues that surrounded them. The man with the peacock eyes regarded the headless dancers with something that almost resembled reverence. His voice lowered, smooth as silk dragged over bone. "They were the last of the *Ashvini* rite. Dancers who remembered too much. Before Kalkini rose, they sought to imitate her—to touch the flame she called divinity. But fire doesn't tolerate imitation."

He walked among the statues, his fingers tracing the cracked stone hips with the delicacy of a sculptor. "Some say they summoned her; others say she devoured them and wore their movements as her own. Either way..." he looked up, his eyes gleaming with a light that didn't belong to the chamber, "they became part of the dance. Flesh burned. Names erased. Only rhythm remained."

"Why are they headless?" Advait asked, his voice echoing too loudly in the silence. The man smiled faintly. "Because to hold the whole rhythm is to lose the self. Mind and memory cannot coexist with the truth of the dance. So they offered their heads to the rhythm. *To remember is to dissolve*." Before Advait could speak again, Aadhya gasped. She dropped to her knees, clutching her chest just below the collarbone. Her breath came in sharp bursts. "It's burning," she choked. "The spiral—it's…"

Advait rushed to her side, pulling at her shawl. Beneath the cloth, the faint spiral mark throbbed - not red this time, but black: a shadow-light, consuming rather than glowing. It pulsed in rhythm with the phantom sound that now filled the room—the faint, unmistakable ring of anklets moving somewhere beneath the stone. Bhairav's face paled. "The seal," he whispered. "It's responding."

"To what?" Advait's voice cracked. The peacock-eyed man's tone softened into something mournful. "To recognition." He crouched beside Aadhya, pressing a finger gently to her forehead. "The seal remembers her. And memory always claims what belongs to it." The moment his skin touched hers, Aadhya went still. Her back arched, her eyes rolled white—and then her lips moved. The voice that emerged was not hers. It was deep, resonant, reverberating through the chamber walls like a thousand echoes collapsing into one.

"Tisra tala. Kriya avartana. Jwala pravesh… Kalkini… jaag rahi hai." (Third rhythm. Act of returning. Entrance of flame. Kalkini… is awakening.)

The air convulsed. The statues trembled. A deafening hum filled the chamber – a vibration not of sound but pressure, a low drumming felt inside the ribs; the ground shifted beneath their feet; Dust rained from the ceiling. Then came the ghungroo: it began faintly - metal against bone, measured and deliberate. Then louder, faster, until it became a rhythm the earth itself seemed to mimic. The chamber darkened, though the opening above remained. The daylight was devoured. Shadows danced where light should have been.

Aadhya rose, her body no longer her own. Her movements were sharp, unnatural, yet impossibly precise. Her arms curved in spirals; her head tilted, spine bending backward until it almost broke. Her feet traced a perfect mandala in the dust. "Aadhya!" Advait shouted, lunging forward, but Bhairav blocked him with an arm. "Don't," he hissed. "If you touch her now, she'll take you with her." "She's not her!" Advait yelled. "She's—"

"She is becoming her," Bhairav cut him off, his eyes fixed on the girl. "The rhythm remembers. The vessel answers." The peacock-eyed man stepped closer to Aadhya. "You see now?" he said softly. "She was never meant to escape it. The flame always returns to its source."

"Stop it!" Advait roared, but his words were swallowed by the drumming. The statues began to move. At first it was only the smallest twitch—a finger curling here, a toe flexing there—but soon, the motion grew deliberate. One of the dancers tilted forward, her stone spine cracking with the sound of splintering wood. Her headless form extended an arm toward Aadhya, frozen mid-mudra. Another followed. Then another. Bhairav's face hardened. "They're teaching her," he said quietly.

The peacock-eyed man's tone turned reverent. "No, priest. They're remembering through her. Each step she takes restores a piece of what was lost." Aadhya's body jerked violently, as if strings were being pulled from within her bones. Her lips moved again, whispering fragments of an old language, each syllable bending the air around it.

"Aakalritya... vakra... nritta..." ("Having invoked... the twisted... dance.")

The mark on her collarbone pulsed faster. Black veins spidered outward from it, racing up her throat. Her eyes turned glossy, dark as obsidian. "She'll die if we don't stop this," Advait said, voice trembling. "She won't die," the peacock-eyed man replied softly. "She'll remember. And when she does, none of you will matter anymore." Bhairav slammed his staff to the ground. The carvings etched along its shaft ignited in a blue flame. The vibration shattered, momentarily cutting through the sound. Aadhya froze mid-turn, the ghungroo rhythm halting.

"Come back, *Aadhrika*," Bhairav commanded. His voice echoed with a force that didn't belong to him alone. "You are not her. You are the fire, not its shadow." The peacock-eyed man recoiled, covering his face. "You dare fracture the rhythm?" he hissed. "You fracture memory itself."

"She's not ready," Bhairav snapped. "The seal cannot open through her yet!" The chamber began to quake again. From the opening above, sand poured in thick, black streams. The statues' bodies groaned as cracks webbed through them. Aadhya's body tensed. Her limbs jerked once, twice—then she screamed. It wasn't human. It was a sound pulled from an older plane, one that split the air and made Advait's vision blur. He felt his knees buckle under its weight.

Then silence. Aadhya collapsed; feathers from the floor rose and scattered, dissolving mid-air like ash. The drumming ceased. The light from Bhairav's staff dimmed to a faint pulse. Advait caught her before she hit the ground. Her skin was cold, her breathing shallow, but she was alive. Her hands still twitched, small, involuntary motions as if the memory of the dance refused to let go. The peacock-eyed man stood motionless, his expression unreadable. Slowly, he raised a hand and traced a spiral in the air with his fingertip. The motion left a trail of faint blue light. “You can cage rhythm,” he said softly, “but you cannot kill it.”

Bhairav’s staff flared once more. “Leave this place.” For a heartbeat, the man’s iridescent eyes caught what little light remained—and behind the shifting hues, Advait saw something monstrous. Wings. Feathers. Fire. Then the man smiled, bowed slightly, and vanished—dissolving into a curl of black feathers that drifted upward into the narrowing shaft of light. Bhairav exhaled heavily. His voice was almost a whisper. “He won’t stop. He’ll find another way to make her remember.” Advait’s arms trembled as he cradled Aadhya. “Then tell me what we’re supposed to do.” Bhairav looked at him, eyes heavy with exhaustion and knowledge that weighed like stone. “Pray she forgets - because the next time she remembers, the desert won’t survive.” He turned toward the wall and pressed the staff against the stone. Symbols flared briefly, and a passageway appeared—a narrow stair ascending steeply back to the surface. Advait hesitated. “Can she walk?” Bhairav’s answer was quiet, almost reluctant. “She must. The earth won’t let me carry her.” And as if the words themselves were command, Aadhya stirred. Her eyes fluttered open, dazed and glassy. She looked from Bhairav to Advait, confused but present. “He was in my mind,” she whispered hoarsely. “The man with the eyes. He wasn’t watching. He was… guiding.” Advait steadied her. “Do you remember the dance?”

Aadhya shook her head slowly. “No. Only how it ends.” They began to climb. The air grew warmer, drier, easier to breathe, until at last they emerged into the bruised violet of twilight. Behind them, the desert stretched silent and unbroken. When Advait turned back, the opening they’d climbed through was gone. The sand was whole again.

“Where was that place?” he asked. Bhairav drew a spiral in the sand with his staff. “Buried not by earth, but by memory. That chamber existed between the present and what was forgotten. We trespassed where thought should not return." He looked at Aadhya. "And yet she brought it back." Aadhya wrapped her shawl tighter, her voice barely above a breath. *"I don't want to dance again."* Bhairav's gaze shifted to the horizon, where a red sun was bleeding into violet clouds. "Then we move. Quickly. Before the desert starts to hum."

The air inside the chamber thickened until even breath felt sacrilegious. Aadhya's chant had become rhythm incarnate—the pulse of a world that no longer remembered its own birth. Each syllable curved through the air like smoke trying to take form. Bhairav's voice thundered over it, raw with command.

"Enough!" His staff struck the ground once more. A shockwave rolled through the chamber, scattering black sand like a dispersing flock of birds. The echo of the impact climbed the walls and struck the open skylight, where a sliver of dying light bled through. Aadhya's body jerked violently—then stilled. Her hair hung across her face in dark, wet strands; her arms remained frozen mid-mudra. The mark on her chest flared, dimmed, and then, mercifully, faded to a dull ember. The drumming ceased. The statues quieted. For one suspended heartbeat, it seemed as if even the desert above had stopped breathing.

Then the wind returned, whispering through the fissures with the mournful timbre of something denied. Bhairav lowered the staff, the wood now scorched and trembling in his hand. "It's done," he murmured, though his eyes betrayed no certainty. Advait knelt beside Aadhya. Her skin was clammy, her pulse uneven. "She's burning inside," he said. "She always was," Bhairav replied. "The seal remembers through pain. It must feed on it to stay asleep." The peacock-eyed man watched them silently, his expression unreadable. At last, he spoke—softly, like the desert speaking to itself. "You think this is mercy? You bury her each time she begins to breathe. Every age needs its dance, Bhairav. You cannot silence rhythm."

Bhairav turned, fury rippling through his composure. “If rhythm returns, the world ends in flame.”

“Perhaps that is the only way it remembers its shape,” the stranger whispered, and with that, he dissolved into shadow—no sound, no trace, only the faint shimmer of peacock hues vanishing into the cracks of the stone. The chamber groaned once, and all fell still. They climbed back toward the surface through the passage Bhairav carved open. The tunnel was narrow, filled with dust that glittered faintly when the torchlight brushed it—dust that looked almost alive.

When they emerged, the horizon had forgotten the sun. The sky hung between colours—bruised violet fading into molten copper. The dunes seemed to breathe. Aadhya leaned against the rock face, her knees shaking. “He was inside my head,” she said quietly. “Guiding the movements. I didn’t want to follow, but my bones… they remembered.”

“Do you recall the full dance?” Advait asked. She hesitated. “Only the ending. The moment she fell. The moment I—she—sealed the fire.” Bhairav drew a spiral into the sand with the tip of his staff. “Fragments,” he said. “Fragments are enough to wake what sleeps.” Aadhya’s voice faltered. “I don’t want to dance again.”

“Then we must move,” Bhairav replied, eyes turned westward. “Before the desert begins to hum.” Night came like a bruise spreading across the sky. Their small encampment glowed faintly beneath the fractured moon. Silent men, Bhairav’s contacts, arrived with jars of brackish water and bundles of cloth. They spoke little, their faces streaked with ash and ochre, as though language itself were forbidden here.

Aadhya collapsed into uneasy sleep. The mark on her chest no longer burned, yet it throbbed beneath the skin with a quiet insistence—like a second heartbeat learning to mimic her own. Advait did not sleep. He watched the fire sputter, shrinking lower each hour. Bhairav sat across from him, the staff resting on his knees. “There is a pattern,” Bhairav said at last, his voice barely above the wind. “The scriptures once called her Kalkini not a goddess but a wound. The dance is her blood remembering itself.”

He lifted his gaze to the dunes beyond. “She doesn’t remember yet. But when she does… you’ll have to choose.” Advait’s throat tightened. “Choose what?”

“Whether to pull her back—or let her finish the dance.” No more was said. The fire sighed and collapsed inward, casting long, nervous shadows across the sand. The wind slipped around them, cool and uncertain. Then—movement. Far out in the dunes, the sand rippled. Not from breeze, but from something shifting beneath. Advait rose, heart hammering. Bhairav didn’t move. The sound came next. Faint, delicate, impossible.

A single anklet bell rang once, clear as crystal; then again - an echo stretched by miles of emptiness. The rhythm was patient, almost tender. Chim… chim… chim. The dunes seemed to answer. Their surfaces quivered in slow undulations, as if something beneath them had begun to turn. Bhairav exhaled through his nose, whispering to himself: “She’s still dancing. ”Advait turned to Aadhya. Even in sleep, her fingers flexed as though tracing invisible patterns in the air. Her ankles twitched—small, perfect movements, timed to the distant chime. Another gust swept through camp. The lanterns flickered sideways.

Somewhere between the dunes, a woman laughed—softly, mournfully—and the desert wind carried her name.

Kalkini. Then silence returned—vast, endless, waiting. The dunes settled. The sky dimmed. Only the desert breathed. Not broken yet. But close.

Chapter - 12

Desert Teeth

The wind had changed. It no longer howled across the Thar like it once did - shrill and hollow - but moaned. Low. Wet. As if the sand were not being lifted by wind, but exhaled from something beneath it. Something with lungs. Something that had learned to breathe through centuries of ash and bone.

Aadhya felt it in her molars first - a dull, steady pressure, as though a finger pressed through the roof of her mouth. She opened her eyes. They had set up camp hours west of Kuldhara's outskirts, near a stretch of cracked mesas locals called *Pyaasi Chaati—the Thirsting Chest.* The name suited it. The terrain was a wound in the desert's spine, a labyrinth of parched gullies that moaned when the wind passed through. Every sound here had weight. Even silence.

She sat up slowly. The fire had shrunk to faint embers, casting skeletal shadows that stretched and trembled across their belongings. Bhairav was awake, sitting cross-legged, his staff laid across his lap like a weapon and a prayer. His gaze was fixed on the dunes. His eyes didn't blink. Advait slept beside his satchel, one arm curved protectively over it, as though the scrolls and relics within were fragile organs he could not afford to lose.

Aadhya didn't wake either of them. The moan was louder now. Not above the ground—but beneath it. She pressed her palm into the sand. It was cold. Not the clean, empty chill of desert nights—but the cold of flesh that had forgotten blood. No warmth. No memory of the sun. The sand felt embalmed – cold and emptied of its sun.

A shadow moved along the dune to her left. Quick. Too quick for a jackal. Too thin for a snake. Her breath snagged. She stood, brushing grit from her palms. The sand gave under her feet—too easily, too deep—like wet flour. Her soles tingled. No… it itched. Deep, under the skin. She clenched her jaw against it. Another shadow darted between two of the tent poles. This one wasn't thin. It was tall. And it was still. She reached for the lantern Bhairav had left by the fire pit, lit its wick, and turned slowly toward the dune's edge.

It was standing there. Half-submerged in the sand - as though it had grown from beneath rather than arrived. A humanoid shape. Gaunt. Elongated. Carved from blackened stone that glimmered faintly, like fossilized wood slicked with oil. Its surface was etched with ridges, each one curling inward toward the hollow of its head. It had no face - only a deep spiral, where eyes should have been.

And teeth - dozens of them - lining the spiral like a maw built of memory. Not bone teeth—but desert teeth: jagged, mismatched, yellowed things that looked ripped from the mouths of strangers long buried. They didn't bite. They waited.

“Aadhya?” Advait’s voice, hoarse with sleep. She didn’t turn. “Don’t move.” He stepped beside her, rubbing his eyes. The moment he saw the figure, the fatigue left his face. His voice dropped to a whisper. “What is that?”

“I don’t know,” she murmured. “But it’s watching.” He swallowed. “It has no eyes.”

“Still watching.” The figure shifted—not in movement, but in presence. The air around it thickened. The flame in Aadhya’s lantern bent—not with wind, but with weight, as though gravity itself bowed toward the thing. Bhairav appeared behind them without a sound. “I was wondering when one would appear,” he said, voice low. Advait turned sharply. “You knew this would happen?”

“I suspected,” Bhairav replied. “The further we move from the chamber, the more the desert tries to take something back.”

“What is it?” Bhairav approached until the hem of his robe brushed the swirling sand. “It’s not a who,” he said. “It’s a when.” Aadhya frowned. “What do you mean?” He gestured toward the spiral mouth. “Each seal has guardians—not demons, not gods, but memories that refuse to fade. When you stepped into that dance, even for a heartbeat, you tore a stitch. Now time itself is trying to balance what was lost.”

The figure began to tremble. Its spiral mouth widened, though no sound escaped. The teeth moved—grinding, not clicking—as if forming rhythm out of pain. The sound deepened until it was no longer heard but felt. It wasn’t sound anymore—it was pressure. A thudding beneath the sand, steady and relentless, like the after beat of *Kalkini’s* long-dead dance. Bhairav’s jaw tightened. “It’s asking to finish the sequence.” Advait’s voice was barely audible. “It wants her to dance again?”

"No," Bhairav said grimly. "It wants her to complete what was begun. That doesn't always mean dancing." The sand at the creature's base began to sink - spiralling inward like a drain. Something vast shifted beneath the dunes—turning, waking, testing the weight of its hunger. "We're leaving," Bhairav said sharply. Aadhya tore her eyes from the figure. "Where?" He pointed to the eastern ridge. Faint against the horizon stood the broken ribs of a forgotten structure—ruins of an ancient well, half-swallowed by dunes. "There. It's a holding chamber. Salt-warded. It won't hold memory for long, but it'll buy us time." They moved quickly, breaking camp in silence. The thing never followed. It just watched as they climbed the ridge, its spiral maw still turning faintly, the teeth trembling as though speaking without voice. When Aadhya looked back one final time, it wasn't alone. Three more had risen beside it—each half-buried, each swaying to an invisible rhythm. Their spiralled mouths glimmered faintly in the moonlight. The dance had not been completed. *And the desert remembered.* The eastern ridge looked closer than it was; in the moonlight, distance deceived - what appeared a few hundred paces away took nearly an hour to reach. The dunes sloped upward in long, aching arcs, and each step sank deeper than the last, as though the desert were swallowing them one breath at a time.

No one spoke. Even Bhairav's anklets were silent. The air thinned as they climbed, until sound itself felt muffled, smothered under a pressure that didn't belong to the night. The ridge rose like a scar—a jagged fissure of dark stone splitting the sand. The ruins of the well jutted from its summit, its octagonal mouth rimmed with pale bones calcified into the stone. It was not round like most wells; it had edges. Sharp, deliberate edges, as if geometry itself had been invoked as a barrier. The wind died as they approached. Aadhya's ears rang from the sudden stillness. The air had a taste—metallic, like the inside of an extinguished lamp.

Bhairav reached the rim first. He dropped a charred twig into the darkness. No echo. “Sealed with bone-dust,” he murmured. “Good. It held.” He moved aside a square slab of sandstone beside the well’s edge, revealing a staircase spiralling downward. Aadhya felt a faint pulse of air rise from it—dry, bitter, old. “Go,” Bhairav said. They descended one by one, the torchlight shuddering against walls slick with crystallized salt. The deeper they went, the colder it became—not with freshness, but with the stagnant chill of something that had not been disturbed in centuries.

The passage ended in a chamber—narrow, low-roofed, shaped like a hollowed lung. Its walls were etched with a single symbol repeated nine times: *a downward spiral pierced by a vertical line.* The pattern gleamed faintly, as if etched with crushed bone. Salt coated the floor in thick layers. Each step crunched softly, like brittle frost. Aadhya brushed her fingers against one of the carvings. A shock went through her palm—like touching a sleeping pulse. She withdrew, instantly.

“What is this place?” she asked. Bhairav didn’t look at her. “A remnant of the Rebellion. When the first bearers of Kalkini’s memory began to awaken, their minds had to be cleansed. The fire priests built this chamber to scrape their memories clean. What could not be erased was buried here instead.”

“You mean… her descendants?”

“No,” Bhairav said softly. “Her echoes.” Advait frowned. “Echoes?”

“They’re fragments that repeat through time. Not born, not reborn. They don’t live—they recur. Memory wearing flesh like a mask.” He opened a small pouch and began sprinkling black ash in a ring around them. The ash hissed the moment it touched the salt. “You’ll both rest now,” Bhairav said. “I’ll keep watch. Do not dream if you can help it. Dreams are doors in this place.” Aadhya lay down, staring at the low ceiling.

Her pulse thrummed unevenly beneath her ribs. The spiral mark on her chest had dimmed since the encounter on the dunes, but now and then it itched—as though something beneath her skin were trying to whisper its way out.

She did not close her eyes. Above them, faint but distinct, came a new sound. Click. Click. Click. But it wasn't the old rhythm of Kalkini's anklets. It was slower. Heavier. Each click echoed through the salt like a nail being tapped into stone. Then another. From below. The chamber's air thickened. It pressed against her skin like water. Aadhya sat up, glancing at Advait—still half-asleep, murmuring under his breath—and then at Bhairav, who sat cross-legged by the entrance, eyes open but glassy, his face lit from beneath by the faint glow of the staff resting across his knees. The iron at its tip steamed faintly, as though resisting an invisible frost.

The clicking grew louder. Not one source now, but many. A dozen, then more. From the ceiling. The floor. The walls. She pressed her palm to the ground. It was trembling—not with quake, but with rhythm. The same pulse she had felt in her teeth earlier, moving through the salt like blood through veins. She rose.

"Bhairav…" He didn't answer. She turned toward him—and froze. He was standing. Stiff, unmoving, his staff at his side. His eyes wide open, but vacant, as though something else were looking through them. His lips moved soundlessly. "Bhairav?" When he finally spoke, his voice was cracked – foreign, hollow. "She buried it here." Aadhya's stomach twisted. "Who?" "The one before you," he said. "The last echo that walked. Kalkini's rhythm called to her. She danced it halfway through. But she stopped—here."

The carvings on the wall pulsed faintly with a wet red glow, seeping from their etched grooves like reopened wounds. The clicking outside the chamber deepened into a kind of speech—

no longer random, but patterned, tonal. Primitive. As if something ancient was learning to pronounce words through the jaws of sand. Advait stirred, startled awake. “What’s happening?” Bhairav blinked rapidly, as though coming out of trance. “She’s waking it.”

“She?” Aadhya said sharply. “I haven’t—”

“Not you,” he said, finally meeting her gaze. “It. It was waiting for someone to remember. And it thinks you do.” The mark beneath her collarbone flared. Not with light—but with heat. She gasped, stumbling back. The vision slammed into her like a wave. A stone hall, identical to this one. Dozens of lamps burning low. A woman danced inside a salt circle—barefoot, wrists dripping red, movements frantic but precise. Seven figures watched from the shadows, their faces veiled in spirals of ash. One of them had the spiral symbol carved directly into his skin. The dancer turned—and Aadhya saw her own face. Then something rose from beneath the salt. A hand, skeletal and crystalline, its fingers made of teeth. The vision shattered. She screamed. Advait caught her before she hit the ground. “You’re burning up—what did you see?”

“I saw someone,” she whispered. “She was me. But not.” Bhairav moved quickly, prying up a rusted iron plate in the wall. Beneath it, something wrapped in blackened cloth gleamed faintly through layers of pitch.“ This chamber isn’t just a sanctuary,” he said. “It’s a tomb. A seal memory is hidden here—and something wants it back.” He unwrapped the cloth. Inside lay a mirror - not glass, something darker; liquid and solid all at once, rippling like frozen water. Its surface was ink-black, absorbing light instead of reflecting it. The moment it was exposed, the air shifted. The mark on Aadhya’s chest flared in recognition.

Bhairav held it out to her. “She left this for you.” he said “Who did?”

"The one you saw. The echo that failed to finish the dance. She trapped her unfinished memory here—the consequence of her failure. That is what the desert has been calling for." Advait's voice trembled. "What happens if she touches it?" Bhairav hesitated. "Then she'll see what should never have been remembered. But if she doesn't… it will find another way out." The clicking intensified—no longer a rhythm, but laughter. Dozens of voices, high and wet, like children imitating joy. Aadhya swallowed hard, then reached out. The moment her fingers touched the surface, the cold spilled into her bones.

And the chamber disappeared. The chamber below the well held its silence like a wound—tight, swollen, on the verge of breaking open. Aadhya did not sleep. She lay curled against the stone wall, the salt-stained floor cold through her shawl. The itching beneath her skin had worsened. It wasn't just the mark on her chest now—it thrummed through her veins, her arms, her spine, the roots of her hair. A pulse not her own, steady and insistent, drumming like something pacing beneath her flesh. Across from her, Advait had fallen into a restless half-sleep, muttering fragments of words that had no meaning in this age. Bhairav sat cross-legged near the sealed entrance, unmoving, eyes open yet vacant. His staff rested beside him, its iron tip faintly steaming from the heat of the salt ring that enclosed them.

The chamber seemed to listen. Even the salt had gone still, its faint shimmer fading beneath the wavering torchlight. Somewhere above, sand shifted—a muffled, uncertain sigh—as if the desert itself had leaned closer to hear what slept below. Aadhya held her breath, sensing movement that wasn't quite sound, a pressure that pressed against thought rather than ear. The air grew heavier, touched by something that remembered warmth but had forgotten mercy. Her palms tingled where they met the floor. The silence thickened—alive, waiting, patient.

Aadhya stepped forward. The wall seemed to breathe. A thin exhale of fetid air escaped the spirals, brushing her face. It smelled of stagnant blood and forgotten prayers, a decay that had learned to live on memory alone. She gagged, stumbling back. "Bhairav," she whispered. He was no longer sitting. He stood facing the same wall, his pupils dilated, his body rigid as stone. His lips moved soundlessly, as though answering a question she couldn't hear. "Bhairav," she said again, louder. He blinked once. His voice came thin, almost hollow. "She buried it here."

"Who?"

"The one before you—the last echo who walked. Kalkini's rhythm called to her. She danced halfway through... and stopped here." The spirals flared crimson. The clicking from beneath the salt grew faster—less like sound, more like speech. Primitive. Tonal. A language older than form. Advait jerked awake, disoriented. "What's happening?"

"She's waking it," Bhairav whispered. Aadhya spun toward him. "Who? I haven't touched anything—"

"No," Bhairav said softly, his voice sharpening into focus. "Not you. It. The memory. It's been waiting for someone who remembers." The mark on Aadhya's chest ignited. Not light—heat. A searing burn that pushed beneath her ribs. Her breath caught as her vision fractured: A stone room—this same chamber, centuries younger. Fire bowls lit along the walls. A woman danced inside the salt ring, wrists bleeding, feet raw. Around her stood seven silent watchers, each marked with spirals carved into their skin. One bore the symbol across his entire face—cut deep, bleeding still.

Then the earth split. Light bled upward from the fissure—not bright, but dense, as though it had been buried too long and forgotten how to shine. The salt around the crack hissed and blistered, forming shapes that looked like faces pressed against glass. Their mouths moved soundlessly, gasping in a rhythm that matched her pulse.

Aadhya stumbled backward. The chamber seemed to tilt, its walls bending inward as if the space itself were drawing breath. The red spirals throbbed along the stone, their glow pulsing with the rhythm of something trying to climb through the floor.

Advait shouted her name, but his voice came in fragments—shattered by the hum beneath the ground. She tried to answer, but the air turned liquid in her lungs; every breath felt borrowed. The fissure widened, and from its edge rose not a hand but a silhouette—a woman made entirely of salt and smoke, her movements slow, deliberate, unfinished. Her face was hidden behind spirals of ash.

Aadhya's vision fractured. She saw the woman's wrists twist in a familiar rhythm, saw the same mark burning faintly at her collarbone. The figure turned toward her, and for one heartbeat Aadhya felt her own bones shift in answer, as though her body remembered what her soul denied.

The salt cracked beneath her feet. She fell to her knees, trembling, watching as the figure reached for her—not to harm, but to offer something unseen, her hand hovering inches from Aadhya's heart. A whisper threaded through the roar of the fissure, faint but distinct—a language without words: *Finish what I could not.*

Then the light folded in on itself. The fissure sealed with a dry gasp, leaving only a streak of red dust across the salt floor. The ground steadied beneath her palms, though the salt still shivered—as if the earth had only paused its breathing.

Aadhya collapsed, coughing, her skin damp with sweat that smelled faintly of iron. Advait caught her mid-fall, the air trembling between them. “Tell me,” he breathed, “what did you see?”

Her voice trembled as it came. “She was there. Not a reflection, not a ghost—*a memory that pretended to breathe.* She tried to hold the seal together, but the desert pulled her under.” The mark beneath her collarbone flared again, softer now, echoing the pulse of the fissure that had closed. The air around them hung thick, humming faintly—like something waiting for permission to return.

Bhairav turned sharply toward the wall, his expression unreadable. “It knows her shape now,” he said. “The desert remembers who she was—and who you are.” The red spirals flickered once, dimming. For a long moment, no one spoke. The silence stretched thin—the kind that breaks only when something new wakes.

Bhairav moved fast, dragging a rusted iron plate from the wall. Beneath it, something wrapped in pitch-soaked cloth waited—an object pulsing faintly through the fabric. “This chamber was never just a shelter,” he muttered. “It was a crypt. One of the seal memories is buried here—and something wants it back.” He peeled the cloth away. Inside was a mirror. But the surface wasn’t glass. It rippled, black and fluid, as though forged from frozen water. The air around it vibrated faintly, bending toward Aadhya like iron to magnet. Her mark pulsed once. The mirror pulsed back. “She left this for you,” Bhairav said. “Who?”

“The one you saw. The echo who failed. She trapped her memory inside this mirror—locked her unfinished dance within it.” Advait’s voice trembled. “What happens if she touches it?” Bhairav hesitated. “Then she’ll see what no mortal should remember. But if she doesn’t… the memory will find its own way out." The sound above changed. The desert teeth had begun grinding now—not clicking, but moving in rhythm. A dry, heavy pulse, like bones learning to breathe. Aadhya took a breath. And touched the mirror. Cold flooded her arm instantly - not surface cold, but soul cold. Her hand sank an inch into the rippling surface, which gave like thick water. Pressure closed around her wrist. And then—

She wasn't there anymore. The chamber vanished. She stood in a basin ringed by dunes shaped like ribs. The sky was green, the light unnatural. The air was still, listening. Around her stood hundreds of figures—stone bodies with spiral mouths, each filled with jagged teeth. They were frozen mid-dance, their hands reaching upward toward a central altar made of fused bones and calcified palms. And upon that altar lay a woman. Her. Not dead. Not breathing. Her eyelids were carved with spirals. The wind spoke her name: *Anantaja*.

Aadhya turned. Kalkini stood behind her, faceless but grinning with rows of teeth that gleamed like ivory blades. "Finish it," she said. The world folded inward. Aadhya screamed. She was back in the chamber. The mirror clattered to the floor. The salt hissed where it touched, the air suddenly alive with laughter—small, wet, childlike. Advait grabbed her as she staggered. "What happened?"

"I saw the last one. The echo who failed. She's not gone, Advait. She's waiting—and the seal isn't dead. It's alive. It remembers." Bhairav's face went pale. "Then the desert won't wait much longer." From above came a crash of shifting sand. Then a sound. A single voice. High, soft, and terribly young.

"Anantaja...Anantaja..." The voice grew louder, shaping itself into rhythm. Not echo. Invocation. Bhairav snatched the mirror and wrapped it in pitch-soaked cloth again. "We need to leave. Now. It's mimicking her name. It knows she's awake." Aadhya clutched Advait's arm, trembling. The pain

beneath her ribs had turned into a heartbeat. The ancient thing beneath the dunes had tasted her memory—and wanted more. “Where do we go?” Advait asked. “We’re sealed underground.”

“There’s another exit,” Bhairav said. “But it was meant for the end—when the seal finally breaks. If we open it now…” The ground shook. Not like footsteps—like breaths. Slow, enormous. Coming from below. Bhairav didn’t finish his sentence. He drove his staff into the wall. The salt cracked open, revealing a black passage. The stench that rushed out was thick and wet—the smell of old teeth steeped in saliva and time. “No time,” he barked. “Move.” Aadhya hesitated, glancing once toward the sealed mirror. A part of her—something deep and ancient—ached to return to the vision. To the body that looked like hers. To touch what she had once been. But she turned. And followed Bhairav into the dark.

The tunnel was narrow, barely enough to crouch. The walls pulsed faintly with light, carved with spirals that seemed to twist inward the longer one stared. Teeth jutted from the stone—some yellowed, others wet and new, glistening faintly. Advait swore under his breath. “These walls are alive.”

“They’re fed,” Bhairav said. “Every fifty years, the desert sleeps between mimicries.”

“Mimicries?” Aadhya asked. He turned briefly. “When someone tries to unseal the dance before its time, the desert takes payment. It copies them. Their face, their breath, their choices—twisted, inverted, hungry.” A deep thump shook the tunnel. Dust fell from above. “No one’s ever escaped once it begins,” Bhairav whispered. They reached a wider chamber—shaped like a jaw. The ceiling and floor were lined with spiralled teeth. In its center stood a cracked pedestal shaped like a ribcage, open like a shrine. Inside it sat a small urn sealed in wax and ash. Aadhya stared. “What is that?”

Bhairav's eyes flickered. ***"The fragment of the first seal. Don't touch it."*** Advait stepped closer—and froze. A laugh echoed from behind them. Light. Delicate. A child's laugh. Then another. Closer. "I'm still dancing…" A shape emerged from the darkness. It looked like Aadhya - but wrong. Her eyes were too wide, her mouth too long. When she smiled, her lips split into fissures, revealing teeth that grew sideways. Her feet left streaks of ash where they touched the ground.

"Hello," it said sweetly. Advait reached for his blade. The mimic tilted its head. "I know what you'll say," it whispered. "Because I already did." Its spine cracked backward with a wet snap. The smile widened to her ears. Rows of teeth filled the split. *"I'm still dancing…"* it sang. "Why won't you dance with me, Aadhya?" The walls pulsed with the rhythm. Voices joined in. Dozens. All her own. We remember you. You left us behind. You buried us in salt. But we found your feet. We found your blood. Bhairav stepped between them, muttering words that sounded like broken glass and smoke.

The mimic hissed. "Too late, gatekeeper." It moved—sliding across the stone like mercury. Bhairav struck his staff. A ring of blue fire erupted around them, burning the salt to flame. The mimic shrieked and recoiled, flesh bubbling. Aadhya's mark blazed again. She fell to her knees. The vision returned: the altar, the bodies, hundreds of her—crying, laughing, burning. Each unfinished, each carved with the same spiral. The mimic screamed too—mirroring her agony. Bhairav shouted, "You're linked! It can't take you because you've seen too many selves!" Advait yelled over the sound. "Then how do we stop it?"

"Only she can," Bhairav said. "I'm not ready," Aadhya gasped. The mimic smiled, its skin cracking. "But I am." It raised its hand, revealing the same spiral mark—but inverted. White. Burning inward. "That's a false mark," Bhairav roared. "It's baiting the seal to open early!" Aadhya rose. Her body trembled, but her eyes had gone still. She stepped into the burning ring. The mimic lunged.

She whispered: ***"Rinam Kritam. Nrityam Ardham."*** *("The debt is made. The dance is half.")* The words burned through the air like scripture. The mimic froze mid-lunge. Its limbs shattered. The teeth in its mouth cracked one by one, falling like hail. It collapsed into dust. Then, silence. Aadhya swayed. Bhairav caught her. "You forced it into collapse without the dance," he whispered, awe in his voice. "I didn't break it," she said faintly. "I just remembered how not to fail." The pedestal behind them cracked. A thin line of smoke drifted upward from the urn. Bhairav's face darkened.

"It's starting," he said. "Midnight is near. The first seal is watching." They fled upward through the tunnel, emerging into the open air. The desert was no longer still. The dunes had shifted into shapes like ribs, the stars above tilted unnaturally—as though the sky itself was being watched from below. Bhairav looked east. "We have less than a day." Advait helped Aadhya to her feet. Her breath came in shallow bursts, her eyes glassy but alive. "Then we make it count," she said.

The wind rose, carrying a new rhythm with it—soft, patient, pulsing beneath the sand. The clicking was gone-but the beat remained. The Dance of Kalkini had not ended.

It had only paused.

Chapter - 13

The Seal Breaks at Midnight

The desert did not sleep. It only waited. The wind crawled over the dunes like breath held too long - exhaled, not blown. Each gust carried a whisper, not of sand shifting, but of something remembering how to move. Kuldhara had fallen silent hours ago, yet the silence had weight—like the desert itself was listening for a sound it had not heard in centuries.

Aadhya walked out of the crumbling haveli with her pulse still echoing in her palms. The mimic's remains had turned to dust—no blood, no sinew, no trace of what once mimicked her flesh. Only the faint metallic scent of heat lingered, as though something alive had been smelted into air. Behind her, Advait emerged - face pale, eyes hollow, still half-expecting the mimic to rise again from its own ashes. It did not. The wind saw to that—scattering what little was left across the night like burnt pages from a forgotten book.

Bhairav Singh walked ahead, his torch low and dying, the flame trembling though there was no wind to trouble it. His voice, when it came, was coarse and measured. "Kalkini hasn't finished," he said, not looking back. "She doesn't need the full circle now. The mimic's death was enough to awaken the remainder. The seal has begun to weep." The words fell like stones in the stillness. Aadhya blinked slowly, her body heavy with exhaustion, though her heart beat too fast to rest. Her skin still carried faint heat from the mimic's disintegration—as though fire had brushed her without burning. "How long do we have?" she asked, her voice thinner than she intended.

"Until midnight," Bhairav replied, continuing across the sand. "That's when the seal's time was written. Not by Devas. Not by Kalkini. By something that predates them both." Advait looked up at the sky—the stars were too far apart tonight, scattered thin like ash over ink. No moon, only the faintest shimmer of starlight dancing on salt dust. They moved in silence through the outskirts of Kuldhara, where the ruins dissolved into desert and the desert into a kind of memory. Here, even footprints refused to remain. "The Stepwell," Bhairav murmured. "That's where we're going."

Advait frowned. "There's a stepwell here? In this wasteland?"

"There wasn't," Bhairav said. "But now there is." They reached it as the wind stilled. Between two ridges of sleeping dunes, the land curved down into a spiral - the earth had turned inward upon itself. There it was—a vast, geometric wound carved into the desert's spine. The stepwell was older than the ruins surrounding it, black stone descending in perfect symmetry, each level darker and quieter than the last. Aadhya stared down into it. Water shimmered faintly at the bottom—dark as oil, reflecting no stars, no faces. "The seal's beneath," Bhairav said. "Kalkini's final mark. It waits under that water." Advait crouched near the edge. "This wasn't here yesterday."

"No," Bhairav said simply. "It appears when the seal remembers." The three descended in a spiral. The air thickened as they went down, the temperature rising even though no flame burned. The steps grew slick beneath their boots—not with moisture, but with something like breath, the residue of presence. By the time they reached the water's edge, even the faint light from Bhairav's torch seemed to hesitate before touching the surface. Then came the sound. Not a hum—a resonance, deep and without language. A vibration that lived between hearing and feeling, that pressed against the bones like someone speaking directly into marrow. Aadhya crouched by the water's edge. What stared back was not her reflection.

It had her face — only older; ash and copper dust, eyes rimmed with kohl, lips cracked from prayer. The figure mimicked her movement but always a second too late, as though the reflection remembered the gesture only after watching it. The torch flickered. Advait's breath hitched. "Aadhya… do you see—?"

"Yes," she whispered. Bhairav's face tightened. "Aadhrika," he said softly. "The seal remembers its keeper." The name was a key turning in the air. The reflection smiled, faint and wrong. Behind it, the water rippled—something black moved just beneath, gliding fast, like a spine shifting in liquid shadow. Aadhya flinched backward. The reflection didn't. "That's her," Bhairav murmured. *"Kalkini's guardian of the first seal."*

"You said the mimic was her guardian," Advait said sharply. "The mimic was her last human offering," Bhairav replied. "She stitched others from the bones of those who tried to break her circle. They guard what flesh can no longer remember." Aadhya felt warmth under her feet—a pulsing, rhythmic tremor, like the well itself had a heartbeat. Advait glanced at his watch. *"11:27."* Bhairav inhaled deeply. "Then we begin the interruption."

"The what?" Aadhya asked, her throat dry. "When the seal cracks, it follows a pattern—invocation, release, devouring. We cannot stop it now. But if Aadhrika's presence fills the gap before the third cycle, the crack diverts. It will not devour this land. It will seek the next." Aadhya stared at him. "And that's supposed to save us?"

"It will save what can still remember fire," he said. She looked at the water. The reflection still smiled. "Touch it," Bhairav said. "Let it remember you." The surface shimmered. The hum deepened. Her body moved before her fear could speak. She crouched and extended her fingers toward the water—the air around her wrist felt heavier, bending inward like a breath being drawn from within her veins. The water moved first. A black tendril whipped up - slick and fast - and wrapped her wrist with burning force. Aadhya screamed, trying to pull away—but the tendril held firm, pulsing with a heartbeat of its own. The reflection shattered, spinning into a spiral of light. Her vision fractured. Flames. The smell of blood on wet stone. Women chanting as the walls of a temple trembled. A priest falling to his knees before fire. And in the center, a woman—herself—burning, laughing, praying all at once. *Aadhrika.*

The tendril released her. She stumbled backward, clutching her arm. Five symbols scorched her skin—black at first, then smouldering into faint red. They curved like ancient script, curling into each other like the geometry of a curse. "It marked me," she whispered. Bhairav knelt beside her, eyes sharp. "No. It accepted you. The seal listens now. You've bought us minutes. Nothing more." Above them, the desert shifted. The air itself began to vibrate. Drums—faint at first, then stronger—echoed from every direction, though no drum existed. It was rhythm without instrument. *Dhumm. Dhumm. Dhumm.*

The sound of a dance beginning again. Bhairav stood abruptly. "We must leave this well. When the final drum strikes, the guardian rises. That will not be something we can reason with." Aadhya's body trembled as she stood. Her arm burned with memory. Each of the symbols pulsed, and in the space between heartbeats, she thought she heard a voice inside them whisper her name. They climbed the spiral steps quickly. The higher they went, the more the air thickened, and by the time they reached the surface, the night above had changed. The desert was no longer dark—it shimmered faintly with ash drifting in the wind.

The stars were distant now, blurred behind a haze of rising heat. The stepwell below was still, but the water gleamed like a pupil—dilated, watching. Advait looked toward the east. "What happens at midnight?" Bhairav's expression was a shadow. "The seal doesn't just break. It calls. And what answers may not remember mercy." The wind shifted again. It was no longer dry—it carried the scent of wet iron, of rain that had never reached this land. Kuldhara breathed once. And the dunes began to move. The fire refused to burn straight. It twisted in small spirals, like the air itself was uncertain which direction time was flowing in. The night above Kuldhara had changed—no stars now, only a thick sheet of pulsing darkness, as if the sky had grown a heartbeat.

Aadhya sat motionless by the flickering fire while Bhairav traced sigils into the sand with the tip of his staff. The symbols glowed for a second and vanished, eaten by the shifting grains. Advait watched them both, his jaw tight. The desert had stopped sounding like wind; it now breathed like a throat clearing itself before speech. "The seal's pulse has quickened," Bhairav murmured. "When it begins to hum beneath the dunes, you will hear her."

"Kalkini?" Advait asked. Bhairav nodded once.

"The dance begins long before she arrives. The sand remembers first."

Aadhya's hand still burned. The five symbols etched into her arm had turned the colour of dying embers. They pulsed softly, one after another, in rhythm with her heartbeat—not in pain, but in cadence. She could almost hear something beneath the pulse, a rhythm she shouldn't have known but somehow did. "What happens if I don't interfere?" she asked quietly. Bhairav looked at her from across the fire, his blind eyes gleaming like wet stones. "Then you'll finish what Aadhrika started. And this desert will open like a wound."

He stood, brushing sand from his robes. "Come. We move." They walked in silence, following Bhairav through dunes that looked increasingly unnatural—curved into crescents, angled like the ribs of something colossal buried below. The wind hissed through the gaps, carrying faint whispers. Words that didn't sound like speech, but like memories spoken backward. Advait kept glancing at Aadhya. "Your arm," he said finally. "It's glowing."

"I know."

"Does it hurt?"

"No," she said. "It's… listening." When she looked up, she realized Bhairav had stopped. They stood at the edge of a wide, hollow spiral in the sand. The formation was massive—half a mile across, curling inward like a fingerprint pressed into the desert. Bhairav raised his staff. ***'This is Vehr-Taal, -*** *The Rhythm of Vengeance,'* ***he said. "Where the fifth gesture begins."*** The air trembled. Aadhya felt it first in her knees—a low vibration that climbed upward through her spine, setting her teeth on edge. The dunes began to hum. The spiral beneath them deepened, sand slipping inward like liquid. "Stay still," Bhairav whispered. "She remembers movement."

Then came the sound—anklets. Not ringing, but dragging, heavy with rust. Each chime echoed with the weight of centuries. *Dhrr…dhrr…dhrr…* It was not a melody. It was a sentence. From the center of the spiral, the sand began to rise—not explode, but lift, as though something beneath was exhaling. And then it formed shape. Kalkini emerged. At first, she seemed human—tall, lithe, her form wrapped in cloth darker than night. But as the firelight flickered, the illusion unravelled. Her skin was carved with spirals that moved—not tattoos, but open wounds, uncoiling in slow motion. Her arms seemed doubled at the joints. And her face—it shifted constantly. One moment a dancer's serenity, the next a hollow-eyed skull. But her eyes remained constant: enormous, black, rimmed in crimson, shimmering like oil.

The dunes stilled. Even the wind bowed. Aadhya felt her lungs seize. Kalkini's movements were both fluid and wrong—her joints bent too far, her gestures too slow to be human, yet too graceful to be beast. She danced without music, yet each step struck like thunder under sand. "She isn't here," Bhairav said under his breath. "Not fully. We are standing in her remembrance." Aadhya didn't respond. Because Kalkini had turned toward her. The dancer's body froze mid-step, and her shifting face calmed. The mouth curled into what might have been a smile. And then Aadhya heard her—not in the air, not in sound, but in her head. You left me in the fire, Aadhrika.

The words were not accusation. They were affection, twisted and intimate, like something said between sisters who had died together. Aadhya's pulse stuttered. "I don't—" You do. Her legs moved before she could stop them. One step forward. Then another. The marks on her arm flared bright, the skin sizzling with faint smoke. Advait grabbed her shoulder. "Stop!" She didn't. She couldn't. Her body remembered steps her mind didn't. The rhythm filled her blood now. Every heartbeat became percussion. Every breath a chant. She saw flashes—a temple of red flame, seven dancers circling an altar of bones, a black peacock feather burning in air.

She whispered, "The fifth gesture." Bhairav's staff trembled in his hand. "You're walking into the memory! If you finish her dance, the seal will tear!" Kalkini extended one long arm. Her hand, delicate but clawed, traced a spiral in the air. The sand beneath them responded, glowing faintly red. You remember now, Kalkini whispered. *You were the vow, Aadhrika.* I was only the rhythm. Aadhya gasped. Her knees buckled, and her palms hit the sand. The world fractured — the desert vanished. She was inside the temple again. The smell of burning oil filled her nostrils. Chanting roared in her ears. Aadhrika—her other self—stood within the flames, body marked with the same five sigils, eyes wild.

"Stop her," Advait shouted, his voice breaking through the mirage. "Bhairav, do something!"

"I can't!" the priest barked. "She's not here anymore!" The wind screamed. The spiral's center began to glow, forming the yantra—the sacred diagram carved into the earth itself, veins of fire weaving into its edges. Kalkini's body froze in her final pose—her left foot raised, her toe trembling above the center of the spiral. The air pulsed with unbearable pressure. And then she looked straight at Aadhya. Her voice came not as words, but as a sensation—a memory pressed into flesh. You sealed me to save them. Now you must open it to save yourself. Aadhya screamed as the ground split beneath her. A fissure tore through the spiral, spilling light that was neither fire nor lightning, but memory—raw and liquid. The dunes convulsed. Bhairav fell to his knees, chanting old words that melted on his tongue.

Advait dragged Aadhya back, but the sand clung to her like hands. The sigils on her arm burst into flame. Her voice broke as she shouted something she did not recognize—a mantra older than language:

"Vatnash… Ayomukh… Aadhrika shravanam karoti…"

"Vatnash…Ayomukh…Aadhrika shravanam karoti.. (Vatnash.. Ayomukh stirs, Aadhrika listens.)"

The desert shuddered. The light surged higher, a column piercing the sky. And then came the voice—deep, rusted, slow.

"Aadhrika... awaken." Bhairav's eyes filled with tears.

"The seal is opening."

The dunes collapsed inward. The spiral disappeared into itself, leaving only a vast pit glowing from below. From its depths, a shadow began to rise—not shaped like Kalkini, nor human, nor beast. It was the silhouette of something ancient—a memory given flesh. Aadhya stood at its edge, her face lit by the glow, her hair whipping around her in the wind that had finally remembered to scream. Her eyes gleamed like molten copper. She remembered now. All of it. The fire. The betrayal. The oath. And the name of what had waited beneath the desert for her return.

The desert did not move, yet everything was shifting. Aadhya stood within the scorched sand-ring as if the world around her had peeled back like torn skin. Her breaths were shallow, but her body no longer trembled. She remembered now—not in fragments or whispers—but in completeness. The memories of Aadhrika unfolded through her veins like fire revisiting its origin: the altars of black stone slick with ash; the bleeding moon that once hung above Daitya shrines; the fire that curled around her fingers like it recognized its master. She remembered the vow—the one that had burned through lifetimes. She remembered how it had ended.

The ground beneath her pulsed like a drum beneath the desert, and Bhairav stood just beyond the circle, his staff sunk into the trembling sand. He did not move or speak, but his eyes gleamed—not with shock, not even with fear, but with the terrible serenity of someone who had waited too long for this very scream to return to the world. ***"You were the last to hold them back,"*** he said hoarsely, his words trembling through the wind. ***"And now, you will be the first to set them free."*** Aadhya's gaze lowered. Her skin was no longer just flesh—it shimmered faintly, translucent in parts, as though light was trying to leak through the cracks in her humanity. Her veins glowed like thin threads of molten copper. Around her, the ritual circle—the salt, the ash, the bones—had melted into a perfect spiral, drawing inward toward the ancient yantra that pulsed in a dim, red luminescence beneath her feet.

The air grew thick, heavy, still. The wind outside the circle stopped. The dunes beyond held their breath. And the moon—full and luminous a moment ago—now seemed to pulse in rhythm with her heartbeat. Then, without sound, without warning, the world fell into an impossible quiet. It wasn't silence in the ordinary sense. It was the stillness that occurs when creation itself halts to remember what it once buried. The kind that suffocates even the idea of movement. The kind where time folds its hands and listens. The fire torches on the dunes froze mid-flicker. The air between breaths solidified. Aadhya felt the pull then—soft, deliberate, unyielding. The seal beneath her feet was calling her name, but not the one she used now. She stepped forward.

The yantra welcomed her. The carvings that had once seemed like shallow etchings now bled, glistening red as though veins beneath the stone had awakened to life. The pattern shifted—spirals tightening, circles folding inward like eyes opening after centuries of sleep. And from deep within her chest, the old chant returned. Not through memory, but through instinct. The words came from somewhere older than language.

"Vatnash…Ayomukh…Aadhrika shravanam karoti…"

("From the depths, Vatnash breathes…Ayomukh stirs…And Aadhrika listens once more.")

The air cracked. The sand convulsed.

"Daanav-vamsa uttishtantu…"

(Let the bloodline of the Dānavas arise.")

Bhairav bowed his head. Advait shielded his face from the wind that wasn't wind at all but breath exhaled by something ancient. *And Aadhya whispered the final phrase:*

"Yenidam rakshitam, sa mayā chhidyate—idānīm."

("That which has protected this— is now broken by me.")

So let it be broken. The world answered. A sound erupted—not a scream, not thunder, but the groaning of the desert's own soul. The yantra split open with a jagged, luminous crack, spilling a light so violent that it tore through the night sky like a blade. A pillar of molten brilliance rose from the earth, twisting upward until it struck the moon and fractured its reflection in the water at the stepwell's base. The blast rippled outward.

Sand dunes imploded, collapsing like waves folding backward. The bones buried beneath Kuldhara churned in their graves. The ruins cracked, their walls bowing outward as if in reverence. Bhairav dropped to his knees, shawl drawn across his face, but he did not avert his gaze. Advait was thrown several feet back, the force knocking the breath from his lungs. The air around Aadhya shimmered like a mirage of fire—her hair whipped in spirals, her silhouette a flame sculpted by wind and will. The fire circled her. And for the first time, she didn't resist it. *Her eyes, once human, now mirrored the desert—wide, burning, endless. Her voice, when it returned, was no longer her own.*

The first seal had broken.

But what emerged from its core was not a creature, nor an explosion, nor the chaos of unleashed power. It was memory. The memory of everything the world had once been before the gods learned to lie. The wind carried its fragments—echoes of the Treta Yuga's blood-soaked dusk. The clash of steel and prayer. The shrieks of Daityas impaled on divine spears. The wailing of priests whose chants turned to fire in their throats. Aadhrika standing amidst corpses, her voice unwavering. Kalkini spinning on an altar of ribs, her dance both worship and rebellion. And beyond them all, a fifth figure—hidden by smoke, laughing with seven mouths, its eyes hollow yet knowing.

Then, abruptly, silence again. The light dimmed. The fire receded. What remained of the yantra was a spiral carved into glassy, fused sand—its center cracked open like an eye half-blinking. From within that fracture came a faint sound. A heartbeat. Or perhaps, the echo of one. Something had been released. Or worse—something had been summoned. Bhairav rose to his feet slowly, his face a mask of exhaustion and dread. ***"You will not be safe in this land anymore,"*** he said quietly. ***"The Dev-lok has been watching. It will feel this fracture before dawn."***

Aadhya stood dazed, her chest rising and falling rapidly, her human exhaustion returning in waves. The flames in her veins dimmed to a dull ember. Her voice shook. "What… happens now?" Bhairav didn't answer right away. Instead, he reached into his satchel and drew out a brittle parchment—creased, weathered, smelling faintly of smoke and sandalwood. It looked impossibly old, as though it had survived being buried under centuries of salt. On it was an inked trail that wound westward—from Rajasthan to Mumbai. At the endpoint, a sigil had been seared into the paper, a mark that seemed to pulse faintly when Aadhya touched it.

"Go west," Bhairav said. "There is one in the city who listens to ghosts. She doesn't know what she listens to yet—but she's been hearing them through machines." Aadhya's lips parted. The name rose unbidden from her mouth, as if whispered into her ear by someone unseen.

"Divyakshi."

Bhairav nodded solemnly. "She's not one of us. But she's being pulled toward you… toward what you've awakened." Advait, his voice raw, stepped forward. "What did we just release?" Aadhya turned to him slowly. Her pupils shimmered faintly red for a heartbeat before fading back. "Not a demon," she said softly. "Not a god." She glanced toward the horizon, where the desert still trembled under its own shadow. "A truth older than both." The ruins behind them groaned. Somewhere deep within the dunes, something howled—neither beast nor human—and the sound twisted into laughter before vanishing into the cold wind.

Bhairav's torch flickered out. "We leave before dawn," he said. ***"Mumbai is waking."***

Kuldhara Halt was a broken platform with no name left on its board. The train arrived at exactly 3:33 a.m. bore no markings either. Its windows were too dark. Its engine made no sound. And yet, it accepted them like it had been waiting. Aadhya sat by the window, clutching the parchment Bhairav had given her. The fire in her veins was dim now, but not gone. She felt its rhythm with her heartbeat. A second pulse. Beside her, Advait stared at the desert dissolving behind them.

"You knew this would happen," he said finally.

"I didn't," Aadhya replied. "But she did." She closed her eyes. And for a moment, the crack in the seal echoed in her mind like a heartbeat. Like thunder under stone. The journey ahead felt coiled with something larger than either of them could speak of yet. But even without words, they both understood: Mumbai would not welcome them kindly.

Far ahead, in a city of millions, Divyakshi Naik woke from sleep with blood at her ears. The screens in her lab, which had long been scanning for ghost frequencies and stray voice patterns, suddenly began to flicker in unison. Symbols she'd never programmed danced across the monitors. Frequencies reversed. And from one speaker—crackling through the static—a voice whispered. Not in Hindi. Not in any language Divyakshi could name.

But her bones remembered it. A name. A chant. A call from something old and waking.

"Aadhrika...utthāpanam...samay ho gaya hai."

("Aadhrika… the time for awakening has come."**)**

A faint giggle followed - not hers, not human. She backed away slowly, but the signal didn't stop. It had already bled into the walls. Into the wires. Outside her window, the sea heaved unnaturally.

Something had begun.

Part – 3

Himachal & Mumbai

Gathering Shadows

Chapter - 14

The House with No Corners

Time: 8:47 PM – Versova, Mumbai

The train had pulled in nearly two hours late. They had left Kuldhara at exactly *3:33am* when the desert wind was still humming with something broken—like the seal had not only cracked but screamed. The express crawled from Rajasthan's sands in a silence soaked in ash, then gathered speed through the wide northern plains, as if fleeing what it had just witnessed. By the time it reached Mumbai—delayed by monsoon floods and what the conductor vaguely called "static failures"—the city was already wrapped in rain.

8:47 PM. The digital clock above the platform blinked its red numbers like a wound refusing to close. Chhatrapati Shivaji Terminus loomed behind them, its Gothic spires flickering with damp light. The air smelled of wet metal, old tracks, and restless electricity, like a lamp left on too long. Aadhya stepped down first. Her boots made no sound against the slick, tiled floor. She hadn't spoken since Baroda—not after what she remembered. Advait followed, eyes scanning the crowd.

The faces were ordinary—porters, commuters, women with plastic rain covers—but everything seemed… stretched. Each sound lingered longer than it should have. Each face held to the edge of his vision before dissolving.

"Do you think she'll be waiting?" he asked quietly. "She isn't waiting," Aadhya said. "She's been listening."

The cab ride to Versova was wordless. Mumbai's arteries throbbed with rain and light—auto headlights refracted into bleeding halos, puddles gleaming like molten glass. The city pulsed - alive and unbothered - yet something in its rhythm felt off-beat, as though time itself stuttered between one breath and the next. As they turned into the narrow lanes near the coast, the traffic thinned. The streetlights flickered—not from faulty wiring, but in a slow, rhythmic pattern. Like breathing. The taxi rolled to a stop before a moss-covered building. Aadhya leaned forward. The signboard bore no name, no number—just a faint metallic chime echoing from somewhere above, as if in greeting.

They got out. The street smelled of seawater, rust, and faint burning—though no one around seemed to notice. A narrow alley led them to the back entrance of a pale, three-storey building, its walls webbed in tangled wires. Antennas jutted from balconies like insect legs. On a terrace above, a woman was whispering into a landline that had no cord. They climbed two flights. Outside Flat 3C, they stopped. The name plate read D. Naik. The paint was peeling, the brass dulled to green. A small circle drawn beside the peephole—vermillion, freshly smeared—glimmered faintly under the corridor light.

Before Advait could knock, the lock clicked.

Divyakshi Naik stood in the doorway. She looked like she hadn't slept in days. Her curls were gathered loosely behind her head - a pencil tucked into the coil like a forgotten wand. She wore a grey tunic over flannel pyjamas, both stained with ink and soot. Her bronze skin had the pallor of someone who lived too long in electric light. Her eyes—sharp, assessing—flicked between them, not suspicious, but calculating.

"You're late," she said simply, then stepped aside. The apartment was dim, lit only by the glow of monitors and a single amber lamp in the corner that pulsed gently, like a heartbeat. The air felt thick—not warm, not cold—just… inhabited. "Shoes off," she said without looking back. She glanced at Aadhya "And no iron inside that room."

Advait hesitated. "Take it off," Aadhya murmured. "She knows." He unbuckled his belt silently.

Divyakshi had already returned to her chair—an ergonomic relic with torn padding—and was typing furiously across six monitors. The screens displayed spirals of data: waveforms, rotating 3D spectrals, geometric sigils that twisted the longer one stared at them. The window was open despite the slanting rain.

"This place smells like...sea static," Advait murmured. "It is sea static," Divyakshi replied, still typing. "That's the name I gave it." She motioned to the floor cushions near her console. The living room was sparse. A low table cluttered with copper coils, tangled wires, and tuning devices. Above the altar shelf hung a string of black feathers, and beside it—a framed photograph of a woman in a red saree. Below it, etched into a copper plate, were the words: *Don't listen too long. They know when you do.*

Divyakshi turned at last. Her face was calm—clinical—but there was a quiet reverence in her tone, the way priests speak after opening tombs. "Three weeks ago," she began, "I noticed interference in the *Aural Mapping Array.* I built it to record ghost frequencies—residual audio trapped in static—mostly from graveyards and old battlefields. But on the 9th of this month, all my devices started broadcasting the same pitch."

She tapped a key. One of the speakers crackled alive. The sound wasn't quite sound—it was breath, reversed. An inhale turned inside out. A rhythm that existed more in the body than in the ear. *"Every day since then," she continued, "the frequency has been rising. I thought it was tectonic—a faultline resonance. But exactly at 3:33 AM this morning..." She looked directly at Aadhya. "It changed. It became intentional.* Like something stopped hiding."

Advait leaned forward. "You mean it was waiting—for something to trigger it?" Divyakshi nodded slowly. "And I think you broke it." She crossed to a whiteboard covered in spectral patterns and equations. One circular diagram resembled the Vatnash Mandala from Varanasi. Another showed a waveform shaped like a fingerprint—alive, moving. *"This isn't just a frequency,"* she said. *"It's a summoning code.* Each pulse carries layers—echoes that don't decay but fold back into themselves. Like a mantra built to call something home."

Her gaze returned to Aadhya. "When you entered this house, one of the coils shorted. That only happens when a circuit tries to complete itself." Aadhya's expression didn't change, but her eyes glinted faintly, as if something ancient inside her had already known. "And it's not just here," Divyakshi added, turning back to her monitors. "Northern echoes have started mirroring this frequency—Himachal, perhaps. But the reverb from there feels older. Buried. Like it's coming from beneath the mountains."

Advait swallowed hard. "How did you even know we'd come?" Divyakshi's voice softened. "I didn't. You found me. When the pulse shifted, it spoke your names. They appeared in the waveform—stitched into the static." Thunder rolled outside, low and wide—like a door sliding open across the clouds. Inside, no one moved. Divyakshi broke the silence. "There's something I need to show you both. Not tonight—

tomorrow. A place under the old salt docks. But for now...you must rest. This house bends time when you don't sleep."

Advait looked up. The walls met at strange, uneven angles. Corners that weren't corners. Edges that refused to exist. *"There are no corners in this room,"* Aadhya whispered. Divyakshi's lips curved slightly. "Exactly," she said. "It's the only way they can't listen." And then the amber lamp dimmed. The sound of the sea rose—not waves, not rain—just a low, continuous chant. *And in its depths, something began remembering their names.*

Time: 6:19 AM – Versova Jetty, Mumbai

The rain had finally paused, but the air still smelled of thunder—metallic and sharp, as though the clouds above had just sheathed their weapons. The city before dawn was half-awake, its streets breathing in steam. Water dripped from telephone wires, from signboards, from forgotten gods perched on building ledges. They walked in silence. The narrow lanes of Versova were washed clean, reflecting blurred streaks of streetlight that stretched like veins along the asphalt. Stray dogs stood in doorways, heads low, eyes tracking them—but none barked. Somewhere in the distance, a drain gurgled, not from rainwater but with a noise too steady, too rhythmic, like something beneath was learning to breathe.

Divyakshi led the way. Her hair was tied tighter today, her steps precise, as though each one was measured against a frequency only she could hear. The device in her hand—a palm-sized sphere of glass and brass—ticked faintly every few steps. The needle spun with no fixed direction, jittering as if torn between magnetic poles. Neither Aadhya nor Advait had slept properly. The apartment had twisted in the night—subtle shifts that mocked the logic of space.

Corners melted; doors led to shorter hallways than before. Time pulsed like a fever—stretching, retracting. When Aadhya closed her eyes, she saw rust-coloured mandalas spinning under her eyelids, chanting in geometric rhythm. Advait dreamed of a tunnel lined with mirrors that inhaled and exhaled like lungs—and woke with the taste of salt on his tongue. They hadn't spoken of it. Some silences are better shared without words. Now, as they reached the end of a broken iron fence, Divyakshi stopped.

"This is where the city ends," she said. "And something older begins."

Ahead lay the Versova Salt Docks—long abandoned, half-swallowed by the new city. Once, these grounds had shipped salt from the drying flats up the coast, but progress had buried them beneath bridges and ferry routes. Yet here, where the land still tasted of brine, the docks survived. Broken planks jutted out like ribs into the sea. The tide was low, revealing staircases that descended beneath the stone wharf, barnacled and bone-white, as if the sea had grown teeth.

"This used to be a gateway," Divyakshi whispered. "Gateway to what?" Advait asked. She hesitated. "Not for ships - for sound."

They followed her past a rusted board that once read *PRIVATE—ENTRY RESTRICTED BY COASTAL AUTHORITY.* It hung crooked now, split neatly down the center, as though it had been struck from within. The wind shifted again. The salt here was different—heavy, dense, as if it had a pulse. Even the iron chains mooring the pier had crusted into delicate crystals. Aadhya brushed one absently and pulled back at once—the salt was warm, almost feverish. "Watch your step," Divyakshi murmured as they descended the moss-slick stairs under the jetty. "This part of the city was never finished. It remembered something too early."

The stone tunnel below was narrow and dark, its walls breathing moisture. Thin streaks of phosphorescent moss lined the ceiling, glowing in faint green veins. The air smelled of copper, salt, and something else—like old prayers gone stale. At the far end, the tunnel opened into a vast, submerged loading cavern. The sea whispered against broken platforms. The space resembled a throat—arched and hollow, flanked by pillars on the entire side. The silence was too engineered.

Advait froze. "Listen," he whispered. There were no waves. No birds. Only a faint drip. And beneath that— voices. Not spoken aloud, but mirrored. Reflections of words, turned inside out, slowed and reversed as though time itself had been folded. The syllables crawled out of the water, unmoored from their sources. Aadhya heard it too.

Her name—Aadhya—but pronounced backward. Each repetition came softer, closer, until she could feel it brushing the edges of her skull. Divyakshi raised her device. The needle quivered violently, spinning in erratic circles. A dim green orb pulsed at its center. *"I mapped this chamber for six months,"* she said, her voice low but steady. *"No GPS works here. Phones die within minutes. But this place has memory—deep broadcast memory. It* replays what the sea forgets." She walked to a rusted control panel built into the far wall. When she opened it, there were no wires—only copper strands looped in perfect spirals. The metal glowed faintly red, arranged in a pattern that made Advait's stomach twist.

Daitya script.

"You asked how I knew this was connected to them," remembering about it - but her hand trembled slightly, because she had seen that same hand in her dreams since Varanasi. "The signals have been layering for three nights," Divyakshi said, adjusting the dials. "The first layer is a chant. The second—a name. The third…"—she hesitated—"…a path. A tunnelling echo reaching north. Himachal."

Advait's throat tightened. "You mean—it's moving?" Divyakshi shook her head. "Not moving. Remembering. The earth itself is remembering." She unfolded a paper map—creased, water-stained, annotated with red ink and spirals drawn in black. "Every anomaly I've tracked—signal drops, wave distortions, heat spikes—they all converge here." She tapped the map. "Versova. Then another mark—"And here." Deep in the Himachal range. "Whatever was buried connected these two points—the ocean and the mountain. When the seal broke in Rajasthan, the sound reached the sea. The sea… replied."

Aadhya stared into the water again. The reflection no longer mirrored the sky above. It showed another horizon—a twilight of unfamiliar stars. Two moons hung in stillness over a mountain that seemed to breathe.

*"You said this was a gateway," she murmured. "To where?"*Divyakshi didn't answer. Instead, she reached into her coat and pulled out a shard of glass—black, opaque, curved like a broken scale. "Here," she said, pressing it into Aadhya's palm. "We found this under the dock stairs. It isn't volcanic. It doesn't belong to any known mineral set. But when certain people hold it—" The shard pulsed. Once.

"—it activates." Aadhya's pupils dilated. Her breath shortened. For a moment, the cavern dissolved. She stood in another place—an open plain of salt, surrounded by figures cloaked in grey smoke. Their hair moved like serpents, their faces hidden behind veils of ash. They were cutting their palms and whispering her name. Not "Aadhya."

"Aadhrika." The vision broke. The shard went cold. "I don't think this is a gateway," Aadhya said, her voice low, distant. *"It's a memory loop."* Divyakshi smiled faintly, almost proud.

"Exactly." They fell silent for a while, listening to the pulse of the sea and the faint, reversed chanting echoing beneath it. Then Divyakshi stood. "There's something else. I didn't plan to show you this yet." She walked to the far end of the dock cavern and stopped before a small, iron hatch embedded in the floor. With effort, she pried it open. Beneath lay a narrow tunnel—black and bottomless. "It's closed now," she said. *"But last night, at 3:33 AM, it opened by itself. For six minutes." A faint breeze rose from its depths—cold, dry, carrying the unmistakable scent of burnt sandalwood and ghats.* "I recorded what came through." She handed Advait a sheet of paper—aged, rough, like something printed on a dead typewriter. Three words repeated across its surface, line after line:

"Aadhrika has returned.

Aadhrika has returned.

Aadhrika has returned."

The ink had bled faintly at her touch. Aadhya didn't speak. She didn't need to. The sea had already begun whispering it too. When they finally stepped out of the dock tunnels, the sky above Versova had begun to pale, but, the sun didn't rise—it only pushed the darkness sideways. Divyakshi locked the gate behind them. "You need to go north," she said. "Whatever is remembering you—it's not done." Aadhya nodded. Advait lingered. "Will you be safe?" She smiled faintly. "They don't come to places without corners." And then she vanished back into the fog.

Time: 7:06 AM – Mumbai

The fog behind them moved like a living thing—slow, deliberate, as if it were closing its throat. When Aadhya and Advait stepped out from the salt docks, the scent of the sea had changed. It wasn't just brine anymore. It was older—

heavy with rot and electricity, like something long-drowned had stirred beneath the waves. Divyakshi was gone. Not merely out of sight, but erased, as though she'd been folded into the mist itself. The rusted gate clicked shut behind them, the lock twisting on its own. Advait turned back once. In the shifting fog, he thought he saw her silhouette—a blur with no edges, dissolving between seconds. Then even that was gone.

The city didn't feel like Mumbai anymore. The skyline ahead shimmered faintly, as though water had replaced air. Every street seemed longer than the one before. Landmarks repeated. A neon sign blinked the same word twice. Even the traffic noise had changed pitch, rising and falling like breath itself. By the time they reached the apartment, the air had thinned. The lanes they took didn't feel the same ones they'd walked hours ago. A dog trailed them for two blocks, then vanished between buildings that no longer had windows.

When they entered, the apartment looked untouched—but space didn't feel still anymore. The walls had softened. The paint rippled faintly, as if remembering water. Aadhya traced her fingers along the corner of the main room. There was no angle there now—no clear meeting of planes. Her fingertips slid into emptiness that wasn't quite void, like the house had decided that geometry was no longer necessary.

"Does it ever stay still?" she murmured. Advait was examining the Daitya shard on the table. Its surface no longer black—just translucent enough to show flickers of light moving inside. "It's like the whole place inhales," he said quietly. "Then forgets to exhale." They slept in shifts, though neither truly slept. Aadhya took the first hours, curling near the window while the sea wind whispered against glass. Her dreams didn't start; they resumed - as if continuing a story mid-sentence.

She was ankle-deep in black water. The tide burned cold, tasting of salt and iron. Around her, veiled women moved in a circle. Their robes were soaked in ochre. Their hands, painted in ash, left streaks across their own faces as they chanted without mouths. A fire burned in the sea. Aadhya looked down. In her hand was a curved blade, engraved with runes that pulsed in rhythm with her heartbeat. The sky above her was moonless—but there was light. Something vast moved beneath the water, like a sleeping god rolling in its own dream. A voice brushed her ear, neither human nor memory:

"You are not late. You are returned."

She woke gasping, the taste of smoke on her tongue. Her right wrist burned - no wound, but the smell of scorched herbs filled the air. Advait was awake, watching her silently from across the room. "You dreamt it again," he said. "Yes," she replied. "But this time, it wasn't mine." He didn't ask what that meant. He didn't need to. Outside, the sky had turned a washed grey. The sea roared distantly, but its rhythm was wrong—offbeat, like a heartbeat that skipped time.

At 3:33 AM, the walls began to hum. Not creak. Not groan. Hum. A low, harmonic vibration spread through the house like a tuning fork struck from within. The air thickened—grainy with static, vibrating just beneath the skin. Every bulb in the flat flickered once, then dimmed to red. Advait bolted upright. His phone buzzed violently in his hand, though no signal reached it. "Do you hear that?" Aadhya was already standing. Her palms were bleeding where her nails had pierced the skin from clenching too hard. "Yes," she whispered. "But it's not sound anymore."

The main wall—where the framed sketch of the inverted pyramid had hung—began to bleed salt. At first, it was just damp. Then the salt crystallized, forming veins. And then in the center of it, she appeared. The crystals spread like writing.

A circle. Then a triangle. Then eyes—dozens of them—etched in salt streaks, blinking without lids. And in the center of it, she appeared.

Aadhrika. Not a reflection. Not a ghost. But form—real, impossible, rising from the wall itself. Her skin shimmered like scorched bronze, inked with runes that shifted as if alive. The same face Aadhya had glimpsed in the water's reflection at Versova—only older, regal, terrifying. One hand held a rope of fire. The other—a new born child, silent, its mouth dripping black salt. The air curdled. The fire-rope writhed like a serpent, its flames whispering mantras too old for translation. Aadhya's knees buckled. The floor seemed to breathe. The child's mouth opened. A single note escaped—a sound between chant and scream. The glass windows shattered inward, shards raining in slow motion. The salt on the walls turned black.

And then— Silence. Only the slow descent of blackened crystals settling across the wooden floor like ash. It took them nearly an hour to breathe properly again. Advait's nose was bleeding. Aadhya's right ear rang until it numbed. The sketch that had hung on the wall was now pitch-dark, its lines melted into one solid void. The room had changed again. The angles were wrong. One corner opened into what looked like a hallway that didn't exist—just a passage of shadow receding into nothing.

"I don't think we can stay here," Aadhya whispered. Advait nodded, trembling. "She said the signal is moving north." "Himachal," Aadhya murmured. He looked at her—half question, half acceptance. "Yes." Neither spoke again until dawn. Not from fear—but because words would have felt too small for what they'd just seen. When sunlight finally pressed through the misted glass, the house exhaled. Just once. The hum died. The corners returned—though slightly askew, as if still deciding whether to exist.

By 9:17am, they were packed. The city outside had resumed its rhythm: honking cars, vendors, rickshaw bells. Yet everything felt hollow, like the sound was happening behind a curtain. People turned too quickly when they passed. A child pointed at Aadhya and whispered something to her mother. A stray dog howled—not at her, but at the building they had just left. Advait noticed the note under the door only as they left. A single slip of paper, written in silver ink that appeared only when tilted against light:

Follow the frequency.

But not in straight lines. They are watching those.—D.

Outside, the air was warm again. Ordinary. But Aadhya could feel the weight of unseen eyes on her skin. They boarded the Mumbai–Kalka Express before noon. As the train pulled out of the station, thunder rolled across the western horizon. The clouds gathered in dark spirals above the city, moving faster than wind should allow. Aadhya looked down at her wrist.

The burn had re-formed—not as a mark, but a mantra. One Pandit Mahadev had whispered in his sleep back in Varanasi. A Daitya invocation. The salt on her fingertips had turned black. Advait stared at the window. The skyline of Mumbai receded, the monsoon shadow following them north like a predator. "Do you think it's really over?" he asked softly.

Aadhya didn't answer. She only watched the horizon—where the sea ended and the mountains waited. Far away, in the high Himalayan pass of Jalori, a shepherd awoke to silence. His sheep stood motionless, all facing north. Mist swirled thick around his cottage, taking shape, condensing. A figure unfolded from it—not walked, not formed—unfolded, as though it had been sleeping inside the fog all along. Two eyes blinked open, sideways, reptilian. A whisper followed. "She moves. The fourth sleeps." And then it was gone. By dawn, the sheep were still facing north.

Chapter - 15
Eyes in the Monsoon

By 4:07pm, the Mumbai–Kalka Express had begun its long, weary crawl out of the city. The iron wheels gnawed the steel tracks with a slow, deliberate rhythm - a pulse that seemed less mechanical, more remembered. It throbbed like something alive beneath the ground. The compartment was nearly empty. An elderly Sikh couple quietly unwrapped foil packets of parathas, murmuring short prayers before each bite. Across the aisle sat a wiry man in saffron robes who hadn't blinked since the train departed. Further down, a woman in a fading green salwar kameez rocked gently, whispering to a small cloth doll pressed against her chest.

Aadhya and Advait occupied berths 35 and 36—side lower and side upper. The air inside the coach was cool but heavy with a scent that didn't belong. Disinfectant, boiled milk - and something else.

Salt - not the gentle salt of skin or tears. The other kind. The kind that scours throats and burns nostrils—the kind that belongs to the *Dead Sea,* not the living. Advait noticed it too. "Smell that?" he asked softly. Aadhya nodded, gaze fixed on her wrist. The mark there had settled into a pattern now—three interlocking spirals forming a trident made of flame. She tried rubbing it off, but the skin pulsed instead - faintly glowing under her touch. Rain began to trace thin slashes down the glass beside her, though no clouds had opened yet. Each droplet slid downward in strange, deliberate symmetry, forming perfect hexagons before vanishing.

They passed Borivali by 4:41pm. The saffron-robed man suddenly stood, his movements smooth, unhurried. He walked down the aisle, murmuring to himself, until he stopped beside Aadhya. His lips moved, barely parting. “When you hear the baby crying in the tunnel,” he whispered, “do not answer.” Then he moved on—his saffron silhouette swallowed by the hum of the carriage.

Aadhya’s stomach turned. “Did you hear that?” Advait nodded slowly. “Yeah.”

“But… why say that now?” she murmured. Advait opened his pack and unfolded the note Divyakshi had given them. The silver ink had dimmed since morning, the edges of the parchment charred like heat had breathed through it. The message, once steady, had changed. They’re watching. Not just you—but those you remember. He frowned. “This isnt what it said this morning.” Aadhya snatched the note. Her fingers trembled. “What—?” The words writhed faintly across the parchment. The same lines, the same creases—but the message had morphed, alive in its stillness.

By 6:03 PM, the train crossed Surat. Outside, the horizon dimmed into a bruised violet. Thunder cracked—not from above, but from beneath. The metal rails thrummed out of sync. The ceiling fan shrieked, froze, then spun again as if nothing had happened. At Vapi, the woman with the doll stood and left the train without her belongings. The doll remained, seated neatly across from Aadhya and Advait, its stitched mouth gaping slightly.

Something glimmered inside. A scrap of paper. Ancient, brown, frayed, with script older than Sanskrit. Aadhya leaned closer. "This writing..." Advait's breath caught. "Is that...?" She shook her head. "Not Sanskrit. Proto-Daitya, maybe. The same Mahadev wrote when he was in trance." The train jerked violently - Not a sway or a brake, but a pull. Like something enormous had gripped the tracks. Passengers stumbled. A tray crashed. Someone screamed from Coach S-4. For a heartbeat, the lights died. Emergency lamps flickered crimson, bathing the entire coach in blood.

In that light, the doll's cloth face seemed to twitch. Just once. But enough. By 8:19pm, they passed Ratlam. Dinner trays arrived, steaming and untouched. Advait had been sketching the spiral from Aadhya's wrist, tracing it over and over—each line more frantic than the last. He stopped suddenly. "You know what this looks like?" She looked up. He rotated the page toward her. "A map," he said. *"Three spirals intersecting—Trikona Tantra. The forbidden alignments."*

Aadhya's stomach turned cold. "Those are myths." "Everything is a myth," he said, his tone flat, "until it happens to you."

10:11pm.

Outside Kota, the train plunged into a long tunnel. That was when it truly began. At first, a low sound—like fabric tearing under water. Then a second, deeper resonance—the vibration of something beneath their carriage, humming in opposition to the train's rhythm.

And then—A baby cried. Thin, high, real. It came from somewhere ahead—maybe Coach S-4. The sound wavered, echoing through steel and darkness. Then again. Closer. Aadhya's heart stilled. "Don't answer," she whispered. "Don't move." The cry rose in pitch, distorted, wet. The syllables changed. It wasn't crying anymore. It was speaking.

"...Aaa...dhrik...aaa..." Her name. Half-formed. Half-remembered. Advait clasped her ears gently. "It's not real," he murmured. "It's not alive - not in the way we think." Then—silence. The tunnel ended. The train burst into open night, windows rattling with the sudden wind. Every passenger around them sat still, frozen mid-motion. The Sikh couple's hands hovered over their food. A bottle of water hung mid-air between fingers that did not move. Even the attendants were statues. Time had stuttered. Only the doll had shifted. It now sat on Aadhya's berth. Facing her. They reached Delhi by 7:30am the next morning. Neither had slept. The paper in Advait's bag had changed again. The map breathes beneath Himachal. Do not look directly into the valley's eye. They stepped onto the platform, both moving through a fog of exhaustion and dread. Around them, life went on—chai vendors shouting, engines roaring, porters swearing—but everything felt distant, as if submerged.

Before boarding their next train, they stopped at a café. Screens lined the walls, flickering with advertisements and weather bulletins—until suddenly, everyone went black. Then, for a single second, they lit up in unison. A pyramid appeared—stone, half-buried in fog. And before it, a woman in robes. Aadhya. But with no eyes. Advait's face drained of colour. "Did you—?"

"Yes." Her whisper was barely breath. "It's already begun." And outside, the monsoon arrived. Not with rain. But with eyes. Thousands of them. Pressed against the glass. Watching. Waiting.

8:20am —Platform 9B, New Delhi Railway Station

The Indb–Mctm Express roared awake, its horn splitting the air—a warning, not a farewell. The vibration travelled through the platform like a low growl underfoot. Aadhya and Advait took their seats in Coach B-2, berths 23 and 24. The windows were tinted, yet faint imprints still clung to the glass—not fingerprints, but retinal smears, as though something had looked outward from within. Advait scratched one lightly with his nail. It vanished. Not wiped away—absorbed. Neither of them spoke.

The train pulled free of the capital's chaos, gliding north into a landscape of ashen light. Punjab's plains should have gleamed gold this time of year, but the sun had misplaced itself. The sky was a single slab of pewter, refusing to change. By 10:12 am, they reached Panipat. The train paused six minutes. The fog that met them there was unnatural. It moved sideways—coiling, reversing, breathing in slow loops, as if inhaled by something unseen. On the platform, a boy in a yellow railway uniform stood perfectly still, holding a tray of water bottles.

He didn't blink. Didn't breathe. As the train began to pull away, his head jerked toward Aadhya. His lips moved, forming words she could hear clearly through the sealed window. "You're late - they've already opened the gate." Advait rose halfway from his seat.

"Did you—?" "I saw him," she whispered. "He had - my eyes."

By 12:45pm, near Ambala Cantt, they shared the compartment with an elderly man wearing a Himachali cap. He introduced himself as Keshav, a mechanic returning home. His manner was polite, detached. He asked nothing of them. Then, without warning, he removed his shoes, folded his legs upon the berth, and began to chant softly. The words scraped memory like sandpaper. Advait recognised fragments—syllables too guttural, too ancient to belong to prayer.

Daitya Bhairavi.

The same dialect carved into the Caves of Hiranyakund. "How do you know that tongue?" Advait asked carefully. Keshav opened his eyes. They were calm, unblinking. "I don't," he said. "But I say it whenever I feel something crawling beneath my feet." He tapped the train floor. "There's something under the tracks today," he added softly. "Something that used to live above." Then he smiled, as though he had spoken of the weather. By 6:18 pm, they reached Pathankot Junction. Cold rain greeted them, sharp as needles. The fog was thicker here- alive, brushing their faces like wet fabric. At the exit, a man waited with a black placard that read simply: ***A. Roy – Daitya Guest House, Barot***.

He was tall and narrow, his neck too long for his frame, hair slicked flat against his skull as if glued there by seawater. His eyes flicked over each of them with practiced familiarity. "Welcome," he said. "I am Rathan. Your driver." His voice rasped like gravel dragged through water. The drive to Barot wound through the mountains for nearly five hours—narrow roads hugging cliffs where mist devoured the guardrails. The headlights barely pierced the white murk, yet Rathan never slowed. His hands gripped the wheel loosely, confidently, as if the road remembered him.

Around 8:22 PM, Aadhya asked, "You know the Daitya Guest House?" He nodded once. "I used to live beside it," he said. "Before they buried my mother." No one replied. The words lingered like a bruise. Villages blurred past - windows unlit, temples boarded, no dogs barked. Even the crickets refused to sing. At Jhatingri, a lone blue flame burned atop a distant ridge, perfectly still against the indigo sky.

"That's not a bonfire," Aadhya murmured. Rathan didn't look up. *"They say it burns only when someone arrives who should not."* The car jolted violently; something struck the undercarriage with a hollow thud. Advait twisted around. "What was that?" Rathan's face stayed expressionless. *"Sometimes the valley throws up bones,"* he said. "Don't stop for them."

9:43pm.

The forest swallowed the road. Fog wrapped the car like damp gauze. The headlights carved tunnels through breath and shadow. Then—a stone marker by the roadside. Moss-cloaked, half-buried. Three interlocking spirals were etched into it—the same pattern burned into Aadhya's wrist. Beneath them, a line of pigment still glistened wet, red as coagulated blood: ***She returns. The one who was flame. The one who undid the seal.*** The car lights dimmed, flaring once before steadying. Rathan said nothing. His eyes never left the road.

10:17pm.

They reached the Daitya Guest House. The wrought-iron gate groaned open without a touch. No watchman. No sound of dogs. Only the wind's low lament threading through pine and stone. The building loomed from the fog—an old colonial lodge crouched against the hillside, its grey façade veined with moss and decay. Shuttered windows glistened with condensation. The left wing sagged as though half-swallowed by the earth. One lamp burned above the entrance. Its flame was blue. Aadhya stepped out. Rain ceased mid-fall - not eased but stopped. Time paused with it.

"This place doesn't wish to be seen," Advait whispered. Rathan placed their bags by the threshold. "I will return at dawn." He climbed back into the car and drove off - no headlights pierced the fog. No engine followed. Just silence. And then - from the forest behind them - *Chimes. Delicate. Hollow.* Like bones clinking in a wind that wasn't there.

The child did not blink.

Aadhya froze mid-step. The figure—neither boy nor girl, no older than seven—stood drenched, as though pulled from the depths of a river. Water pooled beneath its bare feet, soaking into the wooden floorboards in dark streaks. Its mouth was sewn shut with black twine - not crudely but ritualistically, deliberate and reverent, as if stitched by someone who believed silence itself was sacred. Advait stepped forward cautiously. “Who are you?” The child tilted its head slightly. Then, without a word, turned and walked down the corridor. Each step was noiseless - no creak of wood, no rustle of wet cloth. Just the soft, unbroken trail of footprints dissolving as soon as they appeared.

Aadhya moved to follow. “Aadhya,” Advait hissed. “Don’t.” But the pull was visceral—an invisible hand tightening around her spine. The air had changed, thickened, heavy with the kind of stillness that precedes a storm. When she reached the foot of the staircase, the lamp on the reception desk hissed once, its blue flame flaring bright—then collapsed inward, extinguished as though swallowed by its own smoke. Darkness fell like a curtain. They found their quarters on the second floor.

Room 203.

The key was already in the lock – as though someone had been expecting them. Inside, the room was plain—two narrow beds, a small desk, and a stone-sealed fireplace that had not breathed flame in decades. The curtains hung heavy and wet. A fractured mirror stared from the far wall, veins of silver spreading from its center like the limbs of a dying tree. The smell was wrong - not old wood or mildew, but salt, iron, wet paper left too long in blood. Advait dropped his bag, flicked the light switch. Nothing. He lit a candle from his pack; its glow trembled uncertainly, barely carving space from the dark.

“The rain stopped the moment we entered,” Aadhya murmured, still facing the window. Advait checked his phone. Dead. Not drained—dead. The screen black, inert. She tried hers. Same. And then the mirror cracked further—not from any sound, but from the quiet itself. The fractures spidered wider, distorting her reflection until her eyes no longer aligned. “Look at this,” Advait whispered. He had opened the desk drawer. Inside lay a stack of torn journal pages—yellowed, fragile, the ink faded to rust. The first page bore a signature:

D.N.—Divyakshi Naik.

He began to read aloud, his voice unsteady.

“Barot breathes. But not like earth. Like something that once drowned.

The villagers deny a flood, but the trees still lean one way.”

“I hear them in the walls. Soft clicking. Fingers learning how to tap again.”

“I think the second seal is near—not open, not yet. But listening.

And memory never sleeps.”

Aadhya’s hands trembled as she reached for the next page. “Tonight, I saw a child with a stitched mouth. It watched from the corridor until dawn. By morning, it was gone. But the bed was wet.”

A creak rippled through the hallway outside. Then another. Not footsteps—a dragging. They stepped out. The candle’s flame wavered. Paintings along the corridor—sepia portraits of long-dead British officers and their wives—hung slightly askew. The shadows of their frames shifted as though the walls themselves exhaled. The sound came again. From the far end.

A door was open—Room 206.

Aadhya reached for the knob. Advait caught her wrist. “Don’t open doors here.” *“She was in there,”* Aadhya whispered. *“Divyakshi. Maybe she left something.”* The air pulsed once—not sound, but pressure. Like the corridor itself had drawn a breath. They entered.

Room 206 was colder. The fog outside had seeped through the open window, curling over the floor like vapour rising from ice. Dust floated in the candlelight, weightless as ash. The room was almost empty—one bed, a small brass bowl on a table in the corner. Inside the bowl, the black salt had congealed into a solid crust. Embedded in it were three objects: *A scrap of cloth inscribed with a Daitya mantra. A cracked shard of mirror. A baby’s tooth, perfectly clean.*

Aadhya’s breath caught. “She was building something,” she said. “A ritual, maybe.” Advait’s eyes fixed on the bowl. “This isn’t residue,” he murmured. “It’s an anchor. She wasn’t summoning—she was holding something back. Or delaying it.” They backed away. Closed the door gently. But the baby’s tooth inside the bowl was gone.

Back in Room 203, the candle sputtered low. Another was lit. Aadhya’s wrist began to itch. She rolled up her sleeve—and froze. The spiral on her skin was moving. Slowly, rhythmically. Breathing beneath the surface. Advait paled. *“That’s not just a mark anymore.”*

Then—three knocks. Pause.

Three again. From behind the beds.

They turned together. A thin crack had appeared between the wall panels. Behind it—an eye. Yellow. Vertical-pupilled. A goat’s eye, wide and unblinking, staring through the gap.

Advait snatched the lamp and smashed it against the panel. Wood splintered. The eye vanished—but words were carved into the stone beneath: ***"The Seal is Not a Lock. It's a Womb."***

1:13am .

Sleep was impossible. The whole house had begun to whisper—faint, overlapping murmurs that came from behind the walls, beneath the floor, even inside the air. They wandered the corridor again. Every painting was different now; the faces had been scratched from within the inside of the glass, fingernails dragged across varnish from beneath. At the end of the hallway, a wooden hatch. Aadhya placed her palm upon it. Warm. Too warm—like flesh holding breath. "We need to see what's down there," she said softly. Advait hesitated. "You're not going to like it." They descended with one candle. The basement air was thick, wet—sweet with rot and the mineral tang of salt. The walls were basalt, veined with white streaks that glimmered faintly, like veins of bone. Roots dangled from the ceiling, twitching occasionally as if something breathed through them. In the center stood a well. Dry. Its inner bricks were carved with spirals identical to the mark on Aadhya's wrist. Around its mouth, faint impressions dotted the floor—the footprints of children. Bare. Small. Dancing in circles through the salt dust.

The whispers began again—this time clearer. Not words. The sounds of drowning.

Aadhya clutched her temples. Her vision fractured—flames beneath water, mouths opening to scream and exhaling only fire. And above it all—the Rope of Agnivrat, coiling like a living serpent over the mouth of the well. Advait crouched near the bricks and brushed aside dirt. Something was buried there—a small wooden idol. Its face twisted, its eyes two shallow depressions filled with black resin.

"That's her," he whispered. "Aadhrika. You." Aadhya trembled. "Something's waking," she breathed. "Not just memory - something that was never meant to sleep." Then—a sound. Water. Dripping. Then gushing.

But the well was dry. They looked in. An eye stared back - vast, luminous, filled with storm-light. *Not a creature's—a valley's* . The ground shuddered beneath their feet. The place itself was looking at them.

The second seal had begun to stir. They ran. Up the stairs. Through the whispering hall. Every painting was wet now—frames weeping, glass slick with condensation. In Room 203, the air burned. The spiral on Aadhya's wrist seared like a brand. The walls vibrated, humming. And across the mirror, scrawled in lines of condensation:

"Bride of the Blood Valley - she will bleed again to open the door."

Aadhya collapsed to her knees. Advait grabbed her shoulders. "Stay with me. This isn't the end - it's the middle." Her voice shook. "We're not alone." He turned. The child stood in the doorway again—soaked, eyes glowing faintly in the candlelight. This time, the stitches across its mouth were torn open. It exhaled once. And when it spoke, the voice that came out was not a child's—not even human. It was a whisper forged of fire and frost.

"The second seal is listening."

"And she will remember the sound of her own death."

The room trembled. The valley outside groaned. And above Barot, the night sky convulsed—thousands of black birds twisting in unison into a vast, burning spiral. The mark of Aadhrika. The second seal was no longer asleep.

But it had not yet cracked

Chapter - 16
The Rope of Agnivrat

The morning in *Barot* arrived without sunlight. Aadhya woke to the sound of water dripping—slow, deliberate, echoing through the wooden walls like a clock carved from stone. Each drop landed with the weight of something alive, as though the guesthouse itself was breathing in damp, rhythmic intervals. Her fingers were clenched tightly around the bedsheet; her pulse faintly raced. She couldn't remember dreaming. Or rather—she couldn't remember not dreaming.

A cracked bell; a figure wrapped in saffron ropes, buried beneath translucent ice. And the whisper: He remembers the war because he never died.

She sat up sharply, lungs dragging cold air that didn't belong to morning. Advait was already awake, standing near the window. His shirt was damp at the shoulders, darkened in patches as though snow had melted there—but outside, it was only rain. Relentless, monsoon rain that slid down the window like thin sheets of mercury. He didn't look at her when he spoke. "Did you hear it too?" Aadhya asked, her voice a ghost of itself. "The voice?" Advait's reflection flickered in the fogged glass. "No - the chant."

The corridors of the guesthouse were empty when they descended. Their shoes left faint, wet imprints across the dust-streaked floor—dust that hadn't been there the night before. The reception desk bell had cracked neatly in half, and the air smelled faintly of copper and extinguished camphor. Neither spoke of it. The driver who had brought them here, Rathan, was gone. A different man stood beside the waiting Jeep—older, with a face carved by wind and time. An amber bead hung at his throat, tied with red thread, and his expression was as still as the mountains themselves.

"I am Rana-ji," he said simply. "The roads are clear for now." When they asked about the guesthouse staff, his gaze lingered on the distant peaks before answering, "People move on, sahib. The mountains do not wait." He handed Advait a folded scrap of cloth: a hand-drawn map, edges torn, the ink a dull charcoal black. At its center - written in script older than any language Aadhya knew - was a single word: ***Agnivrat***. She traced it lightly with her thumb. "What's this symbol?"

Rana-ji inhaled, as though deciding whether to speak. *"The rope that binds a forgotten god,"* he said finally. *"They say it lies beneath the ice, where vows do not decay."* The road toward Lohardi was almost deserted. Pines leaned low over the track, whispering in a dialect of wind. The fog was thick, folding and unfolding like the hem of a sleeping giant's breath. Somewhere, beyond the trees, came a faint metallic clanging—repeated, rhythmic, always a little ahead of them. Aadhya turned slightly. "That sound… you hear it too?" Advait didn't look up from the map. "It's been following us since last night."

They fell silent again, the Jeep rumbling through switchbacks and forest bends. When they reached a narrow bridge suspended over a roaring current, Aadhya leaned out slightly. The water beneath wasn't clear. It was the colour of rusted iron—dense, too thick for monsoon runoff. It looked like blood trying to remember what it meant to flow. At the other end of the bridge stood an old man.

Barefoot, shirtless; his skin was weathered into parchment, his hair like wet cotton. Around his neck hung a rudraksha bead the size of a clenched fist. When the Jeep approached, he raised his right hand—palm forward. Across that palm were rope burns: deep, blackened, ancient. Rana-ji's voice dropped, sharp as a whisper of warning. *"Do not greet him - he is a memory."* Advait turned slightly. *"A memory of what?"* Rana-ji's eyes didn't leave the road. *"Of betrayal."* They didn't ask more. By noon, the Jeep rolled to a stop before a set of stone pillars—remnants of a ruined temple crouched in a valley curve. Its broken spire leaned like a snapped bone against the clouds. From afar, the structure looked empty.

But as Aadhya stepped across the threshold, her burn ignited beneath her skin. The inner walls were carved with inscriptions that shifted when viewed directly - as though alive. The letters were neither Sanskrit, nor Pali—they curved and twisted like veins of molten iron. Daitya script - but older, wilder. She pressed her palm against the damp stone; beneath the moss her fingers traced grooves not carved by chisels but by fingernails.

"She was sealed here," Aadhya whispered. Advait turned sharply. "Who?" "I don't know." Her voice trembled. "But she had her eyes removed."

He followed her gaze. On the wall, half-buried in grime, was a shape—a woman's face sculpted in agony. Her mouth was open in a silent scream. Her sockets were hollow, and around her, coiled ropes were carved deep into the wall, burning faintly red in the diffused light. Advait exhaled slowly. *"This isn't Deva work. This... this feels older."* The ground trembled slightly beneath their feet. From below, a low hum began to rise—a chant, but too deep for human throats. The air thickened. The light dimmed. In the adjoining chamber, frost clung to the walls like breath turned solid. In its center, imprisoned within a cage of rusted iron and bone, stood a figure.

Not alive. Not gone. He was tall - inhumanly so - his muscles hardened into stone, his skin cracked like frozen bark. Across his chest ropes were coiled in layered bands, fused to the flesh by burn marks centuries old. His eyes were closed, yet his body pulsed faintly, like something remembering how to breathe. Aadhya stepped closer, her throat dry. The symbol on his chest - a spiral enclosed by jagged lines - felt eerily familiar. She'd seen it in Mahadev's notes once, in a passage about Daitya exile rites. Rana-ji stopped at the threshold, his voice low. *"Agnivrat," he said. "The one who watched the Devas from beneath the snow - he refused to forget."* Advait knelt. "Is he still—?"

"Not dead," Rana-ji interrupted. "Frozen. Not by ice. By vow. And rope." The air inside the chamber seemed to throb in rhythm with their breathing. The ropes across the figure's torso shimmered faintly—as if sensing Aadhya's presence. She moved closer. The world dulled. The sound of rain outside faded. Her vision tunnelled, and suddenly—she was no longer hearing through her ears; she was hearing through her veins.

"The second seal will not crack in light," a voice whispered inside her blood. "it will unravel in sleep."

Her knees gave way. Advait caught her as she fell, pulling her out of the chamber's reach. When she blinked, the air was warm again. But behind them, the frozen figure's eyelids fluttered—once, briefly—then shut. They left the temple before sunset. Behind them, the mist hung low and heavy, whispering in half-languages that belonged to no living world. Rana-ji's Jeep was parked where they had left it, engine already running.

"You'll be safe here till tomorrow," he said, leading them to a small wooden hut deeper within the forest. "The rope won't let him rise yet. Not without his flame." Before Aadhya could ask, he handed her a box wrapped in crimson cloth. The weight of it was unnatural—neither metal nor wood. He didn't explain what was inside; he only said, "Dream carefully tonight, Doctor- you are too close to forget now."

And then he drove away into the mist, leaving the faint echo of his words behind. The hut was silent except for the slow percussion of the storm that was beginning to gather. Aadhya and Advait sat facing each other, the box between them like a sleeping thing. For a long time, neither spoke. The air itself felt hesitant, as though the night were listening. Finally, Advait broke the silence. "What if we're not meant to stop the seals?" Aadhya looked up slowly. "What if we're only meant to witness them?" She didn't answer immediately. Her gaze lingered on the crimson box, its cloth faintly pulsing in the lamplight. Her voice, when it came, was quiet.

"What if we're not witnesses, Advait?" she said. "What if we're keys?"

The storm began as a whisper. Then it screamed. Rain lashed the wooden walls of the hut in strange, uneven bursts, as though the wind was a living thing prowling in circles outside. It didn't blow steady—it paused, inhaled, then shrieked again, sharp and deliberate. The lantern flame quivered, not from draft but from listening. Aadhya sat cross-legged before the box. The red cloth clung damply to its edges, darker now as if soaked in breath rather than water. Heat radiated faintly from within—uneven, pulsing like a heart that had forgotten its rhythm. Advait had drawn a thin ring of salt around it. He didn't know why; it had simply felt necessary. The salt was no longer white; its edges had begun to char, turning black like burned parchment.

"Open it," Advait said quietly. Aadhya didn't move. Her fingers hovered above the cloth. "You do it." He hesitated, then reached forward and peeled back the red covering. Inside lay a coiled rope, deep red—so dark it seemed to drink the light around it. It wasn't ordinary rope: its strands were thick and uneven, like sinew hardened into fibre. It glistened faintly, slick with something that wasn't water. The smell hit first—camphor, iron, and an undercurrent of something older, unnameable. The scent of sacrifice preserved. *Beneath the coil lay four objects, tucked carefully into the corners of the box:*

A small mirror, fractured into three shards; a folded, scorched page of script; a bronze medallion engraved with twin serpents; and a single, blackened tooth. The silence around them deepened. Even the storm outside seemed to hesitate. Aadhya reached out, her hand trembling. "I think this belonged to Agnivrat," she whispered. "It's part of his vow." Advait leaned closer, his voice low. "A Daitya warrior… bound by his own promise?"

"Or by someone else's." She ran a finger along the rope's edge. It was warm—alive. "Maybe that's why he never truly died. The rope remembers what the soul forgets." She unfolded the charred page. The writing was barely visible—lines of black ink twisted into a mantra she didn't recognize. The script pulsed faintly, as if aware it was being read. "Don't chant it," Advait said, his tone instinctively sharp. "I wasn't going to." Her voice wavered. "It feels… inverted. Like a prayer said backward."

She picked up one of the mirror shards. Its surface was cold, almost oily to the touch. The reflection shimmered, refusing to hold her face. The moment her fingers brushed it, the world shifted. The hut dissolved. She stood on an endless plateau of ice, the horizon split between white and blood. Each snowflake that touched her skin burned. Across the expanse, figures clashed - Daitya warriors, towering, armoured in flame. Their blood steamed as it hit the ground. At the center of the carnage stood Agnivrat. Alive. Fire curling around his arms like serpents of light. His roar cracked the sky. Behind him, the others fell—creatures with red-gold eyes, their weapons forged of bone and salt. They were being consumed by a blizzard of spears that glowed with divine symbols. He didn't retreat. He turned toward the mountains and hurled his own rope into a fissure of ice. As it disappeared into darkness, a woman's voice echoed across the plain:

"If you bind yourself, they will forget. If you burn yourself, we will return." Aadhya gasped. The air vanished from her lungs. The ice splintered beneath her. And then she was back in the hut, falling forward, choking on the sound of her own breath. Advait caught her. "What did you see?" Her voice trembled, hollow. *"A war. He sealed himself—not to die, but to protect something. He gave his body to the vow so it could live longer than memory."* Advait's gaze dropped to her wrist. The spiral burn had deepened; what had been a faint coil was now a living sigil - three loops forming around a central flame. *"The mark's changing again,"* he said. "It's finishing itself," she whispered. "This rope—it's not just his prison. It's a fragment of that vow. The rest is still around him. This piece… maybe it's the key to waking it."

The storm outside paused abruptly. Silence pressed in, thick and alert. Then—three knocks. Slow. Rhythmic. Both of them froze. A voice followed, muffled through the rain. Feminine. Calm. Ancient.

"You opened the rope. So I must arrive." Advait's hand went to the medallion. "Don't open the door." But the latch clicked on its own. The door swung inward. A woman stood there - barefoot, drenched, her hair white and matted into a single braid. Her skin was the colour of clay after rain. Her eyes—milky, blind—but they moved with certainty, as if she could see everything that dared to exist.

"I am Maati-Jogin," she said softly. "Keeper of the Buried Flame." The air shifted. The storm seemed to lower its voice. Aadhya stepped back instinctively. "What do you want?" Maati-Jogin smiled faintly, not cruelly. "Want? No. I remember. I am memory, child. I keep the names of those who buried themselves to save the world." She walked forward, ignoring the salt ring entirely. Her bare feet did not leave prints. "You have found a piece of him," she murmured, glancing at the rope. "He has waited too long—but not all of him should wake." Advait's brow furrowed. "Then why bring us this?" Her pale eyes turned black for a heartbeat. *"Because forgetting is how the world ends. Every time you remember, the rope loosens; every time you doubt, it tightens."* Aadhya's voice barely held. *"The second seal—it's still bound?"*

"For now." Maati-Jogin tilted her head, listening to something far away. "But not for long. Because one of you has already begun to remember." She reached forward and brushed her fingers over Aadhya's wrist. Pain burst through her arm like fire under skin. The mark flared, bright as molten gold. *"Remember this pain,"* Maati-Jogin whispered. *"You chose flame once before, when silence could have saved you - that choice is close again."* She turned toward the door, the wind wrapping her in its howl. *"The rope will burn in dream,"* she said as she stepped outside. "And when it does, the frozen warrior will rise."

The door closed by itself. The hut was still again. The storm distant now, but never gone. That night, Aadhya couldn't sleep. She rewrapped the rope, sealed it with new salt, tied the red cloth tightly, and placed it beside the dying lantern. But even through the fabric, she heard whispers—breathless chanting, clashing metal, a rhythm of war that pulsed like a heartbeat beneath the floorboards. Lightning flashed outside. From across the ridge, something was watching her. A tall silhouette, unmoving against the rain. Not beast. Not man. Its chest steamed as though fire lived beneath the flesh. And from its breastbone, faint red threads unfurled, swaying in the wind—ropes, breathing.

Aadhya blinked. It was gone. She didn't scream. She only turned toward the window, lit the last diya from Varanasi, and placed it before her. The flame swayed violently but cast no shadow behind her—only in front, as though something at her back refused to exist in light. Across the room, Advait stirred in uneasy sleep. Then his lips parted—and a whisper escaped, but it wasn't his voice.

"Yugantar bhinn hoga… jab aakhri shabd gum ho jaaye."

(Time will rupture when the final word is lost.)

Aadhya rushed to his side, shaking him gently. "Advait." He blinked awake, disoriented. "What? What happened?" "You were speaking," she said. "In a language you don't know." He frowned, dazed. "I dreamt of snow. And a voice beneath it—calling my name." She took his hand. It was ice-cold. They sat in silence. The rain softened for a moment, and in that fragile pause came another sound—from beneath the floorboards. A man's voice. Muffled. Hollow. Endless.

"Unbind me... unbind me... unbind me..." Advait rose slowly, gripping the medallion. It pulsed against his palm like a trapped heartbeat. Aadhya began folding layers of salt around the cloth again, her motions mechanical, ritualistic. "We have

to find him," she said. "Not the body. The rest of him. Wherever his vow was thrown." "Wherever the rope waits," Advait finished. The hut creaked—not from the wind this time, but from weight. Something moved above them. Crawling. Then came the sound of nails—long, hooked, dragging slowly against the roof.

One circle. Then another. Then silence. Neither of them looked up. Instinct older than words warned them not to. Whatever was above had once known fire. But now, it crawled with frost. The scratching stopped. For a full minute, nothing moved—neither inside the hut nor beyond it. Even the storm seemed to hold its breath. Then, softly, a single drop fell from the ceiling and landed on Aadhya's hand. She flinched—not because it was wet, but because it was hot. Advait stepped toward the wall. *"It's melting,"* he whispered. "Not water," Aadhya murmured. She touched the droplet with her fingertip. It smelled of burnt resin and old wax—like the remnant of a ritual that had outlived its priest. She didn't say what she was thinking: it wasn't rain that dripped from above. *It was memory—thawing.*

Overhead, silence pressed down. Then came a long, slow exhale. Not wind. A breath. Measured. Watching. Aadhya's voice was barely audible. "We're not alone." Advait tightened his grip on the medallion, its metal warm now—pulsing like an echo of their own hearts. "Is it him?"

"No." Her whisper trembled. *"It's something caught between."* The floor creaked—not beneath their feet, but below them. As though the earth itself had grown another layer, breathing. Aadhya crossed the room. Her steps were slow, deliberate, her shadow stretching unnaturally against the walls. Near the back of the hut, the wooden panels were uneven—one slightly ajar. She crouched and pulled it aside Behind it, darkness waited. A narrow tunnel, sloping downward, carved not from soil but packed salt and damp clay.

A breath escaped from it—warm, metallic. Not the cold of burial, but the heat of something that remembered fire too well. Advait's voice was quiet. "You want to go in there?" "No." Aadhya's eyes never left the dark. "But we have to." They lit the lantern. Its flame dimmed the moment they entered, shrinking as though afraid to burn here. The tunnel pressed close, forcing them to crouch. The walls glistened faintly, carved with glyphs that moved when the light passed. Inverted mantras - breathing like lungs straining for their first gasp in centuries. The air was wrong—thick, syrupy. Each step felt like walking through the residue of dreams.

The tunnel sloped sharply downward before opening into a small, circular chamber. No torches, no idols—only a single slab of black stone at its center. Upon it lay a rope. Or what remained of one. Thicker. Darker. Coiled tight as a noose. And inside it—something was breathing. Slow, steady, eternal. Aadhya's knees weakened. "This is where it ends," she whispered. "Or begins again," Advait said. His voice sounded distant. He stepped forward, raising the bronze medallion. The rope stirred—not violently, but in recognition. The noose loosened, just enough to reveal what it guarded. A fragment of bone lay at its heart: smooth, blackened, fused into the fibers like a secret burned too long. It radiated faint heat.

"Don't touch it," Aadhya said sharply. But Advait's fingers had already brushed it. The chamber shattered. Light engulfed them - white, then crimson, then the colour of old wounds. They stood in a burning forest. Trees screamed as their trunks split open, sap boiling like blood. The sky was torn in half, and through it marched figures the size of mountains—Daitya warriors, their eyes glowing with the light of dying suns.

Agnivrat was among them. Limping, wounded, his body cracked with fire.

He carried something over his shoulder—a mirror. Not a weapon, but a reflection he refused to drop. He looked toward the torn sky and whispered, *"If I burn now, she lives."* Then he looped the rope around his chest, pulled it tight, and walked into the flames. The world screamed as he vanished. The vision collapsed. They were back in the chamber. The lantern hissed. Advait staggered backward, clutching his hand. Blood dripped from his palm—the rope had lashed him once, clean and precise, as if signing his flesh with memory. The wound formed a diagonal slash that glowed faintly.

Aadhya stared at it. Her wrist-mark pulsed in answer. *"We were meant to see that," she said.* Advait nodded shakily. "He didn't die in war. He sacrificed his afterlife. He bound himself to time." A slow knock echoed through the tunnel above—three raps, deliberate, like ritual punctuation.

They froze. Nothing followed. They turned back to the altar—The rope was gone. The stone was empty. And above them, in the hut, something exhaled—a deep, ragged sigh that felt tired. Advait ran first. Aadhya followed, lantern swaying wildly. They burst into the hut, breathless—then stopped.

The box was open; the salt circle smeared. Standing in the middle of the room was Maati-Jogin. But she wasn't alone. Behind her loomed another figure - taller, cloaked in pale robes soaked through with frost. His arms were bound behind him with crimson threads. His face hidden beneath a warped bronze mask that had half-melted and fused to his skin. The air bent around him, like space itself refused to touch him. Maati-Jogin's tone was calm, but reverent.

"You have found what was buried. So now - he must walk again." Aadhya's throat tightened. "Is that… him?" The masked figure lifted his head. His breath fogged the air—but inwards, as if he inhaled frost rather than exhaled it. The sound was hollow, a void breathing through lungs that had never been meant to. "Only a memory," Maati-Jogin said softly. *"The real one still sleeps beneath Barot's bones. But this—this is his echo. It will lead you to the Seal."* Advait stepped forward. "The second seal—it's still bound?" "For now," she answered. Her eyes dimmed. "But it stirs. Because fire has remembered its shape. And dreams have started to bleed." She crossed to Aadhya and touched her cheek. Her hand was freezing.

"You were his last word." Aadhya's breath faltered. "What?" "He died with your name in his mouth - the name you once had. The name you will remember when the ice breaks." She stepped toward the door, pausing once more. "Do not chant the mantra in full. Not yet. The seal must break only where destiny commands—not here. Not out of fear." And then she was gone. The door opened to the storm; both she and the echo vanished into the rain like breath dissipating from glass.

The rope was gone. The box was empty, but Aadhya's wrist burned anew - three loops now instead of two. The sigil had evolved into a flame encircled by rope, pierced through by a single spear.

"Barot," she whispered. "The temple beneath the hill. That's where the real seal lies." Advait nodded grimly. "And Agnivrat's body." They gathered their things in silence. The chanting still hummed faintly beneath the floorboards, rising and falling with the wind—like something asleep and dreaming of its own birth. Before leaving, Aadhya glanced back once. On the inside of the doorframe, scorched into the wood, a message read:

He who remembers the rope will remember the fire. But not all fire saves.

Her fingers brushed the words once, reverently, before closing the door behind them. By morning, the storm had passed, but the world felt wrong. The air had been peeled clean, as though a layer of silence had been stripped off everything living. The forest stood still. The river below sounded flat, dull—its rhythm broken. Rana-ji was waiting beside the jeep.

"The storm spared the village," he said. "But all the trees around the hut—blackened. Burned without fire."

Neither Aadhya nor Advait replied. As they drove downhill, the mist parted behind them. When Aadhya looked back, the hut was gone. Not destroyed—gone, like a thought erased mid-dream. Only the ground remained, scorched into a perfect spiral. She turned forward. "We need to reach the temple before the seal senses us." Advait didn't question her. Not anymore. His hand rested on the medallion; hers hovered protectively over her wrist.

The second seal had not yet broken, but something within it had opened its eye.

Chapter - 17
The Fever Chant

The road down from the vanished hut coiled like a snake-reluctant to sleep. Fog still clung to the trees, heavy with something more than mist - something that moved when they did not, whispering syllables too fragmented to be language. The jeep rattled over gravel and stone, headlights carving through the grey in fevered slashes that never quite reached bone. Aadhya sat in the back seat, her gaze fixed on the spiral of scorched earth where the hut had stood. It was already receding into the folds of the mountain - a memory peeling away from the world. Beside her, Advait held the medallion wrapped in the scrap of Maati-Jogin's salt veil. It throbbed faintly. Not pulsing—breathing. Like something underground, dreaming through soil.

"We're close," Aadhya murmured, more to herself than to either man. *Rana-ji* glanced at her through the mirror. "How do you know?" She didn't answer. Her wrist ached again - not burning, but singing. *The glyph's three loops had begun to curl into each other, shimmering faintly beneath the skin. Warm, not with fever but with rhythm—an ancient pulse that beat out of time with her heart.* Advait unfolded the charred scrap of paper from the box. The reversed mantra had darkened further; its letters curled like embers on a dying wick. "This script," he said quietly. "It's not just Daitya. It's inverted Sanskrit—flipped, like a prayer meant to bind instead of bless." Aadhya leaned closer. "What does it say now?"

He traced the line with his finger. "'When the rope remembers the flesh, the chant will return. Fever is the gate; bone is the key.'" Her eyes narrowed. "Fever," she repeated. "That's what the dream was." He looked at her sharply. "You saw it again?"

"Not asleep," she said. "While awake - after he touched the rope. I saw a child made of mirrors, carried through a burning forest. I think Agnivrat was trying to save her." Advait's brow furrowed. "Or bury her - to keep what she carried from being found." The road narrowed into a single curling lane, hemmed by pines that leaned inward like eavesdropping monks. Their branches didn't sway with the wind; they listened. The jeep's engine coughed once, then steadied, growling as it climbed. When they crossed a wooden bridge, the air changed again. Beneath them, the water churned thick and red-brown, like silt mixed with blood.

At the far end of the bridge stood an old man, barefoot, his hair matted with frost. Around his neck hung a rudraksha pendant the size of a heart. He raised one hand as they passed. The palm was scarred with deep rope burns—centuries old and black. Rana-ji slowed but didn't stop. "Do not greet him," he said tightly. "Who is he?" Advait asked. Rana's eyes stayed on the road. "A memory," he murmured. "Of what?"

"Of betrayal." They drove on in silence. The road curved again, and the forest parted to reveal the ruin they sought. The temple stood crouched within a bowl of stone - half buried, its ribs of column and arch breaking through earth and moss. From a distance it looked deserted; up close it breathed. The ground was damp beneath their boots, humming faintly as if the soil still remembered chanting. Aadhya stopped before the first pillar. Her wrist burned through the cloth of her sleeve. “He’s near,” she whispered. Advait brushed dust from a half-fallen wall. The carvings were Daitya script - but rougher, sharper, etched by hand rather than chisel. Beneath one inscription was a smaller scrawl in red pigment. He wiped away moss until the full line emerged:

To enter is to remember; to remember is to burn. He looked back at her. “This was never meant for worship. It’s a warning.” Her gaze had already shifted toward the central archway - a gaping mouth, carved with teeth-like ridges. Above it, a defaced frieze showed kneeling figures before a masked warrior holding a rope of flame. The warrior’s face was gone. Chiselled out—or erased by something hotter than iron. The wind died. Even insects stopped. “Fever,” Aadhya said softly. “It isn’t illness. It’s memory. Burning its way back.” They entered. Inside, the temperature rose. The air was thick, metallic—like blood evaporating. The passage sloped downward; the floor slick with condensation that was not water. The walls pulsed faintly with veins of light, each glyph glowing like a heartbeat under skin. Advait ran a palm along the wall. “The symbols… they’re alive.”

“They’re remembering,” she corrected. The deeper they went, the louder the sound became—a murmur of countless voices chanting in reverse. It wasn’t echo. It was resistance: a ritual being sung backwards to hold something down. Aadhya slowed. “It’s the reversed mantra.” Advait nodded grimly. “The one meant to suppress. Someone carved it into the stone itself.” The air trembled with heat. Sweat streaked down her temple, though the space had no fire. Then they reached the chamber. The chamber was circular and sunken; rope-like veins stretched from wall to wall, converging upon a platform blackened with scorch. Upon it lay a skeleton -massive, horned, its bones translucent like cooled glass. Where its chest had shattered, the fragments still shimmered faintly with light. In its palm rested something that should not have endured.

A mirror - not reflective but alive; its surface rippled like the skin of boiling water. Aadhya's glyph flared crimson. Her knees weakened. She stepped closer. Advait caught her wrist. "Don't. What do you see?" Her eyes were wide, unfocused. "A child. No - me. But not this me: Aadhrika. She's trapped inside it." The fever in the air spiked. The bones vibrated - a groan moving through the chamber like a living pulse. The ropes shuddered; one slid an inch across the stone. The mirror cracked - just once, a single line through its center. The chant stopped; silence hit like a blow.

Then the ropes began to move again, coiling and twitching toward her feet like serpents relearning their bodies. Advait yanked her back. "We have to go!"

"It's the seal," she gasped. "This is where it sleeps."

"Not breaks," he said, pulling harder. "Not here. Not now." The mirror flared, then dimmed. The skeleton stilled. The heat collapsed into still air. Whatever had begun had only paused. They fled upward through the narrowing corridor, lungs burning, until the pale wash of daylight met them again. At the temple's mouth, Aadhya turned one last time. The setting sun struck the entrance, and for a heartbeat she thought she saw it change - stone muscles tightening, teeth closing.

The mouth had sealed itself.

They didn't speak as they climbed the steep incline, roots clutching at their boots like desperate fingers. The forest behind them remained unnaturally silent—no rustle, no animal calls, no breath of wind. Only that faint, subterranean hum, as if the earth itself had a heartbeat struggling to remember its rhythm. At the ridge's summit, Aadhya bent forward, palms on her knees, her forehead glistening with sweat despite the mountain chill. Her wrist was inflamed—the glyph no longer glowing, but raised as though carved by heat. The fever chant had fallen quiet, yet its echo clung inside her skull, pulsing with every heartbeat.

"I don't think it was just a vision," she whispered, her voice half-lost in the wind. Advait looked up from where he crouched, brushing moss from his sleeves. "You said you saw yourself."

"I saw Aadhrika," she corrected. Her tone was distant, almost reverent. "Younger. Caged behind something. Like she wasn't meant to awaken—like something's holding her memory hostage." Advait unfolded the mantra parchment again. The ink had blackened into faint metallic sheen. "This isn't an invocation," he said, tracing the reversed script. "It's suppression. A containment hymn. Maati-Jogin didn't mean to release the seal—she was stopping someone else from unbinding it."

Aadhya's gaze sharpened. "Kalkini." He nodded slowly. "The box, the mirror, the rope—all sent to you before it was too late." Her lips tightened. "But we are too late. The mirror cracked."

"Yet the seal didn't break," he countered gently. She looked away. "Not yet. But it's stirring. I felt it breathe." The sky had begun to melt into violet and blood-orange, the dusk thick enough to drown colour. The forest warped with it. Trees seemed to bend inward, their silhouettes no longer resembling wood but limbs—distorted, beckoning. The earth felt spongy, as if exhaling beneath their steps. By the time they reached the clearing where Rana ji had parked, the last of the light had thinned. The driver emerged from the shadows, his eyes wide and hollow.

"I waited," he said quietly, his voice trembling. "Something told me not to call out. The forest... it was listening." He looked beyond them, toward the direction of the ruins. "Did you hear it? The singing?" Aadhya froze. "The fever chant?" Rana nodded. "Low, like a hive inside the soil. My teeth hurt from it." Aadhya placed a hand on his arm. "You're not fevered?" He shook his head. "Not yet. But the mountain's burning inside. I can feel it." They climbed into the jeep. The engine groaned as it turned, struggling against the incline. As they descended, twilight thickened into an unnatural dark. Even the headlights seemed weaker, the beams swallowed by fog that pulsed like breath.

The air smelled of salt. Rana slowed. "The sea," he murmured. "There's no sea here," Advait said. "I know," Rana replied. "That's why I'm afraid." The smell grew sharper—wet iron, sweat, and brine. The same scent as the guesthouse floor, as the blood-marked rope. Then the engine stuttered once. Twice. Died. "Not again," Rana muttered, slamming the steering wheel. The headlights flickered, then cut off completely. "Wait," Advait whispered. "Listen." Footsteps. Dozens of them. Light, deliberate. Encircling. Not human. "Turn off the lights," Aadhya said instinctively.

"They already are." The forest began to move - not sway, not wind. It shifted. Figures drifted between the trunks, their outlines stuttering like film caught between frames. The sound followed - a dry, rhythmic clicking, bone against bone. They emerged from the fog - small, childlike silhouettes cloaked in tattered hides, faces masked with clay and ash. Each mask was cracked across one eye; from the breaks seeped faint trails of steam. Rana's breath hitched. "What are they?" Aadhya's whisper was almost inaudible. ***"The Feverlings."*** They stood in perfect silence, dozens of them. Watching. Listening. Then one stepped forward. It lifted a small hand, pale as wax.

Resting in its palm was a shard—jagged, reflective. A fragment of the cracked mirror.

Before Advait or Rana could react, Aadhya stepped out of the jeep. "Wait!" Advait hissed. "Don't—" But she was already moving, drawn as though by gravity. *The Feverling raised the shard and pressed it gently to the glowing glyph on her wrist - no pain, only heat.* The shard merged into her skin, vanishing like a drop of water into sand; a soft hum rippled through the clearing. And suddenly she could hear it. The chant. Not through her ears—through her bones.

"Nara-agnaya-daitya… Paap-vratya-jagran…"

(Fire of Man, Fire of Daitya… Awake, O Vow of Sin.)

Ancient syllables, looping backward, their cadence like fevered breath. The words bypassed her mind entirely, carving through the marrow of her memory - not hers but Aadhrika's. *The Feverlings tilted their heads in unison. Then, as if summoned by something distant, they turned toward the hills and scattered into the forest - vanishing soundlessly between trees.*

Aadhya staggered, dropping to her knees. Her skin glistened with heat, the glyph smouldering faintly like metal cooling after forge. Advait rushed to her. "Are you hurt?"

"No," she gasped. "*But something just... awakened. The mirror wasn't meant to show—it was meant to connect.*" She lifted her wrist. The shard was gone. Absorbed. "There's more," she whispered, her breath shallow. "That wasn't the seal. That was its guard - the fever chant itself. Someone's trying to reverse it." Rana turned the ignition. The engine roared back, obedient now.

Aadhya climbed inside, trembling. “We need someone who understands chants older than the Devas.” Advait nodded grimly. “Then we go to Joginder.” Rana’s knuckles whitened on the wheel. “You mean the mad shaman?”

“Not mad,” Aadhya said softly. “Exiled. For knowing too much.” Rana exhaled. “He lives past the old dam. Near the petrified orchard. No one goes there.”

“Then that’s exactly where we’re going,” Advait said. The road narrowed again, dissolving into dirt and shadow. The road out of the orchard wound through a silence that felt alive. The trees loomed like dark sentinels, dripping resin that smelled faintly of smoke and rot. Beneath the wheels of the jeep, the mud hissed softly, as if releasing breath trapped for centuries. No one spoke. The shaman’s warning still clung to them—tight, suffocating, like a noose made of thought rather than rope. The fever chant hadn’t faded; it followed, laced through the wind like a whisper spoken just below hearing. It curled beneath their boots, into their throats, into the marrow of silence itself.

Even the air felt feverish now—thick, humming, restless. Rana ji drove slower than usual, both hands gripping the wheel, eyes fixed on the road as though afraid it might vanish. The headlights carved brief tunnels through the mist before dissolving into blackness. Aadhya sat in the back seat, staring at her wrist. The glyph there pulsed faintly, not glowing, but alive—listening. The red rope wrapped around it had begun to dry, the once-wet fibers stiffened into threads that looked almost like veins. “The cave,” she murmured. Her voice trembled but did not break. Advait turned slightly, his face pale in the reflected light. “He said it’s past the frozen stream.”

"The burial verse is there," she said. "Something strong enough to drown the reversal chant." Rana ji didn't answer. But his knuckles whitened against the steering wheel. By midnight, they reached the edge of the old dam. Beyond it stretched a valley carved by shadow and frost, where the world seemed stripped of all colour. The stream below wasn't marked on any map. *Locals whispered its name like a curse—Siti Nala, the Whistling Stream. But tonight, it didn't whistle. It hummed. Low. Ceaseless. Like something deep within the mountain was remembering a song.* The jeep could go no farther. Rana ji parked beneath a ridge and shut off the ignition. The sound of the engine's dying breath merged seamlessly with the humming from the valley. They stepped out.

The cold bit instantly. But it wasn't clean mountain cold—it was fever-cold, paradoxical, hot from within. The air shimmered faintly as they moved through it. Their flashlights dimmed after a few paces, their beams smothered as if swallowed by the fog. They carried only what mattered: the rope from the box, the cracked mantra parchment, a coil of regular rope, matches, and a small copper lamp from the guesthouse. The snow underfoot was blackened; the frost did not glitter - it absorbed light.

When Aadhya crouched, she noticed movement beneath the frozen stream. Shapes. Human—but wrong. "Do you see that?" she whispered. Advait nodded slowly. "Yes - something under the ice." She brushed away the frost, revealing a face. A human face, eyes wide open, mouth mid-chant. Her stomach lurched. "They were singing when it froze."

"Or frozen because they were singing," Advait said grimly. They moved in silence after that. The trees here were warped, their trunks bending backward as if resisting gravity. Some were melted halfway down, frozen mid-collapse. A few still leaned over the stream, their branches blackened into claws.

The path wound through them, narrow and winding, until it opened onto a ravine. At its far end yawned a dark cleft in the rock—a cave mouth half-collapsed, rimmed with salt and moss that grew upside down. It looked like the mountain had tried to spit it out. Aadhya tightened the red rope around her wrist. "We go together. No separation."

They entered. The light from their lantern dimmed immediately, as though it were being inhaled. The walls of the passage were slick not from water but from something viscous-dark sap that pulsed faintly like the veins of a buried heart. Every step released a faint hiss, the sound of air escaping wounds that weren't there.

The passage turned sharply, carved not by tools but by something molten, twisted, deliberate. The hum grew louder the deeper they went. Then the tunnel widened. They stepped into a chamber ringed by towering standing stones—black, glassy, and wet to the touch. On each pillar, faint Daitya glyphs shimmered, their meaning half-swallowed by erosion and time.

At the chamber's center lay a platform. *And upon it—a body. Maati-Jogin* - her skin was ash-grey, lips blue, hands folded around a wooden box identical to the one she had given them. Her eyes were open—yet empty, as if her soul had dissolved mid-syllable. Aadhya's knees weakened. "She came here before us." Advait's voice was a low whisper. "She tried to stop it." Beside the box, etched into the stone with fingernails, were verses written in twisted Daitya script. Not carved, but scratched—desperate, deliberate. Advait knelt, tracing the markings gently. "It's written to be sung." He translated slowly, reverently.

"Na nidra, na aagni, na rudra ka vaad,

Raksha kare jo, vohi bhool jaaye yaad.

Svar palat jaayein, jab naav doobe gyaan mein,

Ghar lo khoon se mantra, ya chhodo veerān mein."

(Neither sleep, nor fire, nor Rudra's word shall guard you. The one who protects, forgets what must be remembered. When syllables turn upon themselves, and the boat drowns in knowledge, Either inscribe the mantra in blood, or abandon it to the wasteland.)

Aadhya's breath shuddered. "The burial verse." It wasn't a spell; it was a choice - a vow between remembrance and oblivion. To speak it was to surrender memory. To sing it was to bury oneself alongside what was meant to be sealed. "She meant for us to find this," Aadhya whispered. "To decide whether we end the chant—or become it." Then came a whisper. From behind the standing stones. Figures emerged—tall, skeletal, their bodies draped in salt-stiffened cloth. Their faces were cracked with ash. Eyes hollowed to pits that glowed faintly like dying embers.

The nearest one stepped forward. "You carry the glyph." Aadhya did not flinch. "And you carry the hunger." The figure's voice was like paper tearing. "We are what remains of the verse. We sang it once—and lost our names to its ending."

"What happens if I sing it now?" she asked.

"You bury the second seal for another age," the figure rasped. "But you also bury your name—the one that calls the fire."

"Aadhrika," she whispered. The figure shook its head. "No. Your own name." Advait's voice broke the silence. "You don't have to do this." But she was already stepping forward. "I do." The red rope began to glow faintly as she climbed the platform, kneeling beside Maati-Jogin's body. The air turned feverish, trembling as though the mountain itself braced for what came next. And Aadhya began to sing. Not loudly—softly. Like a lullaby meant to calm something far older than grief. The language was alien, yet it moved through her effortlessly, spilling from her throat like smoke from a dying flame.

The walls groaned. The pillars vibrated. The whispering figures began to sway—not in menace, but mourning. The burial verse crawled through the air like a serpent of light, binding the chamber in a slow, rhythmic pulse. The fever chant—once so loud—fought to rise again, clawing from the earth. But the verse drowned it, line by line. Salt streamed down the walls like tears. The glyph on her wrist dimmed. The red rope frayed. She kept singing. Her voice broke once, then steadied again - gentle, defiant, human.

Slowly, the fever chant fell silent. Stone by stone, the chamber cooled; the humming ceased. The standing figures bowed their heads, dissolving into dust that glowed faintly as it scattered. When she opened her eyes, the cave was still. The second seal had not broken- it slept. Outside, the frozen stream cracked once—a deep, resonant sound like a long-held breath finally exhaled. The air grew clear. The fever smell faded. They emerged before dawn, pale light breaking through mist. The horizon was washed in shades of ash and rose. Aadhya's voice was raw, her throat streaked with dried blood.

"We buried it," she whispered. Advait nodded. "For now."

"But it's not over." She looked down at her wrist. Only one thread of the red rope remained. "Maati-Jogin died to delay it," she said quietly. "And someone else is still trying to awaken it." Rana ji watched the paling sky. "Then where to now?" Advait answered without hesitation. ***"Vindhya."*** Aadhya's gaze was fixed eastward. "Where the blood remembers. And the next echo waits."

The fever chant was gone. But something else - something deeper - had begun listening.

Chapter - 18
The Circuit of Fire

The mist over Barot had changed. It was no longer fog - it had texture now, a coarse, suffocating density that clung to skin like scorched breath. The sky above had shed its monsoon blue. Everything lay muted under a pewter haze, as though the sun itself had dimmed in hesitation - unwilling to bear witness to whatever had begun moving beneath the mountain's surface. Rana-ji drove without a word. He had not taken them back toward the main highway but down an older, half-forgotten trail. The road wound through skeletal pines and crumbling earth, swallowed in places by roots and slick mud. The steering wheel trembled beneath his hands. He drove as if guided - not by sight - but by something whispering directions only he could hear.

In the back seat, Aadhya sat rigid, her fingers coiled around the loop of red rope that still clung to her palm. It was only a single strand now - the last one Agnivrat had not burned. The burial verse still reverberated faintly through her chest - not as a melody but as an aftertaste, an ache that refused to fade. Advait watched the trees blur past the window. "He said the fire must be walked," he murmured. She turned slightly. "Who did?" He did not look at her. "The voice, when the fever chant ended. I heard it - it said, 'Fire cannot be buried; it must be walked in circuit.'"

Aadhya nodded slowly. "A ritual - like a yagna, an endless repetition meant to contain." From the driver's seat, Rana ji's voice broke the quiet. "There's a temple ahead," he said, his tone low and rough, as if dragged from memory. "It was not always ruins." He paused, eyes never leaving the mist. *"They call it Chakravaah Mandir - the Temple of the Circuit."* Advait leaned forward. "You've seen it?"Advait asked. Rana's jaw tensed. "Once. My father made me swear never to return. It burned three times in one night - without smoke, without fuel. But last night, I dreamed of it again: of its steps, of ash where no ash should have been."

The silence that followed was heavy, broken only by the steady growl of the jeep's engine. Aadhya's hand tightened on the rope. "Then that's where we're meant to go. The second seal isn't buried - it's watching." Rana made a trembling sign across his chest. By the time they arrived, the light had soured. Noon should have been bright and thin, but instead the sky was stained orange - the colour of a day dying too early. It was as if sunset had arrived out of order - called prematurely by something ancient and wrong.

The temple stood - or rather, sank - at the center of a hollow. Most of it had been claimed by the hill around it. The stone shikhara was cracked and half-swallowed by soil, ribs jutting upward like the bones of a colossal carcass. The air stank faintly of iron and burnt resin. Not a single bird called. Even the wind refused to enter. They climbed out of the jeep. The moment Aadhya's boots met the ground, she felt it - a vibration just below hearing. The air itself was charged, trembling faintly, as though they were standing inside a bell just after it had been struck. Her skin prickled. The hair on her arms stood upright.

Advait lifted his camera, but the lens fogged instantly, the mist blurring every outline into static. He wiped it once, then gave up. They descended a set of fractured steps, each one darker than the last. The staircase curved inward, leading into what had once been the *garbha griha* - the sanctum where a deity should have stood. But there was no idol here, no image - only a pit. It was perfectly circular, ten feet wide; the stone around it blackened as though from fire - but there was no trace of ash, no residue of smoke. Seven stone markers surrounded the pit in a ring, each equidistant from the next.

Aadhya's breath caught. The air around each marker shimmered faintly, distorting the light. Advait crouched beside one. The symbol carved into its surface was not Daitya not Sanskrit - something between the two, older than either. "These aren't names," he said. "They're actions." Aadhya moved to another. *"Circuits," she whispered. "Ritual motions. Invocation patterns - not prayers."*

"Invocation of what?" Advait asked. Before she could answer, Rana ji spoke from behind them, his voice softer, almost reverent. "Not of a god."he said. He hesitated. "Not even of a demon." They both turned. Rana's eyes were fixed beyond the clearing, toward the forest's edge. His pupils were dilated, unfocused, as though something unseen had stepped out between the trees. His face had drained of colour. "Then what?" Advait asked. Rana didn't respond. His lips moved, but no sound came. Aadhya followed his gaze. The forest was utterly still—but within that stillness was pressure, as though the trees themselves were holding their breath.

Then, without warning, a gust of hot wind surged through the clearing. It coiled into the circle like a living thing, spiralling downward into the pit. The ground shuddered once - then the pit ignited. Flames shot up. Not flames that rose toward the sky, but flames that poured downward - spiralling into the earth like molten silk. Gold and crimson intertwined, too pure to be natural. The light didn't *illuminate*; it devoured. Aadhya staggered back. The heat wasn't on her skin—it was inside her, like her blood had started to boil. Advait shielded his eyes. *"It's—burning in reverse!"* The fire licked the rims of the seven markers, each one flaring for a heartbeat before cooling again. Then one of the stones began to whisper. It wasn't sound—it was thought, pressed into their skulls. Aadhya froze. Advait stepped closer. "Did you hear that?"

"Don't," she warned sharply. But he was already kneeling, his face inches from the glowing sigil. The voice hissed—soft, metallic, unmistakably sentient. He who circles once, sees the truth. He who circles twice, forgets the lie. He who circles thrice… awakens the fire beneath. Advait rose slowly. "We're meant to walk it." Aadhya's pulse hammered. "Walk it? Why?" He turned to her, the reflection of flame dancing across his face. "To bind it—or to test it. The fever chant was a call. This… is the response." Before she could stop him, Rana stepped forward. Without a word, he crossed into the circle.

The flames didn't burn him. They bent. As if bowing in recognition. Aadhya's throat tightened. Rana walked slowly, clockwise, tracing the inner rim of the ring. The sound beneath his steps deepened—a resonance like a drum made of flesh. He completed the first circuit. The earth shivered. Then he stopped, eyes distant - looking older, skin drawn, shadowed. *"I remembered something," he said hoarsely. "Something that never happened. My mother... screaming. A mirror in my throat."*

The words sent a chill through Aadhya's spine. She stepped forward next. The rope looped around her hand pulsed faintly as she entered the ring. The flames hissed at her ankles but did not harm her. *A voice bloomed inside her - not around her, but within. You bled once in a field of salt. You knelt before the wrong name. You must not forget what the fire forgave.* Her vision blurred. Each step felt heavier, the air denser, the world trembling faintly underfoot. She reached the end of the first circle, knees trembling. In the pit's mirrored light, she saw a face - her own, but not hers: a face she recognized from a life not lived.

"Aadhrika," she whispered. The flame rippled, pulsing once in response. Advait entered last. His movements were cautious, deliberate. He made the first circle, then the second. At the third he faltered, collapsing to his knees. When he looked up, his eyes were wide, haunted. "I saw my father," he said in a choked whisper. "But he didn't know me. He was under stone. Chanting." Aadhya didn't speak. She couldn't. The wind stopped. Then all seven markers glowed at once. Their symbols aligned, burning bright. From the pit's heart, something rose—slowly, deliberately.

A blade – charred, curved, heavy as if forged from bone and smoke. It hovered above the fire for a breath, suspended in impossible balance, before sinking back into the pit with a sound like stone weeping. A voice followed. Neither male nor female—something between echo and breath. The circuit has been made. The name remembered. The flame now waits for blood. The fire collapsed. The light vanished. And silence swallowed everything. Aadhya looked down at her hand. The last thread of the red rope was gone—turned to fine ash. The glyph on her wrist had cooled to black.

The seal had not broken. But its memory had returned. And now, something beneath the earth was stirring again, not chanting, not calling, simply deciding whether to wake. The silence that followed was not peace; it was residue - ash without flame, smoke without scent. Every sound seemed to fold into itself, trapped in the air like something sacred and smothered. Even their breathing felt intrusive. The temple of the Circuit no longer looked ruined; it looked emptied.

Aadhya stood on the outer rim of the circle, her fingers grazing the place where the red rope had seared her palm. The skin there had not healed. It was darker now—marked like a faint scar shaped into the loop of an extinguished fire. The glyph beneath her wrist was no longer bright; it had cooled into a dull black spiral, as though even the symbol had grown weary. Advait remained kneeling at the pit's edge, his reflection faintly visible in the sheen of cooled stone. His face was ghost-pale, his lips colourless. "We didn't stop it," he said softly.

"No," Aadhya replied. "We reminded it we are here." Rana ji hadn't moved since the flames died. He stood with his hands limp at his sides, eyes clouded in a trance-like haze. For a long moment, he didn't even blink. Then—suddenly—he gasped, as if surfacing from deep water. "I heard her again," he whispered. Aadhya turned. "Who?"

"My mother,"he whispered, voice trembling. "But she wasn't as I remember her. She was screaming in a language I didn't know; yet I could feel the meaning. She was trying to hold something in - not from escaping the world, but from escaping me." Advait frowned. "In you?" Rana shook his head, lost. "No. In someone else. A room of salt. No windows. Just walls sweating white." The word salt sent a small shiver through all of them.

It had followed them everywhere. *The salt in the Fever Chant*. The salt in the buried flames of *Agnivrat*. Even now, the scent clung faintly to the wind. Preservation. Memory. Sacrifice. Whatever they were dealing with, salt was both its boundary and its blood. Rana's voice broke the quiet again. "Then I saw a tree - no leaves, only ropes tied to its branches. From every rope, hung a tooth: hundreds of them, swinging in wind that did not exist." He fell silent. Advait exhaled slowly. *"A tree of vows,"* he murmured. Aadhya looked toward the pit, expression unreadable. "Or of punishments."

She stepped closer, peering into the black circle. The stone within was not smooth anymore. Something beneath had shifted, pushing faint cracks through the surface like veins under flesh. "This temple," she said slowly, "was not built to worship anything; it was built to contain. Every circuit walked here was a message - a reminder. It's less a shrine than a lock." Advait nodded grimly. "Then the question is—what was so dangerous it had to be sealed inside a flame?" Before anyone could answer, the ground sighed. It wasn't an earthquake. It wasn't even a vibration. It was a pulse—steady, rhythmic, deliberate.

They froze.

Aadhya felt it through the soles of her boots first. A steady beat, almost like a slow drum – no, like a heartbeat, but older. Not the rhythm of blood. The rhythm of something buried alive. Rana's whisper trembled in the air. "The earth's breathing." Aadhya's voice lowered. "No. It's remembering." A hiss of steam burst through a fissure near the pit's rim, curling upward in thin tendrils. The smell hit them first—sharp, metallic, almost sweet. The scent of boiled iron. Advait covered his mouth. "That's not smoke."

"No," she said. "It's exhalation." Another fissure opened. This one bled a black fluid that shimmered unnaturally, as though infused with shifting light. It slid across the ground toward the center of the pit, moving with the intent of a living thing. Advait reached for his bag. "We should record this, take a—"

"Don't," Aadhya cut in sharply. "It's not material." Rana blinked. "Then what is it?"

"Memory," she said. "This is how Daitya seals work—they remember. Every oath, every death, every betrayal leaves a residue. It's what binds them. The moment we touched the circuit, it began to recall."

"Recall what?" Advait asked. Aadhya looked down. "Us." The black fluid pooled in the center of the pit, swirling as though stirred by an invisible hand. Then - suddenly - it stopped. The air changed. Every sound receded until only one remained—a slow, arrhythmic thump rising from beneath the earth. It wasn't loud, but it was absolute, as though everything else existed only to echo it. Rana took a cautious step backward. "That's not a heart." Advait's gaze was locked on the pit. "Then what is it?" Aadhya's eyes flickered with realization. *"A chant without words. A song remembered by the bones of the world."*

The seven stone markers began to hum. The distortion around them thickened - the air folding, bending, warping. Each stone seemed to shift shape, not in form but in perception, as though what they saw was struggling to remain consistent. Then, with a sharp crack, one of the markers split clean down the center. From within the break a second stream of that black, glimmering liquid oozed forth. It moved slowly but deliberately, slithering toward the pit like blood returning to a heart.

Rana's voice was thin. "We should leave." But the path behind them was no longer visible. The mist had folded inward, closing like a fist. Aadhya's hand found Advait's wrist. "Don't move. Don't run - it reacts to motion." He swallowed. "What does?" Her gaze was fixed on the pit. "Whatever we woke." A new light rose from beneath the fissures—not red this time, but gold. Liquid, radiant, ancient. For an instant, it painted the pit like molten glass, revealing what lay beneath.

A shape - curled. Bound: a figure, half-buried in darkness, its limbs wrapped in something that looked like muscle but glistened like rope. Its hair spilled across its face in matted black streaks. Then its eyes opened. They were not eyes but voids - two wells of perfect obsidian that reflected nothing. Aadhya's breath caught in her throat. Rana staggered backward, muttering prayers under his breath, the words fractured and desperate. Advait's voice broke the silence. "Was that—?" Aadhya shook her head. "Don't say it."

But she knew. Deep inside her, beneath the ache of her wrist and the echo of the burial verse, she knew that face. Not as a stranger's. As something older. Something once sworn to her. The air trembled. The figure vanished. Then the pit exhaled -a blast of heat that threw them back. The seven markers exploded, shattering into fine black dust that lifted and spun, forming a spiral of ash around them. The forest roared to life. The wind screamed, carrying with it hundreds of overlapping voices. Mantras. Prayers. Curses. They collided into a cacophony that no human ear could decipher. The sky above them darkened to slate. Clouds spiralled into a vortex.

"Back to the car!" Rana shouted. But when they turned, the road was gone. The way they had come had been replaced by twisted trees, their trunks gnarled into impossible shapes—like ribs growing from the soil. The forest had changed as if reacting to the awakening. Aadhya's eyes burned. *"We have to complete it," she said suddenly - "The circuit. We have to walk it again."* Advait stared at her. *"It's suicide."* She shook her head. "No. It's a seal. It needs closure. If we stop now, it'll rise fully."

Rana's voice trembled. "You mean to finish what it started?" Aadhya's expression was grim. "No. To confuse it. We give it something it can't remember. A paradox." Advait understood instantly. "A contradiction in its own memory. The only thing that can put a curse back to sleep." They stepped into the circle once more - what was left of it. The stones were gone; only the ash ring remained, faint and crumbling, but still warm.

“Together,” Aadhya said. And they walked. Not clockwise, not in unison, but against each other - paths crossing, steps colliding, patterns breaking. The pit shuddered. The air convulsed. Then came the sound—a scream not from lungs, but from the mountain itself. The flames erupted again, only to be torn apart by their movement.

The world bent inward, and then - stillness. The smoke froze. The roar died. The circuit sealed itself with a soft, audible click, like a door latching from the inside. Above them, the swirling clouds began to uncoil. Light seeped through again—weak, pale, trembling.

The forest stood silent. Whatever had stirred beneath the temple… had blinked. And gone back to sleep. For now. The Circuit of Fire. The wind fell still.

Even the torches that had survived the temple’s breath seemed uncertain, their flames quivering mid-sway as if the air itself had forgotten how to move. Aadhya stepped forward, her footsteps echoing longer than they should, fading and returning like ripples in a frozen pond. The ground beneath her boots was no longer stone - it sounded hollow, as though she were walking across the skin of something that was merely pretending to sleep. Advait followed, his face pale in the dim red light that bled from the cracks in the sanctum walls. Together they moved toward the center, toward the circular plinth that dominated the chamber. The copper ring embedded into the stone looked newly scorched, though no fire had touched it. Burn marks spread outward in jagged spokes-five of them - branching from a central depression like veins cut open.

"The circuit," Aadhya whispered. Advait nodded, his voice low. "It's a ritual circle. Maybe even a gate." The carvings surrounding them had shifted again. They were no longer Daitya glyphs. The language had melted into pure geometry: spirals within spirals, eyes blooming from flame, chains unravelling into vines. The air hummed faintly, a sound between a sigh and a heartbeat. At the exact center of the copper ring lay what remained of Agnivrat's rope.

Or rather, its shadow: the crimson thread had blackened completely, transformed into a single brittle strand of ash. Yet even in death, it pulsed faintly, as though remembering what it had once been bound to. Aadhya crouched beside it, her wrist throbbing. The glyph beneath her skin glowed faintly, as if the rope's memory and her own shared a pulse.

And then—the rope began to hum – a sound was not audible in air but internal, resonating through bone, vibrating the spaces between thought and heartbeat.

It wasn't just alive; it was listening. Aadhya withdrew the mirror shard from her satchel. The same one that had survived every ruin, every fever, every chant. The moment she lifted it above the copper circle, its surface misted - fog swirling within like trapped breath.

"Do it," she said quietly. Advait took the bronze medallion and stepped to the edge of the circuit. His movements were careful, reverent. Kneeling, he dipped the pendant into the center of the copper ring. For a heartbeat, nothing happened. Then—the floor shuddered. A faint light, deep and red, pulsed beneath the copper veins. The spokes glowed one after another - south, east, west, north - and finally the hidden fifth direction beneath their feet. Aadhya's breath hitched. The mountain groaned. The rope fragment disintegrated into dust, its last breath curling into smoke that sank rather than rose.

Then came the sound—a low, guttural rumble that was not thunder, not wind, not even the earth itself. It was older than any of them could imagine. The mountain was exhaling. The torches flickered once and died. Only the under light from the circuit remained, casting their faces in crimson shadow.

"Aadhya," Advait said softly, "your arm." She looked down. The glyph had changed again. What had once been three interlocked loops was now a complete sigil—crossed by a spear and encircled by five inward flames. The pattern was whole. ***The second seal had not broken. But it had cracked.*** And through that crack, something ancient had begun to whisper. It wasn't language. It was pattern. Images rose behind her eyes—memories that weren't hers.

A child's hand dipping into a bowl of ash.

A woman kneeling before a mirror that did not reflect.

A mantra spoken backward, each syllable unravelling light.

A rope igniting around a figure who refused to scream.

Then—a name. A name that lived on her tongue before she could think it. The earth screamed. The sanctum doors slammed shut, dust raining from the cracked ceiling. Aadhya and Advait stumbled as the circuit flared to blinding red. When the light dimmed, a mark had appeared where the ash rope had lain. A handprint where the long-fingered, skeletal, fused with fire. It glowed for a moment white-hot, then cooled to black. Advait stared at it. "That wasn't here before."

"No," Aadhya said softly. "It's a warning." He looked up. "From what?" She turned her gaze toward the dark corners of the sanctum, where faint, rhythmic breathing had begun again—distant, like wind moving through a hollow chest. "Not from the seal," she said. "From whatever guards it." Then came the whistle. A piercing, metallic shriek—not from an instrument, but from air compressed into violence. It echoed through the stone, ricocheting off the walls like something ancient being summoned.

All six torches reignited simultaneously, their flames unnaturally high and steady, painting the walls with dancing shadows. Black smoke coiled upward, merging into a thin column that twisted toward the ceiling. In the rising smoke, for the briefest moment, an image took shape—an eye. Lidless. Enormous. Watching.

Aadhya froze. It blinked—and vanished. She turned to Advait. Her voice was barely a whisper. "We're not alone anymore." He nodded, eyes wide. "The seal was never unguarded. It was waiting. And now—it's aware."

The heat in the sanctum intensified, pressing down on them like a physical weight. The air felt alive, thick with static and memory. Even the shadows seemed to breathe. Before leaving, Aadhya reached out and brushed her fingertips over the handprint in the copper ring. It burned her skin instantly—but she didn't pull back.

The pain felt familiar. Recognized. Like an old vow calling her by name. They turned toward the exit. The tunnel they had entered through had narrowed again, its walls now trembling faintly, the stone sweating moisture that smelled faintly of sulphur and salt. When they emerged outside, dawn had begun to stain the horizon. The forest was silver with mist, but unnaturally still.

Not even the wind stirred. Rana ji was waiting near the jeep, his face drawn and pale, wiping sweat from his forehead though the morning air was cold. "You're lucky," he said quietly. "The ground shook half the night. My compass stopped working. The birds flew in circles until they fell from the trees. Even the river near the village turned red for two hours—and then clear again." Neither Aadhya nor Advait replied. Rana looked between them, eyes hollow. “You went into the bones, didn’t you?”

Aadhya nodded. “And something looked back.” He didn’t ask what. He just stared at the trees and murmured, “Some doors stay closed for good reason.” As they climbed into the jeep, Advait turned once more toward the hill. The forest behind them was already changing—branches curling over the path they’d taken, sealing it off like scar tissue closing a wound. It was as if the land itself had chosen to forget them. But the air had not. A voice rode the wind—soft, cold, and unmistakable.

Just one word. Not spoken aloud. Whispered into the back of Aadhya’s mind. Aadhrika. She froze. The name.

The same name Maati-Jogin had spoken.

The same name Agnivrat had died holding in his mouth.

The name that now bloomed like fire behind her eyes.

Not yet remembered. But no longer unknown. She raised her wrist. The glyph pulsed once more—not with pain, but with recognition. The second seal had not broken, but it had heard her - and it would remember.

Chapter - 19

The Second Seal Cracks

The second seal remained unbroken, but the world around it had tilted.

Since the sanctum, something had shifted - not with a cataclysmic sound, but like a floorboard coming loose under a careful foot. A patient, inexorable loosening. Even the sunlight felt altered - thinner, as if someone had pared back its edges. Aadhya stood at the ridge's lip where the pines bled into shale. Below, *Barot* looked like watercolour left out in rain - roofs half-hidden in mist, rivers dulled to pewter. The stream they had crossed two nights before had changed colour, as though some dark thing had leeched into it from the deep.

Advait came up behind her with the slow caution of someone who expects danger in the ordinary. He did not speak at first. He simply fell into place beside her, hands buried in his jacket, eyes fixed on the switchback road. "We're not done," Aadhya said. "No," he answered. "The seal's whole, but it's been stirred." She nodded. The glyph on her wrist had settled into a different temperature - not flame, but metal left in snow, implacably cold and watchful. The pattern no longer beat. It listened.

"Maati-Jogin's death wasn't the curtain," Aadhya said. "It was a bell." Advait's jaw tightened. "We heard the chant, and something answered." She drew the small, half-black mirror shard from her pocket. Its surface had a new reluctance - reflections slid as if reluctant to cooperate. For a moment she thought her own eyes blinked in the glass - but she had not moved. The shard's image lagged by a breath. Rana-ji was loading the jeep - fuel cans, wool blankets, and a small bundle of preserved food.

The dashboard radio coughed and spat with interference, then fell into a ragged, constant static. Through that crackle a voice emerged - low, female, ancient. A cadence Aadhya and Advait both understood the tongue: old Daitya, remade into a blood-rhythm.

Her wrist flinched. The glyph throbbed once, then stilled. "It's time," Aadhya said. "For where?" Advait asked. "For where the stone remembers," she answered.

"The Confused Stepwell. Vibhraant Kund."

He gave a small, humourless sound. "Maati-Jogin did not say go there to be clever." "No," Aadhya said. "She encoded it in the dying words. The chant pointed us there. That's where the second seal was laid - not sealed, not broken, but laid, like a scar across the earth."

Rana-ji refused to follow beyond the tree-line. "The animals avoid it," he told them. "Even the wind skirts that path." He handed them a charcoal map drawn by a hill monk, the ink smeared with rain. There: a black dot and a name: Vibhraant Kund—no one's place. By noon they were at the first circle - a ring of white ash laid perfectly around a black stone dais. The air itself felt denser, as if someone had put a lid over reality. Insects had stopped making sound; even the trees seemed to hold their breath.

Aadhya stepped to the platform's center and set the mirror shard upon the stone. It vibrated as though in sympathy. "Back," she said to Advait. He stepped away. She knelt, sliced her palm along the shard's edge, and let three drops of blood fall in a small, deliberate arc onto the stone. The glyph on her wrist flared hot, and the platform answered - not with a collapse but with remembering. The surface opened inward like an eye that had been plucked gently and restored.

A square aperture yawned. Narrow stairs spiralled down into velvet dark. From below rose the smell of wet moss and smouldering rope - old incense burned and never finished. Aadhya led the descent. Each step seemed to pull them a century backward. No sound came up from below; only an absence, the hush of memory. At the fifth tread she stopped. The fifth stair - every prohibition had clustered around that step. On the wall, scratched in reverse so it would reveal itself only in reflection, was a sigil - five loops forming a spiral knot, tongues of flame curling inside each loop. She held the shard up; the glyph resolved into something like a lock.

"The second seal," Aadhya breathed. "Still closed, still resisting."

"And below?" Advait's whisper came close behind. They had not reached the water - the echoing had already begun: footsteps behind them. Deliberate, one pace behind each step they took. When they turned, there was nothing. A voice floated from somewhere above - her voice, or the memory of it - saying in a loop: "Aadhrika. Aadhrika. Aadhrika."

The shard cracked. A vein of red light ran up the stone. The seal had begun to fissure. They descended into a chamber that was not a well's bottom so much as its inversion - tiers rose around an open heart, the architecture spiralling upward into darkness, as though the well had been a mouth turned inside out. At its center sat a copper urn crusted with black salt, bound by three coils of rope.

The ropes were not merely twine; they were braided from vine and hair and they had been burned tight into place. The top coil was frayed, the second twitching as if something inside drew breath. At Aadhya's first step into the chamber, the floor thrummed—not a seismic fury but the cadence of a sleeping thing. She knelt. The urn's ropes were warm to the touch in a way that belonged to living muscle. Around the pedestal were fresher markings—new hands had carved protection after the Daityas themselves were gone. Someone had tried to hold the thing in place and had failed to shred the memory entirely.

"This is not a seal," Aadhya said, voice low. "It's a prison." From the ceiling a face outlined in absence unfolded - hair like ash, lips sewn. It was not a surface marking; it was the memory of a woman fixed into the vault like a palimpsest. The face belonged to the thing the seal had been meant to hold - *Aadhrika.*

Memory flooded Aadhya - visions not her own: a younger woman handing the urn into a circle of Daityas, whispering the words that braided the ropes, dyeing them with her own blood. The younger woman looked up. She saw Aadhya—or what Aadhya would become—and mouthed, without sound, "You will break it, not now, not yet. You must carry it." The room bucked. Dust fell in curtains. Somewhere in the spiral, fissures opened and shut like the blinking of a too-large animal. A sliver of red mist escaped the urn, wandering like a tiny creature hungering for the edges of the chamber. It wore many eyes and fixed them on Aadhya.

"They know now," she whispered. "The awakeners," Advait breathed. "Those who set the seal to sleep may be rising." From overhead came a third sound: rope tearing, and somewhere distant, a cry that was less a voice than the suggestion of one. The second coil split very slightly, hairline at first; a ribbon of red mist uncoiled and slithered upward, saturating the air with a metallic sweetness. They climbed in silence, each step a small prayer. The stairwell lashed with whispers and then reformed behind them, stone swallowing its own tracks as if the stair itself wished to forget who had walked it.

Outside, the ash circle had been smeared as if by the passage of many feet. The jeep waited, keys where they ought to be, but Rana-ji was gone. In the peat-smell of the roadside lay a single black feather, glowing faintly from within like an ember.

Advait stooped to pick it up, but Aadhya stopped him. “Don’t,” she said. *“It’s a marker -left by something to say, ‘I was here.’”* She felt the air tilt toward the trees. The clouds turned in a slow spiral - not a storm but a signal. From the mouth of the well a column of flame rose - insubstantial, patterned with glyphs - and in its center a figure hovered, absorbing the light like sponge: Kalkini, like a conductor waiting at the center of an orchestra.

At the base of the column the urn cracked and a scream - not a sound but a presence - spilled out, a synesthetic ruin of Daitya voices pressing at the world.

They left as the fire died into silence, the land cooling around them as if it had merely exhaled after remembering how to cough. Barot lay behind them, thick with soot and silence. The second seal had not shattered—yet it had taken a breath. And, somewhere, Rana-ji had been unstitched from the world. Advait’s voice came quiet as a match struck. “Nothing makes sense.” She didn’t answer. She held the last thread of rope the way a mourner holds a token. It blackened in her palm and turned to ash.

In the hills beyond, a prison stirred. Agnivrat inhaled.

They left the stepwell with an urgency that had nothing to do with weather. The sky above *Barot* rolled slow and sullen, clouds arranging themselves into a cresting wheel. The air tasted of salt and soot - an impossible pairing in a mountain valley - and every breath felt like pulling at a thread in cloth that wanted to fray. By twilight the world's edges were thinner. The forest accepted them as if it had been expecting to be walked again. But for all its hospitality, small wrongness's thrummed: bark that never grew rings, roots arranged like knotted fingers, birds that circled once, twice, and then dropped beneath the canopy and vanished.

They drove without music. Advait watched the feather in the dirt as if it might bloom. Aadhya kept one hand on the wheel and one on her wrist, feeling the glyph's slow, cold pulse. The last thread of the rope was gone. *Agnivrat's* tether - shredded, but not absent - had been swallowed into the sanctum's memory, where something listened and timed its breath. "How do we find whoever is unbinding it?" Advait asked at last. His voice was flat, the way people speak when they name something irretrievable.

"We don't find them," she said. "They find us. Or the place does. The seal remembers shapes; it calls to their shape." They stopped near the village's edge. The lane to the jeep's left was worn into grooves deeper than a season should make, as if heavy feet had trod it countless times. The villagers they passed eyed them the way small creatures study a burst of light: cautious, superstitious, alert. No one asked questions. In regions where memory holds a physical weight, questions are prayers and prayers are dangerous. They found a shelter by the ford and slept in segments: one hour on, two hours off, windows bricked against too much sound. When Aadhya slept, the world unstitched.

She dreamed of rope - thick, wet, braided with hair and ash - and a man who tied it around himself like a vow. The dream burned like a physical thing and left her palm smelling of smoke. At noon a woman came to the threshold. She called herself Kanta - grey hair bound in a plait, an apron stained with tea and salt. Her son had been taken two years earlier, she said simply, words falling into the air like coins into a well. He'd walked the kund at dawn and never returned. She had seen strange lights in the valley since.

"People forget in this place," she told them, eyes blank. "They go in and leave something of themselves. Return empty. Or worse - they come back with other names in their mouths."

Advait took out his notebook and sketched the sigil on Aadhya's wrist. Kanta watched, then smiled without humour.

"The marking remembers what you refuse to say," she said. "It will not leave you alone."

At dusk they followed the river to a low dam where Joginder - exiled shaman and custodian of ash-lore - was said to wait. His hut was an earthen mound with strings of bone hung like wind chimes. He smelled of herbs and old paper. His eyes were painted white and the spiral glyph on his forehead was inverted.

"You disturbed the sanctum," he said without greeting. "So the valley turned its face."

Aadhya offered him the mirror shard. He took it, turned it slowly, and the surface shuddered, showing joggers of memory: a crown of rope, the flaring of a fire, a woman who did not know whether she had burned others to save or saved others to burn. He let the shard go and hummed. "We have hours," he said. "The coil splits and the chamber breathes. Whoever opens the urn will not find what they expect. They will find that the seal remembers a name - and that name will ask to be answered."

"Who will answer?" Advait asked. "You will not choose who answers," Joginder said, "the land will. People who carry old shapes awaken. The chant has been reversed. It is feeding names back into the world, like throwing bread into a hungry river. And who comes to take it—those who remember better than we do." That night the fever chant rose along the stream—soft at first, as if someone were unthreading a garment, then surging into a chorus that set teeth on edge. Aadhya dreamt of the urn below. She saw the second coil begin to part like a jaw.

They left before dawn. The road to the next ridge curved like an arthritic finger, and the valley below shuddered as the sun bled through cloud. On the jeep's dash, the radio played nothing but a long low tone that felt like a struck bell. They reached a ruined farmhouse at the foot of an old pilgrimage path. The farmer had seen a black-feathered figure pass the well the night before and had woken with the scent of ash in his mouth. He gave them boiled barley and watched them with the slow suspicion of a man who has learned to believe less than he sees.

They made a plan: divide places to look. The map *Joginder* gave them was a scatter of old sigils: the petrified orchard, the ruined dam, the ash-marked pathway where the villagers said shadows walked even in midday. Each place carried its own echo of the second seal. They parted at the fork in the trail: Advait to the orchard, Aadhya to the dam. Rana-ji had not returned. A silence for his absence existed in the jeep's seats like another passenger.

At the orchard the trees were blackened to the sky. Fruit had petrified in mid-bloom, as if the world had been paused and not resumed. Advait walked the alleys until he found burned rope tied to a trunk—charred threads that smelled of iron and hair. Beneath it, a footprint that was not quite a human - toes splayed like a hand. He took a sample, wrapped it in cloth, and paused. All the trees seemed to be listening. A choir of small noises collected behind him: the faint, dry rattling of something inside bark.

Back at the dam, Aadhya crouched beside the frozen sluice and found a child's boot half-buried in the silt, leather cracked but warm. A single feather lay near it, black and warm as coals. She did not touch it. She understood, suddenly, that the feather marked not just a place but a path someone had chosen - a marker to say, follow me into remembering. At twilight the valley's heat changed. Birds stopped. Even the river's voice quieted to a careful, small sound. And the sky… the sky held a ring of ash like a lid.

Aadhya felt the sigil on her arm burning now not with pain but with pressure, an insistence that something had found the edge of its binding and had begun to test how far it could stretch. The broken rope thread in her pocket pulsed like a small, dead heart. She sat on the dam wall and watched the water move through the sluice. Underneath the surface, shapes drifted—one here, one there—like the underside of a map. Each moved with intent. Each was listening. A whip of wind brushed her neck, and for a single, terrible second, she heard a chorus of voices singing the same name—not from the well, not from the stone, but from the world itself: "Aadhrika… Aadhrika…"

She did not shout. She did not move. Her mind stepped outside itself and watched, in a calm removed from fear, as the valley answered back. The second seal - that cruel, patient thing of rope and urn and memory - had begun to crack. Night settled fast, like a lid. The valley's edges tightened and the trees bent inward as if to listen. The air felt suspended: small things stopped their tiny motions and waited. Aadhya and Advait reunited at the ford, their faces lit by each other's exhaustion. They found two fresh boot prints leading away from the well and into the scrub. *Rana-ji's keys lay on the jeep seat; he had left them there as if to say, I will return. He had not.*

"Everything that was anchored is loosening," Advait said. *"The watchers are stirring."* Aadhya touched the glyph on her wrist. It had rearranged itself again—the emblem of three loops now crossing with a spear and laced with five inward flames. She could feel the room outside her ribs where the seal's memory nested: a hollow, humming with expectation. The first sign came as taste. A metallic tang that made their tongues feel like pages. The second as sound—soft and popping—like old film being rewound. Then came the smell: rope burning slow, not with hungry flame but with a slow, ceremonial cauterizing.

From the pines a song rose: not human, yet something had learned to stitch vowels between branches. The melody folded in upon itself and carried names. They walked toward it. The road narrowed to a goat-path and then ceased. The trees had rearranged in the dark, making the path into a corridor of trunks. A figure glided ahead—not walking, more drifting—her robes torn into strips of ash and red. Ropes looped her wrists like bracelets; their ends smouldered and hissed on the earth.

She moved backward, as if pulling the world with her. Her veil opened a fraction. Eyes—dozens of them—clustered across her face like peppercorns. Each reflected Aadhya in some variant: as woman, as warrior, as burning priestess, as child. Every eye blinked out of time. Advait lurched. He began to say names—names in languages he had never learned. Aadhya clapped her hand over his mouth.

"Don't answer," she hissed. But the woman of ash—Kalkini's herald, or Kalkini herself—had done more than sing. She was returning names to the air as if feeding the valley. One of the eyes blinked and Aadhya's name pulsed a painful light in the space between her ribs. The woman opened her mouth and the voice that issued was Aadhya's own, speaking languages she did not yet know.

Aadhya felt the rope's last thread in her bag like a lived thing. Without thinking, she drew it out and held it up. She said a word that belonged to no tongue she had spoken: ***"Ālavaṇṭaḥ!"*** and hurled it like a command. The ash-woman convulsed inwards and collapsed into salt that hissed on the ground. For an instant the chant broke. Silence rushed back in like an ocean hitting shore. Advait collapsed to his knees, hands pressed to his temple. Blood trailed from his nose—he had swallowed some of the valley's names. *"She's feeding it," he rasped. "Kalkini's feeding the split."*

Aadhya tasted something metallic and dark on the air and then slid backward into a vision. She was at the Vibhraant Kund again, but not as she had known it. The well had become a wound, its mouth flayed, the urn cracked open and spilling threads. The seal no longer appeared as rope so much as a living pattern—spirals, loops, shapes that bit into each other like teeth. From its fissures memory flame spilled, licking through the tiers, burning with colours that weren't meant to exist: bone-white, ash-blue, blood-crimson.

Kalkini floated above the urn, not chanting but receiving. Her arms were wide, her eyes lit. Around the rim shapes recoiled and sighed. The seal had cracked down its center and something peered out: not a daemon nor a god, but the impression of a being that had once been named in a world before words. Aadhya woke with a single, piercing scream. The sound echoed in the trees for a long time after her lungs had gone quiet. Advait turned, eyes wet, hair crisp with pine soot.

"The seal opened," she said. "Not fully—but enough. Kalkini has found the fissure and is reaching her hand through."

Far beneath the vaults of a ruined shrine, ropes that had held a sleeping man began to unwind. Agnivrat's chest, carved in frost and salt and ancient iron, shuddered. The glyph on his breast flared—red to black to something that could not be named. Muscles once resigned to immobility twitched. He inhaled. Ropes loosened a fraction. Back at the ford, the feather glowed. Birds fled the orchard in a disorderly scatter. People's doors in the village creaked like mouths opening. The well's column of flame, high and patterned, had shrunk but left a residue: a fjord of ash and a smell of copper that sat on the air.

They drove out of Barot under a sky that had not yet forgiven them. As the jeep found the main track, Aadhya saw—just once—the pillar of fire at Vibhraant Kund, reduced to a sputtering column, and within it the figure of Kalkini like a conductor listening to a chorus only she could hear. The urn there had been smashed, its ropes fallen away in a cluster of black threads; out of the fissure the Daitya voices had poured—not liberated, not yet—but awake and hungry. They put distance between themselves and the well as the ember-fall lightened the road behind them. Farther on, the sudden blank absence of Rana-ji throbbed in the jeep like a wound. No signs, no tracks. The keys left on the seat suggested he had trusted the world to hold him for a moment and it had not.

Hours later, they stopped on a ridge not to rest but to listen. The glyph on Aadhya's wrist had redrawn itself, the spear intersecting three loops now surrounded by a ring of smaller flames, as if the pattern were adding teeth. The second seal had not shattered into chaos, but it had taken a breath—an intake that felt like a promise.

"Now the others will come," she said finally. "What others?" Advait asked, but he already knew: not the Daityas themselves but their echoes—descendants and vessels, people whose bones carried the shape of old rites. Kalkini would call them, and some would come willingly, others by compulsion. Names would be remembered and people would answer. Villages would wake in the night with foreign tongues on their lips. The world would tilt a degree more.

Aadhya tightened her hand over the last thread of red ash. The rope dissolved between her fingers, a little puff of grey like smoke leaving a candle. Somewhere, far below frozen vaults, Agnivrat moved and remembered his name. They set the jeep to the road again. Bonfires burned in distant hollows. The map *Joginder* gave them was already fat with new notches. "Next?" Advait asked. "Vindhya," she said, feeling the word like an orbit. "Where the blood remembers. Where the next echo waits." He nodded. "Then we go. The war didn't end—it only misplaced itself."

They drove, and as the valley fell behind their taillights, the sky re-knotted into a circle of ash. In a place that had slept beneath ice and rope, a man who had bound himself to silence took a breath - and began to remember how to stand.

Agnivrat inhaled again.

The breath he drew did not end. It threaded through rock and root, through bone and water, a vibration that slipped into places where sound should never live.

In the Vindhya hills a salt wind woke and began to move against itself, carrying with it the smell of rusted blood. A drumbeat answered from the east—slow, deliberate—each strike hollowing the silence a little more.

In far Sikkim, a monastery bell rang once though no hand touched it. The echo returned with another voice inside it: laughter—small, breathless, child-thin.

The earth quivered as if it recognized the sound. Beneath the forests, beneath the salt, beneath the snow, veins of red light stitched themselves into a single, crawling pattern. The mountain exhaled. The light sank back into the soil.

And somewhere between those two breaths—a place the world no longer remembered—

something smiled and whispered a name that none of them had spoken yet.

The wind carried it east.

It would reach them soon.

Epilogue

The Quiet Between Heartbeats

Fire is supposed to consume and be done with it. But some flames learn to remember. They remember the skull that would not burn, the mirror of heat that showed another face, the rope that beat like a vein, the chant that ended with silence instead of salvation. They remember the mountain that bled through its ice; the woman who bore its mark; and the man who followed her into absence.

When the last fever-song broke and the air fell still, the world should have cooled. It did not. It only held its breath - that was how it ended, and how it began again.

What came after that silence would not belong to this story- its echoes would wait in the blood, and in the next telling.

They walked east, where maps forget their edges. The ground there trembled faintly - a slow percussion that was not wind or water. Each step pressed warmth from the soil, as though the land itself were alive and listening. The horizon offered no shape - only a colour between red and black, the hue of sleep denied too long. Behind them, the ashes of old fire drifted upward and froze mid-air - a constellation of dust that refused to fall.

Aadhya felt it first - the faint resistance beneath her skin, the pulse that did not belong to her. The scar on her wrist glimmered once - a pale echo under flesh - and quieted. Her body carried two rhythms now - one human, one remembering. *Advait* walked in silence behind her; his shadow stretched before him instead of after. When he breathed, its vapour lingered too long, curling back toward his face as if unwilling to depart.

The forest rose without warning. Trunks stood bone-white, slick with dew that smelled faintly of metal. Roots crossed the path like interlocked fingers, and between them the soil sighed. Every leaf carried a droplet that did not fall; each droplet caught a faint red shimmer from nowhere. The wind that moved through the branches made no sound - it moved like thought.

They passed a pool of water so clear it seemed absent. Beneath it, shapes stirred - too slow for fish, too defined for reflection. Aadhya knelt; the surface quivered once and steadied. Her face looked back at her, then shifted - a second visage superimposed, ancient, patient, aware. Its eyes held the dull gleam of cooling embers. When she blinked, the image blinked half a heartbeat later. She stood quickly, the pool closed over itself as if ashamed.

The air thickened. Mist gathered in long filaments, weaving from tree to tree until the forest wore a veil. Salt crusted the edges of her boots; when she brushed it away, it re-formed. The scent of iron deepened. Somewhere far below, the ground murmured. It was not speech, but cadence - syllables stretched beyond hearing, the language of stone remembering its first fracture.

Advait whispered, "It's breathing." The words fell heavy, and the mist absorbed them whole. For a moment she thought the silence would shatter under their weight.

Instead it expanded, as if making room for what had been named.

They reached a clearing where light existed without source. It hovered in the air like a held breath - neither bright nor dim, simply certain. Beneath it, the soil was patterned in circles of pale dust - rings within rings, intricate as fingerprints. At their centre, the ground pulsed faintly.

Aadhya crouched and touched one circle.The dust moved beneath her fingers, alive - arranging itself into a spiral identical to the mark on her wrist. Heat climbed her arm - deliberate and slow. She did not pull away. The rhythm beneath the earth matched the rhythm in her veins: two pulses aligned, then merged. When she looked up, the trees were bowing.

A sound followed - low, continuous, too deep for thunder. The air trembled; the mist reddened; the rings in the dust began to revolve. *Advait* took a step forward, his outline flickering against the strange light. The world seemed to hesitate, caught between exhale and return.

Then everything stopped.

Stillness - not peace but anticipation. The light dimmed to a heartbeat's glow; the ground cooled. Somewhere, a drop of clear liquid surfaced through a crack in the soil.

It shimmered, then darkened to crimson. Steam rose - soft and fragrant, the scent of rain meeting blood. *Aadhya's* scar burned once, brilliant as dawn, and went dark again. From the hollow beneath the world came a whisper - too quiet to be heard by ear, too exact to be imagined. It slid through her chest and left meaning without words.

"When the fire sleeps, the blood shall speak."

The forest responded with a single motion - every leaf turned upward, trembling. A wind rose from nowhere, tasting of salt and old prayer. The mist collapsed, folding inward, leaving only the faint shimmer of heat above the soil. In its wake, the air smelled of endings.

They stood very still; even their shadows had forgotten which way to lean. The horizon ahead was neither dark nor light - it pulsed softly, colour of diluted flame. They began to walk again, drawn not by sight but by recognition. Behind them the circles of dust smoothed themselves flat, erasing every trace of the pattern. Night did not end. It simply turned its face - and in that turning, something beneath the earth remembered her name.

Blood remembers what fire forgets.

End of Book 1 – Daityagarh: Awakenings

To be continued in Book 1.5 – Daityagarh: Blood Echoes

The night did not end.

It only turned its face.

And in that turning,

something beneath the earth remembered her name.

Author's Note

Some stories arrive quietly.

Daityagarh didn't.

It came like a voice I couldn't ignore - in dreams, in silences, in the moments when the world around me slept. A city built on ash. A woman who could remember lives she never lived. A mountain that refused to forget.

For months, I didn't even know what it was trying to become - a myth, a warning, or just an echo of something I had carried for years without realising it. I kept rewriting, reshaping, researching, until the story began to breathe on its own. It didn't belong to me anymore; it was writing through me.

Daityagarh took nearly a year—but it also took a piece of me. I spent long nights building it line by line, chasing the right words until they finally stood still. There were times I wanted to stop, to silence it - but it wouldn't let me. Some stories aren't written - they demand to exist. This was one of them.

This book became a mirror of everything I've ever questioned - faith, memory, identity, and the strange spaces between life and myth. Through Aadhya's eyes, I explored what it means to inherit something ancient and unfinished - what it means to be haunted not by ghosts, but by destiny itself.

Every place in this book—the ghats, deserts, forests, glaciers - came from real soil, real history. I walked through many of them, listened to their silences, read inscriptions that time tried to erase. Somewhere in those silences, I found the pulse of Daityagarh.

There were moments when I felt as if the book was leading me instead of the other way around. Sentences appeared before I thought them. Scenes changed on their own, as if the story were remembering itself through me. Maybe that's what writing truly is—listening, not creating.

If this book found you, I hope it stays. Not as fear, but as memory. Not as darkness, but as recognition - of something ancient, unspoken, still breathing beneath our world.

To everyone who stood by me through this journey - my family, my readers, and the people who believed even when I doubted - thank you. You gave this story its spine.

And to you, holding this book now—thank you for walking through its silence with me.

The story doesn't end here. It waits, like Daityagarh itself - patient, watchful, alive.

Because stories like this are not endings.

They are beginnings disguised as echoes.

— Dhara Shah

www.ingramcontent.com/pod-product-compliance
Lightning Source LLC
Chambersburg PA
CBHW041301210926
51847CB00010B/103
* 9 7 8 9 3 7 4 2 6 2 8 7 0 *